The Bicycle Kick

The Library of Congress has cataloged this edition as follows:
Dooley, Ted, 1948 – 2006
The Bicycle Kick

ISBN: 9781790138999
Book cover and interior design by Doreen Hann

First Edition, December 2018

The Bicycle Kick

A Novel by

TED DOOLEY

This book is dedicated
to the memory of Ted Dooley: his energy,
words, humor, and love.

"They build you up till you fool yourself that you're something else and it's like a curse . . ."

—Joan Jett

It is a remarkable photograph. Shot from knee level, it raises the central figure to monumental stature: a young woman in white playing soccer, framed by a green field with a crowded grandstand in the background. Behind her, two players in red look up at the ball near the top of the frame, their faces surprised, probably at the height the girl in the foreground has achieved to reach the ball. The girl in white is perfectly upside down. One leg extends straight up; her foot with a gold cleat has just struck the ball. Her long chignon of gold hair is about to whip against her back in the next moment. The player's expression as much as her stunning inversion makes the picture so striking: her face has a calm, almost faraway look, as if her eyes are focused on a distant point somewhere beyond the goal in front of her.

The shot, called a *bicycle kick* because the player must spin a full revolution like a bike wheel to take it, is not uncommon at the game's highest levels, though at any level it is spectacular. The girls in the photo are all fourteen years old. The team in white is the U.S. National U-15 age-group team, while the team in red is from Norway. The photo first appears in *Sports Illustrated*, in a story about Title IX and young women in sports. The caption under the shot reads simply, "Bicycle Girl." A letter in a subsequent issue asks for another picture of the player and the editors comply: next to the reprinted bicycle shot, a bone-thin girl with long blond hair and blue eyes frowns over the same caption.

The photo will appear often over the next few years, in newspapers and websites covering women's sports. Followers of youth soccer may have heard of Chase Ellis before the photo is published; she is a top national player. But the nickname enables a growing reputation. From one kick caught on film, a fleeting moment of extreme athleticism and unnatural calm, a young player becomes known as the Bicycle Girl.

It seems that every parent has a child playing sports these days and all of them begin as stars. In one way or another, like the girl in the picture, they turn upside down and come back to earth sooner or later.

Part One: Florida, July 2006

1.

What is this slimeball doing giving the up-and-down eye slide to my daughter, right under my nose? Am I invisible? Isn't it obvious to him, as it is to everyone else in the lobby, that these girls are all teenagers – especially mine? Aren't they all surrounded by a bodyguard of list-making, chore-doling, curfew-setting, generally meddlesome and annoying parents? Hey sport, flag up: father here. Like I'm supposed to be impressed that every article of clothing on your entire body is emblazoned with the Nike swoosh?

But the girls are impressed; they've all gone gushy and bug-eyed, whispering behind their hands. They've just unloaded enough equipment from the team bus to equip a small Third-World nation, so their athletic bodies are warmed up and ready to play, and I don't mean soccer. In the frenzy of arrival at our hotel, a few of our daughters have already begun to scatter deep into the corridors while the adults are stuck in line, jockeying with one another to register for our block of rooms. A few other teams have arrived at roughly the same time, though I didn't see any with their own lux-bus like ours. Thank you, Victor Somebody or Other, for showing us poor people how rich you are.

The other teams have noticed Nike Man lurking and leering, though no one seems alarmed at his presence. The adults are as impressed as their jiggly teenagers. A name is quickly bruited about: Javier somebody, from Portugal, or Senegal, or Buggerall. Someone says World Cup and I get it: he's a celebrity soccer player. Great. And it gets worse. He's a coach now, or some sort of appendage of one of the Division I colleges. So he's getting a full complement of female smiles, of all ages, only slightly offset by the more reserved but still impressed looks from the men in the group. Which would all be fine with me, hey, something to brag about back in Boston, you know. Guess who I met at Disney last week? Javier Hunko. Well, hooha to that. Except while half the hotel lobby is recognizing him, he's recognizing my fifteen-year-old.

Surrounded by a platoon of warm-up suits, Javier calls out to her across the atrium and comes skipping over like a bell captain.

"Chase!" he calls, then steps too close to her. "Chase Ellis? Hi!"

His dark Mediterranean eyes do their lechy traversal. I have no idea if he actually knows her, but he acts as if he does. OK, there are whole chunks of my daughter's past life I know very little about, which makes me different from most teenagers' parents only by degree. It is just as likely that he only knows her from her "Bicycle Girl" photos in *Sports Illustrated*. Chase is already taller than he is, and so am I, which pleases me for no good reason. He looks too young to be a college coach; I'd say midtwenties max, but I'm not good at this sort of calculus. He's powerfully built, not handsome, but with a kind of shaved, bullet-headed toughness that when added to the fame thing will no doubt appeal to women, especially the young ones.

I want to intervene and steer her away, even though I know I should leave her alone, but the team manager needs my credit card at the registration desk. One after another, parents are called up to pay for their rooms. Only the parents designated as chaperones get their tabs picked up by the club. While I wait for a cow-eyed clerk to process my card, I try to keep an eye on Chase and the slimeball. Half the time he's talking close to her face, as if she's deaf, and the rest of the time he's talking to the lobby, a lot of which is in fact paying attention.

As usual, Chase is looking at the floor. For all of her six feet of height, she is still more coltish than the other girls on her team. Her long gold hair is tied back in a thick chignon. This afternoon she has an angry pimple on the flare of her nose that I know is killing her because she keeps putting her hand to it, which of course makes it worse. Pimple or not, she is by no means the hot bod in this group. There are girls on her team – and plenty more in the lobby now glomming onto Javier – who look like they could give Hunky all he could wish for and then some. Not Chase. She's a kid. This isn't just daddy-talk, either. She's got a sunken-cheeked gauntness that gives her appearance almost a worn-out quality. Her shoulders are about as wide as a sea plane but the rest of her is boyishly thin. She doesn't add to her charm by attempting a personality. At best, she manages an occasional half smile, with her mouth taut and her eyes invariably frowning, her signature expression of discomfort usually mistaken for contempt, especially by her teammates.

But she is not contemptuous of him; I can see from thirty feet away that she's beginning to respond. Awkward around adults or most girls her own age, Chase is comfortable with boys and young men, though even then she won't talk much. Instead of pulling away from Javier while her shoulders look as if they are climbing up to her ears, she half turns her long body almost into his, and when she does look up from the floor, she meets him squarely in the eyes. There is nothing more alluring than eye lock.

Jenna, the team's head coach who is also Chase's high-school coach, moves over to one side of the lobby to give out room assignments. Slowly the players and parents gather around her, although Chase is still listening to Javier. Jenna reads the list of room numbers for the girls, gives out a key card to each girl, and tells us she wants chaperones only in the rooms with the girls until they're settled in. Chase will have three players for roommates, including Amy, the Juventus captain. Parents who are not assigned as chaperones – meaning most of us – are given an assortment of jobs, including solving the dinner problem. Jenna makes it clear: everyone travels and eats together, which is a colossal pain in the ass. Try finding a restaurant for a group of forty at Disney during the national championship. Jenna says no girls are to leave the hotel unescorted by chaperones. Some of the girls glance at one another, some titter, most are just waiting to get to their rooms. These girls are all experienced tournament players, as are their parents; they know the drill.

Except Chase, apparently, even though she has more tournament experience than anyone on the team. She's still cornered by Mr. World Cup. One or two of the parents look at me as if I'm supposed to go over and reel her in. But it looks to me like she's trying to get away from him, though she's too shy and unassertive to know how to pull it off. It's hard for any kid to walk away from an adult who's bearing down on them and Javier is definitely bearing down. Chase's teammates don't know her well enough yet to read her. Jenna hands off the rest of the keys to Victor to distribute and walks over toward the two of them.

"Hello Javier," Jenna says, coolly I note, and the two shake hands like distant cousins. He seems to get the message, winks at Chase, and heads off toward the bar. I watch him until I notice Jenna looking at me. I make a mental note to talk to her about him later, but I probably don't need to. Jenna knows Chase in some ways better than I do.

"Why do I always get the Bike Dyke?" Amy asks. She's talking to a small circle of players around her, but she says it just loud enough that those of us nearby can hear her.

Jenna has heard her and glares at Amy with a look so withering it begins to make all of us uncomfortable. From the way Chase is wincing, I can see that she's heard it, too. Amy is popular among the players. Jenna assigned Chase to a room with Amy because she thinks the talkative Juventus captain will draw Chase out of her usual silence. Since when does a talker ever draw out a shy person? The attention from Javier hasn't helped; her teammates are annoyed by Chase enough already.

As the players and parents cluster in small groups or scatter to their rooms, Chase heads off alone, pulling her wheely-bag with two backpacks looped around the handle. I want to run after her and be company for her, use the ol' Magoo, make her feel better, but she's not eight years old anymore. I've learned enough in the past year not to crowd her but to let her go her own way. To a point.

I've managed to bag one of the few single rooms for myself, avoiding having to share beer and bathroom with some other father. The hotel was booked months in advance. I was a late booking and had to use a mostly bullshit connection with the chain's corporate headquarters to get it. Teams from all fifty states are in Orlando for the weekend. This is the national club championship, not the biggest but surely the most prestigious youth soccer tournament of the year. This is saying something, since these gigs have become huge moneymakers and have proliferated like pests without predators. In fact, the whole youth soccer thing is growing like a major industry. Chase currently is on the rosters of at least three different teams, though not all of them play year-round. This is not unusual for marquee players like Chase.

For four days and three nights, thousands of players scattered throughout the Orlando area converge on gigantic field complexes and play up to five games if they last through the eliminations. College coaches watch the play from strategically placed towers at every field. Video will be shot of a lot of the games, especially for the top-ranked clubs. The town will be crawling with Javiers. It ought to be a gas – a weekend at Disney with a lot of sports thrown in. What's not to like? But the heat is on and not just the weather. All of us are seeking the fleeting connections that might lead to the next step in a rite of courtship that is subtle, yet rigorous, and fraught for nearly everyone, with the aches and pains of opportunity and disappointment.

My room is acceptable, even for someone as finicky as me: king bed, stiff sheets, lots of thick towels, TV with cable, AC that clanks and hardly works, no view to speak of, and sliders to a balcony about two inches deep. The AC is a loss since we're in Florida and it's July. I'm near the end of a long hallway in which most of the other rooms are taken up by the girls. Except for the chaperones, most of the parents are a floor above me. The girls bang doors, spill into the hallways, and chase each other for no apparent reason other than noise. I can hear Amy out in the hall clowning with other girls. I know Chase would enjoy being one of them but it's unlikely she's out there; the others would just drift back into their rooms – not by conspiracy or even trying to be unfriendly. They just don't connect with her.

I'm supposed to work on finding a restaurant that will seat eighteen teenagers and twenty-two adults. Good luck with that. I take a beer from the little fridge, suck foam, and wait a few minutes. Sure enough, within ninety seconds Victor calls. The parent of a player from Rhode Island who's been on the club team since she was nine, he owns half of Providence and paid for the luxury bus himself.

"Tommy," he asks, "what do you think about Olive Garden?"

"Perfect. Should I call for a table?"

"I already did. They'll take us all but we've gotta get moving."

"Great. Go for it," I say. I have no idea what this means but it seems to please him and he'll do what has to be done to mobilize people. I ask if he wants to grab a beer.

"We're in room 208. We've got a case of Heineken – come on up."

I go because I'm hoping Jenna will be there. Everyone on these trips, including me, is drawn to the coach like a groupie; but it turns out she's about to meet with the team. Some of the parents are running around dealing with tournament officials and rosters. Others are doing something with the player ID cards, which are guarded like Fabergé eggs. Up in room 208 a group of fathers, a few mothers, and the team's assistant coach are downing beers and talking over the television, turned onto ESPN. Except for me, all of these people have been traveling together for at least several years, which is unusual in the world of club soccer, where players change alliances like swingers in Cancún. This is the core parent group, the old guard, the people who hired Jenna and comprise an assortment of team and parent groups, including the club's board of directors.

The talk quiets a tiny click when I enter. I'm still an outsider, even though we've been connected with the team more or less for the past year. Although Chase officially joined the team last summer, she was injured at the time. Then high-school season kicked in, and club play didn't start up again until December. Chase continued on and off to deal with injuries, like a lot of players. The two of us didn't climb onto the tournament bandwagon until this past spring, so Chase has not yet been sorted into the team's pecking order. New players are always mixed blessings: the more they help the team win, the more invitations the team gets to top tournaments. But better players can gobble up minutes. Chase's problems with her teammates are by no means just because of minutes or being new, but they are a part of it.

"So Chase knows Javier Couto?" a parent asks. Faces turn to me, waiting for an answer.

I shrug and say, "I guess," taking a beer offered by Victor, who is talking into his cell phone. I have nothing more to offer on this subject, but the room wants me to say more.

"Someone from her past, I suppose."

"From Chicago?" someone says, looking to clarify what I'm saying.

"I really don't know." I can see they think I'm guarding a connection like family jewels.

"Better be careful with that," someone says.

"Yeah, he looks like a lech," I say. But this is ignored completely.

Turns out the warning to be careful is about recruitment rules and violations. It seems Javier Couto is working at the tournament as a scout, evaluating players for a whole host of Division I colleges. A woman named Liz asks if Chase's knowing him means that she's all set.

I've collected enough tidbits about college recruitment in the last few months to know that this is a loaded question. Club play is all about scholarships. Most of the girls on Chase's team have just finished their junior year. It's already late July, so if they haven't signed an offer sheet, their parents may already be a little desperate. These people are so bug-eyed about college that they only see a hookup with Javier as a shot at college. I saw the guy look at Chase. He was recruiting her, no doubt about it, but not for college. I may be new at parenting but not at the game he's playing. I say something about Chase just starting her junior year in the fall, so it's a little early for her to be worried about college.

"Right," one of the fathers says with a laugh.

Liz, sitting near me at the door, says quietly, "This is all new to you, isn't it, Tommy?"

"Seriously."

She smiles sympathetically. "Her knee seems OK."

"She wouldn't tell me if it wasn't."

"They all get like that," Liz says. She's from Hopkinton. Her daughter's a defender so Chase isn't grabbing any minutes from her kid. Her husband, who thankfully stayed home, wears an Olympic Development windbreaker to every game and lurks near the goal screaming instructions at his daughter, like Bobby Knight.

One of the other mothers is looking at me.

"Chase has your color," she says.

Which is semi-true: Chase is a dirty blond with hair so thick you could mop gravel with it, while my hair is more red and not so curly, though it has its moments when it rains. If she means skin color, she's nailed us, since neither Chase nor I have any of it: two faces so bloodless pale we both look like skim milk. Except Chase has a spattering of freckles around her nose. Actually, I have freckles, too, though not where anyone here is going to see them.

Off his phone now, Victor is able to convince us we need to head down to the bus if we want dinner. He says the girls are on their way. Olive Garden will have a room for us in fifteen minutes but won't hold it for long with all the teams coming in.

We've been on the bus for a few minutes waiting for stragglers. I haven't seen Chase get on. The team manager works her way down the aisle and kneels next to my seat.

"We can't find Chase," she says quietly. "Jenna has gone to look for her."

My cell is immediately at my ear. A prerecorded voice tells me I've reached Chase, even though I obviously haven't. I call Jenna, who says she's double-checking the room.

Off the bus, as I cross the hotel lobby heading for the bar, Jenna jogs over from the reception area.

"She's coming," she says. She looks at me with a wry smile; the two of us have been through this moment-of-panic drill before. I just smile back. It's a silent exchange that has become familiar between us over the past year, ever since Chase started high school almost a year ago.

Chase appears, crossing the lobby slowly, looking as if she's oblivious to a busload of people waiting for her. When she steps out under the carport, the girls on the bus start catcalling at her, mostly friendly, but here and there with a slight edge. The team manager says "Let's go!" and Chase scowls defensively. Her awkwardness is not apparent to everyone the way it is to me – to others she probably seems arrogant. Chewed out and upbraided by coaches for most of her life, she is still uncomfortably shy when adults who aren't wearing cleats speak to her.

As she climbs on the bus, one of the girls yells suggestively, "Where's Javier, Chase?" Chase's eyes flick at Jenna but she doesn't answer.

The first game for Juventus is at eight the next morning, which means the team has to be on the field by seven fifteen. Backtracking from that point, the wake-up time for breakfast is ridiculous since the field is a half-hour ride from our hotel. I find myself walking around the lobby in the dark doing a *Night of the Living Dead* impression. The girls allegedly went to bed at ten while the parents yakked and drank, great role models all of us. On the bus to the field, the girls seem reasonably awake and for the most part excited to be playing.

On the bus back to the hotel in the afternoon, the mood is decidedly different. The girls are collapsed in the rows toward the back of the bus; all of them are withered, sweaty, prickly with irritation after a day on the field in the sultry Florida heat. Most of the parents are sullen from sun fatigue; we just sit in the cushy bus seats looking out at the part of Orlando that is all strip mall and parking lot. Some are grumbling, some more openly critiquing team play. A few pairs of parents whisper together, leaning across aisles to make comments privately, no doubt about the play of other people's daughters.

In the morning game, Juventus played the Olympic Development team from Pennsylvania, and tied them 1–1. This was disappointing, since Juventus had killed the same team in a Memorial Day tournament just two months earlier. Juventus could not get its offense going and only scored on an early penalty kick. In the second game, Juventus lost 2–0 to a high-ranking club from Sonoma, California, a team that was handily beaten in their morning game against the top-ranked club from Dallas. Juventus had lousy luck in the tournament draw, and now has to get ready for a game tomorrow morning against the Red Devils from North Carolina, the team that won the Orange Classic in December.

Chase is sitting in the very last row on the bus next to the smelly bathroom, the seat next to her piled with team bags. She did not start the first game against Pennsylvania. When she did play, she was undistinguished, making a few solid passes but mostly moving up and down the right side fighting off coverage that collapsed on her whenever play shifted to her side of the field. Her jersey was grabbed constantly, and she didn't move well against aggressive defenders. She never got off a shot. The second game against Sonoma was much the same. Although no one on the team managed a convincing shot against the California club, I've heard Chase's name in conversations after the second game and on the bus. Of those who get the most attention, much is expected. Although I don't actually hear the comments, I doubt they are flattering.

Jenna calls a team meeting in her room before the girls are allowed to shower, and as usual, no parents are allowed. My room is next to hers, so while I can't make out what she is saying, I can tell from her voice that she is chewing out the team. She never screams, on or off the field. But she is intense; I know from past experience that she does not hesitate to single out girls for criticism in front of the others, adding significantly to the pressure they feel, especially when the team is underperforming.

After the meeting, parents drift down to the bar while the girls return to their rooms to shower and primp as if getting ready for a prom – meaning an hour of hair dryers, makeup, and praising each other's outfits while trashing them to others. Chase is held back for a private chew-out with Jenna that seems to go on for nearly as long as it takes the team to shower.

Opening the stairway door to run up to Victor's room, which has become the gathering point for a lot of the parents, I'm surprised to find Chase in the stairway landing. She's alone, still in uniform, leaning against the wall, shoulders drooping as if from exhaustion. I've watched this girl run too often to think that this is just game fatigue.

She's about to cry but fighting it off, and no doubt wants desperately to be left alone. I have to say something.

"You OK?" I ask.

She shrugs.

"You can use my shower if you don't want to wait around."

She ignores my offer. "I'm fine."

I wait to see if she says anything but she just looks at the stairwell carpet.

"Anything I can do?"

After a moment, she looks up at me. Her physical presence is so imposing it's easy to forget she's not much more than a child.

"I fucking hate this," she says quietly.

With that, she abruptly pulls open the stairway door. I watch her walk down the hall to her room, stepping around a few of her teammates who are talking in the hallway. They watch her from the sides of their eyes but continue their conversations.

By the time most people are gathered in the lobby to board the bus for another chain-restaurant dinner, Chase is late again. When she finally arrives and boards the bus, there is no banter from the players. Despite the heat, she's wearing a Northwestern sweatshirt and flannel pajama bottoms, while the other girls are rigged out in makeup, short skirts, and string-tops. Chase moves to the back of the bus next to the bathroom. After a moment, Jenna follows her back, kneeling in the aisle to talk to her, then comes up and sits next to me.

"She's isolating herself again," Jenna says.

"She's late because you kept her after the meeting – did you want her to go to dinner in her uniform?" I say.

"I'm not talking about that," Jenna says.

I can see there is little point in arguing with her. The loss to a team

Juventus should have beaten has irked her. Throughout the past year, Jenna has been a patient ally for Chase, and while she has kept pressure on her to perform on the field, Chase has for the most part responded reasonably well. But Jenna is under pressure now herself; the demands of a national club tournament are considerably worse than those of a high-school season. Chase, curled up in the back of the bus in an old sweatshirt like a homeless person, seems distracted, hardly like an athlete gathering herself for another day of competition.

We are late for our reservation, and instead of a banquet room we have to wait, as smaller tables become available. The players are scattered throughout the restaurant in groups of four and six, while the adults wait in the lounge for spots to open up. By the time we are all seated, spread among several rooms, I lose sight of Chase, and then see her, on the other side of the restaurant near the bar. She is sitting in a booth next to Javier Couto, across from a young man and woman I vaguely recognize as tournament staff. Javier has his arm stretched across the bench seat behind Chase's shoulders. If she could see me watching her, she'd glare in embarrassment.

While the three adults enjoy themselves, Chase looks tense, her eyes alert. Javier leans in close when he talks to her. When he does, her hand starts to come up between her face and his, almost as if she were about to touch his face. It's a young girl's reflex – she's trying to hide the pimple. But it only draws more attention to her vulnerability.

Part Two: Massachusetts, May 2005–April 2006

2.

Chase was not a name I admired. It was one of those WASPy family things that meant so much to my wife, though she was usually quiet about them. Her family tree looked like an interlocking directorate, all the names bouncing from one column to the next, surnames becoming proper names that sounded vaguely male, with all the classic WASP associations: trust funds, sliced chicken sandwiches on white bread with trimmed crusts, everyone a lawyer who wasn't a banker, and all of them stiffs.

My wife's name was Taylor McKinley. Her father's mother was Somebody Taylor, her mother is Maris Arlen McKinley, Taylor's brother is Arlen McKinley, and Maris's mother was Ellen Chase. So in the rigorous algebra of WASP genealogy, our daughter had to be Chase. If she'd been a boy, it would have made no difference. Taylor claimed the origin of the name Chase was French and that it meant *power*, which fit with her aspirations for her daughter. So my daughter was Chase Boyan for the first few years of her life, until Taylor and I divorced and she married a WASP like her, this one named Dale Ellis.

Our daughter became Chase Ellis, a name that survived Taylor's second divorce a few years later. Fortunately or not, Chase always managed to distinguish herself well enough since she first entered preschool to be known simply by one name. She's just Chase, almost the way one name works for Beyoncé or Seabiscuit. Chase and I had only lived in our new town a few weeks before nearly everyone learned who Chase was.

A curly-haired towhead in her early years, Chase now has the thick, blond hair of her mother. While Chase wears it long and tied back, Taylor wore hers ultra-short, like a Hemingway heroine. In the chronology of her puberty, Chase is decidedly a late bloomer, barely entering the early phases of a development that most of her classmates completed much sooner. Yet she is already taller than I am, at five ten, by at least two inches. Taylor was almost as tall. Bone thin, blue-eyed like everyone on both sides of her family, but not beautiful like her mother. Chase can still be pretty if not for her unrepentant scowl. No matter what she is doing, her eyes are invariably cast down, as if she must watch her step in the dark. She is often too knock-knee awkward to be thought unfriendly by most people, though the Chase I know at home can be as surly as a lifer.

It was a little over a year ago that I got the phone call about her mother. While it should have come from Maris, Taylor's mother, it was Taylor's lawyer – her executor to be exact – who called me. It was a hot late morning in May, a Saturday. I'd just come in from a run on the Esplanade in Boston. I was sweating on the floor of my Beacon Street kitchen while pouring Vitaminwater down my throat. I had a one-bedroom condo at the time that I liked quite a lot; it had a view of the Charles River, though mostly what I saw was Storrow Drive. It was close to the Public Garden, a quick jog over to the running paths along the river, and cheap. I'd bought it cheap; I don't make much money, but I regret every nickel I've spent except on my car. The best feature was that the place had a garage, between Beacon and Storrow, a one-stall cinderblock cave that should have been valuable when I put the place on the market. Until that phone call, my car was my baby.

Taylor was dead. The lawyer, a precise, anal type who spoke so slowly he sounded like computer talk, put the facts to me pretty directly, no bullshit. I had to stop him midsentence several times; it was as if I'd entered some dream state and was imagining nonsense. She what? Are you sure? That sort of thing. Even more odd was that she'd died nearly a week earlier. After all, I was the father of her only child. Granted, we'd been divorced for more than ten years officially, and apart for more than eleven. We had occasional contact over that time and all of it about Chase, usually through email. And most of the emails were excuses or explanations for why Chase would not be coming to Boston for the promised weekend, or why it turned out my stopping by while I was in Chicago would just not work. Chase did manage to visit Boston a couple of times a year, usually on her way to her grandmother's house in Connecticut. I would not have expected Taylor's mother, Maris, to call, but her brother, Arlen, was a solid sort of guy. I'd always liked him, as much as it was possible to like a human incarnation of tasteless white bread. Taylor was different: elegant, granite-hard, spoiled like a rock star, humorless to the point of being a little grim, and now dead. It took a while for the computer voice to get me to accept this simple fact.

She'd died in her sleep. Sudden cardiac arrest, the lawyer explained. Apparently she had a very slow heart rate that without other symptoms had not concerned her family doctor given her athletic background.

Then one night two weeks ago, her heart simply stopped. She was thirty-eight, the same as me.

"Otherwise," the lawyer explained, "she was in excellent health."

"You mean like otherwise the war zone was a great place to visit?" He didn't respond. I asked about Chase. My daughter stepped into my consciousness as if a large door had just opened in my head. I started rolling out another stream of questions, and it soon became apparent that Chase was the reason for his making the call to me rather than a member of Taylor's family. Incredibly, Taylor had specified in her will that in the event of her death, custody of Chase should go to me.

"Excuse me?"

He repeated himself, and after that did a pretty fair job of handling the ferocity of questions I pelted at him. I had not been informed before of the will, because Taylor's family had been scattered and only barely made it to the funeral. He did not explain how it came about that I was not told about custody while Taylor was alive. There was now a court date pending. Maris was asking for custody herself and apparently had been caring for Chase in Chicago at Taylor's house. There were complexities to be ironed out in probate. I needed to come to Chicago and appear in court. Yes, a lawyer would be prudent if I did wish to gain custody of my daughter. No, Chase's former stepfather, Dale Ellis, was not a factor in the decision. He'd drunk and beaten up Taylor then fled to Hawaii behind a phalanx of lawyers to protect himself from Maris. Taylor's second divorce was no harder than peeling off a Band-Aid.

Sunday afternoon, the next day, I checked into the Best Western Hotel on the North Shore in Evanston, a few blocks from Northwestern University, where Taylor had worked. Her house was less than a mile from the campus, a small but impressive three-bedroom home with lots of French doors and a yard with a goalpost at the back. Her brother,

Arlen, always decent, a little dull, met me at the hotel and drove me to Chase's home, filling me in on a lot of details along the way.

"So I have to fight Maris for my daughter, is that right?"

Arlen sucked air, concentrated on driving, found a place to pull over safely, gathered himself, then answered, "She wants what's best for Chase."

"And that would be what?"

"I think," he said in slow measures, "we all need to talk this through very carefully. What," he asked slowly, "are your wishes?"

"Do they matter?"

"Of course. Chase is your daughter."

This felt like a rebuke.

"What about Chase? What does she want?"

"She wants her mother back." He looked out the windshield at the lake. "She's been through a lot. She's not herself."

Arlen explained that the court date would not be confirmed until the next morning, pending my arrival, but that the judge would arrange time for us as soon as I was in Illinois. Before leaving Boston, I'd talked to a lawyer who had been an undergraduate friend at Boston College and now practiced in Chicago. He would be available when I needed him and would get copies of everything. My brother, Fergie, who was also a lawyer, was tied up in court in Boston but had already talked to my BC friend. Fergie wanted the name of the judge and made clear he was ready to fly out if there were any problems. Fergie had insisted I give copies of emails between Chase and me over the past few years to my Chicago lawyer. I had no idea why, but I knew Fergie and I took care of it.

I expected a crowd at Taylor's, as if a wake had just ended and the faithful migrated to the family home. Not so. It was just Maris and

Arlen, and Chase somewhere in the house, though not appearing yet. Maris, whom I remembered as edgy, talon-handed, and sharp-eyed, looked older of course, but she still had her edge; she was sitting at the kitchen table, leaning over a whiskey glass full of Chardonnay. She stood and silently greeted me with two hands on my shoulders and a near kiss that whizzed by my cheek.

"So you finally made it," she said.

"I just heard the news last night."

Arlen offered me a drink and I readily accepted. The three of us sat and talked for some time, mostly about Taylor, some about Chase. It was the longest conversation I'd ever had with any of Taylor's relatives. Maris needed to talk, unusual in my experience of her. It may have been the Chardonnay. She was not uncivil; Maris was incapable of that. But when she did speak, she addressed her son, and when I talked, usually asking questions, she ran the tip of her finger around her glass as if making a sound of her own was preferable. When I told her how sorry I was that she'd lost her daughter, she gave a tight little nod of her head but that was all. She was barely holding herself together.

Chase had found Taylor's body, in bed, after her mother had failed to wake up to drive her to school. Apparently she thought her mother was still sleeping at first and went downstairs to watch television, glad to be late for school. When she finally went back upstairs, she realized after touching Taylor that she was dead. She ran out of the house to a neighbor's, who had already left for work, then stopped a car on the street. The driver called 911. The EMTs came and Chase went with her mother's body to the University Medical Center, where nurses called the few colleagues of Taylor's that Chase could remember. Probably mistaking Chase for much older than fifteen because of her height, the attending doctor explained that Taylor's heart had stopped and that they would have to do an autopsy to determine the exact cause. Maris said that since that moment, Chase had one way or another removed herself from everyone.

"She hasn't said two words to me since the funeral," she said to Arlen, who already knew this.

"So we have a court date tomorrow about custody," I said, sticking a fork in the elephant in the room. Arlen told me once again the time of the hearing.

"So what's the fight card?" I asked. I figured it was better to get into it now while we were all a little softened by alcohol.

Maris's eyebrows snapped up her forehead.

"Meaning?"

"Are we about to get into a wrestling match over Chase?"

"There's a lot to be decided."

"As I understood from the executor, Taylor already made that decision." I looked at Arlen. "Wasn't this in her will?"

Arlen looked uncomfortably at his drink.

"You're not putting my granddaughter on a plane like so much luggage and carrying her off to Boston," Maris said coolly. "I don't care what the executor says."

The following afternoon in the judge's chambers, it became clear that Taylor's will was a recent one, so there was no question of whether this represented her intentions at the time of her death. Everyone, including Maris, was surprised, to the point of disbelief, that I had no knowledge of Taylor's wishes. Me, too.

Chase was not in the courtroom. A social worker had visited her at home twice since Taylor's death, including once on the morning of the hearing. Although the woman spent time in Chase's room with her, apparently Chase had not spoken much, if at all. In court, Maris's lawyer asked for a continuance on the custody decision until Chase had time to express her own wishes. There was some back-and-forth between the lawyers on this. My lawyer described my work and living circumstances in ways that made me envy myself. The judge denied the continuance but would consider temporary custody, to be reviewed at the end of the summer. Maris's lawyer promptly asked the court for temporary custody and argued that since Maris had spent considerably more time over the past ten years with Chase than I had, that this would mean the least disruption in Chase's life. Maris said she was prepared to live in her daughter's house to care for Chase through the summer. In answer to a question from the judge, I said I was prepared to stay in Chicago for a few weeks to ease the transition for Chase, but that I would need to return to Boston and my work.

I expected the judge to take it all under consideration and make a decision at some later date, but he looked over the papers briefly and then announced his decision. He said that Chase had visited me in Boston regularly for more than ten years and noted that the two of us corresponded frequently and affectionately over the past few years. He granted me temporary custody of Chase as if it were a matter of course, and set a review date for the end of August.

Maris insisted that it be clear the decision was only temporary, which seemed to irk the judge a little. There were also complexities of probate to be decided, as the executor had suggested to me over the phone in Boston. Taylor had a family trust fund as well as her own assets, and Chase had a trust fund in her name as well. Taylor had been equally clear in her will about the disposition of her assets, but the complexities were mostly about Chase's inheritance and who would control them until she came of age. My lawyer noted that I had no need of these funds and readily agreed to let Taylor's family continue to manage them as they had done during Taylor's life. The judge listened to that and said that until the final disposition of custody was determined, no one would have access to these funds anyway. They all seemed reluctant to talk about amounts, which of course I was curious about. It was as if I was a child like Chase, not to be entrusted with family assets or information.

I didn't give a flier about her family money. I just wanted to do whatever needed to be done to make Chase look less stricken. I'd seen Chase the evening before at home. During the afternoon, she appeared suddenly in the kitchen, pale as a ghost, to get a glass of grape juice, while Maris, Arlen, and I were talking.

"Hi, Sweetie," I said quietly, but she only glanced at me. When I stood up and tried to embrace her she tensed, almost spilling the juice, and I stepped back. I hadn't seen her for almost a year and I was stunned by how much she'd grown. For a moment I felt like I was looking at an adult until I noticed the pajama bottoms decorated with cute little cartoon frogs. Maris said something about a salad in the refrigerator, and before I could say anything, Chase was gone. I went to look for her but the door to her bedroom was closed. Maris had said something earlier about a doctor saying Chase needed time alone, so I didn't knock.

Later that evening, I went to look for her again. Her room was open, but she wasn't there. Feeling like an intruder, I took a step in and looked around, though I was careful not to get too comfortable. The rigorous order of photographs, trophies, and ribbons on display throughout the room was undermined by the litter of clothes, bed linen, and food papers all over the floor. I had several nieces and nephews in

Boston not much older than Chase; it looked like a teenager's room to me except for the number and size of the trophies.

At Arlen's suggestion, I looked for her in the basement. It had the look of most basement playrooms: tile floors and old furniture. I didn't see her at first; the two long couches were empty. I was about to go back up the stairs when I saw the frog pajamas through a doorway to a small utility room at the far end of the basement. She was lying on the floor, on one side, her legs curled up. Her head was resting on the back of one hand against the tile. Her face was wet and blotchy with redness, and her mouth and hand were wet with drool. Her eyes were wide, staring off at a point under the central air-conditioning unit in the corner. Except for the slow breathing cadence of her enormous shoulders, she would have looked dead. Her eyes didn't even flick at the door when I walked in.

I knelt down and put a hand on one leg of the frog pajamas, near her ankle.

"Hi, Sweetie," I said, which repeated my entire conversation with her since my arrival. The motor of the air conditioner rumbled quietly, a comforting white noise. Her T-shirt said Las Vegas Shootout. We stayed just like that for an unbearable amount of time, my hand on her leg, her breathing slowly, her eyes staring across the floor. My knees started to hurt.

"Are you hungry?" I asked, and when she didn't respond, I waited a little, then asked her again. Her only answer was a very slight tremor in her leg. She looked as if she'd been stricken by a horrible paralyzing poison that only allowed her a tiny shiver and a steadily dripping nose. I gave her a tissue from my pocket. Her hand clutched it automatically but she didn't use it, she just continued to look across the floor. I sat back against the wall and stayed for a while, then got up and looked upstairs for a pillow and a blanket to cover her. Arlen distracted me with a request for an assortment of phone numbers. When I found a blanket and a pillow, I went back down to the basement but Chase had gone.

I'd known of course for years that my daughter was an athletic prodigy. Taylor, for all her reluctance to share Chase with me, had not undermined me with our daughter. At least not too badly. After Dale Ellis split for Paradise Hawaiian-Style, Taylor must have felt some need for Chase to have an alternative father figure in her life, preferably from long distance. Chase sent me birthday cards and Christmas cards every year, and Taylor emailed me news clips, almost all of which were about soccer, most of them from the local Evanston paper or a series of youth soccer weeklies and websites. I sent Chase birthday and Christmas presents, as did my brother and sisters, who would never leave a family stone unturned. Chase and I emailed one another with some regularity; I would always respond to Chase whenever Taylor sent something about our daughter, and Chase, dutifully and briefly, would answer back. The best I ever got from her was an occasional HAHAHAHAHA or a YOU'RE FUNNY! if I wrote something goofy. Occasionally, we texted, but her answers were so brief and slow in coming that I had the feeling she couldn't type very well, which turned out to be true.

I wish I could say I felt great pride in Chase's youthful accomplishments. I didn't. I'd been an athlete myself all through high school and college, though as a runner not a team sport player. I would have loved to have a sports star to brag about. Somehow the distance, and the infrequency with which I was allowed to see Chase, made the whole soccer thing a tad bitter for me. I was happy for her. She could have just as easily been a cheerleader or a math whiz like Taylor. I'd never been invited to see her play. To tell the truth of it, the soccer clippings sometimes filled me with a sense of longing that I'd not experienced otherwise in my life. The details of the games felt like stories about a stranger. When she made *Sports Illustrated* (to which I'd subscribed since I was twelve), over a year before Taylor's death, I felt this odd sense of emptiness, as if I'd been cheated out of something; the girl in the magazine was unrecognizable to me.

For two weeks I hung around Evanston, remaining at the Best Western because I didn't want to step into Taylor's life now that she'd left it. Maris stayed at the house. After the first night in the kitchen, we had no more long talks, only the quick essentials about Chase that needed attending. School was still in session; Chase was near the end of ninth grade, but there were weeks left before summer break. No one insisted Chase return to school. People from the neighborhood, from Chase's school, and from Northwestern stopped by regularly, and Maris rallied herself impressively to make them all feel comfortable. Even at her worst, she was a self-possessed woman, with a lifetime of experience as a hostess. I did not hang around the house but tried to be useful where possible. Chase had a way of quietly slipping in and out of the house through a basement door so that no one ever seemed to be sure if she was in the house unless someone went to look.

I needed to put together my own picture of Chase and her life with Taylor in Evanston before we headed east. I pushed myself to call on faculty at Chase's school and to meet the parents of a few teenagers who were Chase's friends. I also managed to talk to several of the girls, who seemed genuinely torn up by Chase's circumstances. I had coffee on campus with a few of Taylor's colleagues, some of whom were grieving while a few of whom seemed mostly curious. I shared a lunch break on a campus bench with a fellow member of the math department, who I learned afterward had begun dating Taylor just before her death. He'd seemed shocked, fumbling with his sandwich paper and eating almost nothing. The most productive conversation I had about Chase was with the coach of her soccer club, who'd known her for several years. He was a blustery jock type who liked to talk about workouts and motivation, but we seemed to hit it off and there was no doubt he was concerned about Chase.

One friend of Chase, a small girl called Suze, came by a few times. But I never had the sense that Chase was in contact with a lot of friends. No one, not even Suze or the coach, expressed any persuasive sadness at the prospect of Chase leaving the Chicago area. Maybe this was simply because they recognized there weren't other options and wanted things resolved for her.

During this time, Chase did three things: she stayed in her room as much as possible and no one pestered her there. She also went to the weight room at a nearby health club where Taylor had a family membership, running the two miles herself. Or she just went out for a run, which she did quite often, wearing an elaborate knee brace that looked heavy and incredibly uncomfortable. When I asked her if I could run with her, she looked as if I'd asked to wear her socks. Once, after she'd gone out for a run, I was ready and followed her, but not for long. She gapped me so fast I went into oxygen debt and turned onto another street, my throat burning from the attempt. There was no way she could have maintained that pace throughout her workout; she just didn't want to run with me.

A counselor from Chase's school came over several times and spent time alone with Chase in Taylor's study. Her only insight from these visits was that Chase was grieving and would need time. She encouraged us to keep as much of Chase's life the same as possible, which of course was not going to work. She gave me the name of a practitioner in Boston and told me in no uncertain terms to arrange for Chase to see her as soon as I returned. She asked my permission to contact the person, which of course I granted, though it felt a little strange to me to have that sort of authority.

It must have felt a little strange to Maris as well. After the court hearing, Maris, while still maintaining the illusion of the gracious hostess, was snappish and occasionally challenging around me. When the school counselor made the point about keeping things the same for Chase, Maris demanded to know how I planned to do that if I was taking Chase to a strange city, away from her home, her school, and her friends. I didn't argue with her, not only because it would make things worse for everyone, but because I knew she had a point. Though I would never acknowledge it to her.

Arlen, who only stayed a few days beyond the hearing, floated the idea of my staying in Taylor's house through the summer to give Chase time to adjust to the massive changes imminent in her life. My job demands, such as they were, seemed insignificant to those of the McKinleys.

"We can manage that," Arlen said gamely.

I knew he was trying to find the right thing to do for his niece. But I had to get back to Boston. Arlen had to return to New York, to his own family and business. I also knew that Maris needed to get home herself, to New Canaan, though certainly not for financial reasons. Her own life had been torn up by her daughter's sudden loss; she needed to be in her own home to begin grieving in earnest. Arlen tried to console her by saying that Connecticut was a lot closer to Boston than Chicago.

No one had a clear idea of how Chase felt about leaving, even as a temporary measure. She just looked at the ground when we tried to talk to her and shrugged.

At their best, teenagers are not generally motivated to share themselves with adults. From what I'd learned about her, Chase was never chatty or social, though a few of the people I talked to said she had a sense of humor that surprised people. Which put her one-up on her mother, who was never social either and had the sense of humor of a piece of slate. Chase had to push herself to overcome a strong natural shyness. Her coach and a few of her teammates said she was different on the soccer field, more assertive and confident, though she'd never been a body banger like most of the girls who played at her level; she relied instead on speed and foot skills. With me, she seemed silent, almost numb. She avoided eye contact with everyone. The school counselor had told me to expect this. Maris and I, along with Taylor's best friend, a woman named Kirsten or Kristen – can anyone keep those names straight? – had tried one night in Taylor's kitchen to get Chase to open up a little.

She'd been so zombie-eyed that we weren't entirely sure she understood she was about to be relocated to Boston. Pressed by Kirsten, she finally snapped, "I get it, I'm going to Boston, what else do you want me to say? My mother is fucking dead." She glared at Maris as she said it. Maris did not react, but something in her face – her tightened lips, her set jaw – told me she was by no means ready to give up custody of her granddaughter so easily. I knew from bitter experience just how much fight Maris had in her.

3.

More than anything, soccer got us through the next few weeks. Check that: soccer got us through the next few months. To be exact, it was the prospect of the sport rather than her actually playing that dominated much of our new life together.

Chase had sustained a knee injury in the fall of the previous year while playing for her private school in Chicago. Her soccer credentials before high school were impressive: she'd played for a series of national age-group teams, one of which resulted in the photograph of her in *Sports Illustrated*, and for a succession of club and Olympic Development teams since the age of nine. Before that she had played on local travel teams since the age of four, often "playing up" – joining teams of older girls. By the time she joined her high-school varsity team as a freshman, she was a known commodity even beyond the Chicago area. She was on her way to earning a rare high-school All-America status as a freshman when her injury happened, knocking her out of the fall season.

The injury was a common one for female athletes, whose growing joints are more vulnerable to damage in sports than men's. She tore her ACL, the anterior cruciate ligament that connects the femur to the tibia in the complicated mechanics of the knee. There had been complications: she'd torn it by hyperextending rather than twisting it, which made her kneecap dislocate, causing collateral damage. In surgery, the damaged ligament was replaced, by tissue from a cadaver, which to me sounded ghoulishly extreme, while other damaged cartilage was smoothed and shaved. Despite Chase's youth, the surgery had taken longer to heal than expected, apparently because of donor problems possibly causing infection. For much of the past winter and spring, Chase spent long hours rehabbing on an assortment of machines and in drills, and had not kicked a soccer ball with purpose since the previous October.

Taylor, as was her way, had been grimly fanatical in pursuing the best doctors and in helping Chase to carry out her rehab. According to her colleagues, Taylor had been the classic soccer mom. She fretted on the sideline at games and practices; moved Chase from club to club for better coaching; worked as a chaperone on tournament trips; and like every good soccer parent, undoubtedly made herself a colossal pain in the ass to every ref, coach, and player who opposed her daughter in any way. She even traded in her slick BMW for a bulbous Acura SUV with extra seats so she could haul more players and gear. Chase's soccer exploits dominated Taylor's conversations. Her den at home had almost as many soccer photos and trophies as Chase's room. This rang true to my image of Taylor: often inexpressive herself, she was intensely competitive and threw herself into new pursuits to the point of obsession, and stayed with them as long as they provided problems for her to solve. Chase must have been a source of enormous pride for her mother.

As soon as Chase and I returned to Boston, I had to start making connections for her to continue her rehab, which would benefit from a local doctor's assessment if I wanted my health plan to cover it. This being Boston, the only challenge was choosing from the wealth of top specialists. I knew people at Boston Children's Hospital from my job, and within two days had Chase set up with what people claimed was the top sports medicine orthopedist in the area. Chase saw him briefly; he said he'd need to see her again once all Chase's films were received from Northwestern. Chase hardly looked at David Friedman, the famous fifty-plus surgeon; it was actually a little embarrassing.

But she seemed to take to a young ortho in his office who had just joined the practice and said hello in the waiting room after the appointment. Carrie Raynor was a knockout: Harvard Med graduate in her early thirties, she had been a serious figure skater through college and now included attending to an Olympic skater in her new practice. Her first interaction with Chase was to tease her about wearing flip-flop sandals that were almost identical to what she herself was wearing. I scheduled the follow-up appointment with her.

Chase had not brought a lot of stuff with her from Evanston. Maris and Kirsten had both advised her to just take what she thought she might need "for now," as if making things seem more temporary might be reassuring to her. In truth, it was more reassuring to Maris. Which was just as well, since my apartment suddenly seemed a lot smaller after four large bags and six feet of teenager spread out across my floor space. The only full bathroom was inside my bedroom. I tried to get Chase to take the bedroom but she wordlessly settled into the alcove off the living room that I used as a den. This was where she had always stayed before, on weekend visits – but she was a little girl then. The daybed in the alcove was now too short for her; I had it hauled out and put an extra-long mattress on the floor instead. Her bags filled all available shelves and closets. She had to use the half bath for most purposes while using my bathroom for showers. It took one quick look around the apartment to see that the two of us could not stay there for very long.

When I apologized for the cramped quarters, she just shrugged.

I did get the soccer channel on my cable TV. Our first night in Boston and for many thereafter, the two of us sat together in my tiny living room, eating chips and salsa and watching European club teams do amazing things on the pitch. I'd never followed the game before. At first it seemed grindingly boring. But Chase would make an occasional comment on the games, sometimes becoming almost animated after a particularly impressive play. Other times her reactions were more dramatic.

A few days before her first visit with her new doctor, we were watching two British teams battle in the final minutes of a close game. Chase favored Arsenal. When a West Ham player drove toward the net to score, he collided with an Arsenal defender, who appeared to hook the attacker's leg, and both went down. The referee called a penalty kick against Arsenal, and the West Ham player quickly broke the tie with a score. Chase, standing wide-eyed in silence before the penalty kick, exploded with a string of expletives about the ref and slammed the coffee table with her foot, sending chips and salsa onto the floor. Before I could react, she retreated to the small powder room off the kitchen and slammed the door. I cleaned up, finished watching the game, poked around the kitchen, and finally went to bed, but she did not reemerge. I didn't know whether to try to talk to her that night or not, and decided to let it go, not really knowing what I would say to her anyway. Even though she was my daughter, she still seemed like a guest in my home.

Because Chase's school in Evanston was private, her freshman year was over in May, so the last weeks of the school year that she'd missed were not problematic. The question hung in the air whether she would return to Chicago, which was really impossible, or stay in Boston, or possibly move to Connecticut to live with her grandmother. There was an unreal feeling to Chase's sudden presence in my life. Just as the apartment looked as if it had been turned upside down, both of our lives were much the same. My routine of working late and eating out with friends had to stop. But when I was at home with Chase, we were like two people waiting in the same train station. I had no idea what she wanted or expected, and my efforts to engage her in even little routine conversations were deadly failures.

Maris called her every evening, but showed no interest in speaking to me. A few times I took the phone from Chase just to insist myself on her. In these brief exchanges, the issue of Chase's future was raised in the context of the school discussion. Maris kept demanding that we move on enrolling Chase in a private school. Technically, Chase was still enrolled in her school in Chicago, but Maris was not about to relocate herself to Chicago over the long haul and didn't expect me to do it either. One evening, after a brief exchange with Chase – in fact her conversations with Chase were always brief, just like mine – Maris asked to talk to me. She had pulled strings, as she put it, and managed to get Chase into a very spiffy school in Connecticut. She announced this as if it were a done deal. She said it was too late for me to get her into a decent school in the Boston area but she had "pull" in Connecticut and had managed a miracle. I said I was not going to abdicate custody just because Maris had a wire into some snob-factor prep school. Maris's voice went icy hard and she said this was not about custody; it was about school.

"I'm afraid you don't understand what has to be done here," she said.

But I'd been married to Taylor, and I knew how to use an ice pick.

"So public schools are not good enough, is that what you're saying?"

Maris and the McKinleys were supposedly liberals, do-gooders from way back who would never want to acknowledge their fundamentally conservative selfishness.

"I never said that," she said. "Chase needs special circumstances."

"You're saying Chase has special needs?"

"No, I did not say that."

"Oh, sorry. I thought you did."

She gathered herself a moment. She didn't want to argue with me; she simply hoped to ignore me and I would do what she wanted. But I don't think she quite knew what she wanted this time – a special circumstance if ever there was one.

"You can't be seriously proposing," she said, "to send Chase to a public school in Boston."

"We're looking at several suburban communities," I lied.

"This is not a decision you can just blithely make yourself."

"Didn't you just tell me you enrolled her in a private school in Connecticut?"

She tried a different tack.

"She sounds miserable with you up there."

"You think she'd be happier in Connecticut?"

"Yes. I do."

I felt a little wounded by her saying Chase sounded miserable.

"Things will get better for her as soon as she can start playing soccer again."

"Oh, please. Don't talk to me about soccer."

"You don't think she should play?"

"She tore her knee apart! She couldn't walk without crutches for months! Frankly, I don't see where all this soccer business is going; it's not like she can make a life out of it. And it's not like tennis or golf. People can play those games all their lives."

Obviously, I'd struck a nerve here; the ice voice had cracked, now it was just nasty.

"I'm sorry but I just don't get it," Maris said. "I know I know, she loves it, she's a good player. Taylor drove me absolutely *crazy* with all the soccer foolishness. Chase could end up crippled for life. Frankly, I'm not at all sure that it's in her best interests."

"Chase is pretty sure about it."

"We don't even know if she can play again."

"Of course she can play again." These injuries are routine; tennis players hurt their knees too, Maris. But since you feel that way, you must see she'd never be happy in Connecticut."

Maris and I had a lot of history from the years I was with her daughter, and none of it good. I was not about to let her win this. But she changed direction on me, probably making a mental note to talk to her lawyers the moment she got off the line, and asked about Chase's diet. Was she eating? Like a horse, I said. But what was she eating? Here I had to improvise. Truth was I mostly ate a lot of crap – pizza, cheeseburgers, junk – and Chase seemed quite comfortable with the quick and easy, and why not, she was a teenager. But Maris zinged me.

"Taylor was always very careful about her diet. With all that exercise she does, you have to be sure she's not just eating but that she's eating well."

I had not even thought about how to deal with this one. Order the flimsy salad along with the McDonald's double quarter-pounders?

"I'm learning to cook," I lied.

"Oh, please."

In early June, Chase had her second ortho appointment at Children's Hospital. Unlike the first visit, I decided to go with Chase into the exam room, feeling awkward while I did it, but what the hell, I'm her father. Chase, silent and zombie-eyed, didn't seem to notice. After a brief wait, Carrie Raynor came in and said, "Hey, flip-flop girl!" Her dark hair framed her thin face beautifully. Her energy in that cheerless little room was like a shaft of light.

She showed us Chase's recent MRI: a series of maybe thirty pictures spread out across two lightboards showing the insides of Chase's knee in black-and-white. The worry in Chicago had been that postsurgical problems had delayed the healing process and that the ligament was not fixing itself properly.

"I've gone over this with three of my colleagues, including Dr. Friedman, and it looks on film like the ligament has adjusted and is settling in fine. Let's take a look."

She then examined Chase, at great length. She pulled her knee, pushed it, made Chase push one way then another, and took great care moving her hands around Chase's leg, squeezing, pressing, looking for aches and pains. When Chase claimed she felt no pain, Dr. Raynor pushed her.

"Oh, come on, girl! That hurts everybody! Are you messing with me?"

Chase smiled, the half smile, with her head turned slightly down, as she did when she seemed genuinely pleased, and then acknowledged here and there that she felt some discomfort.

"Good," Dr. Raynor said. "I was afraid I was examining a horse."

The doctor sat down in front of Chase and smiled, one hand on Chase's leg.

"I can see you've been doing your homework beautifully. You're going to have to continue your PT and keep building yourself up gradually. If you still have tenderness, you may be pushing yourself a little faster than you should."

"Can I play?"

"I'd like to wait for us to make that decision until the end of the summer. For now I think you can start working on lateral movement and maybe even get some touches, but I don't want you in cleats and I don't want you in any contact yet."

She took Chase's hand in hers.

"I know this is very hard for players to hear, so I want you to listen closely to me, Chase. You too, Mr. Boyan."

"Tommy."

"Tommy – OK! I'm Carrie." She smiled. "So how do you know William Tillotson?"

"Bill? Through work, mostly." Bill Tillotson was chairman of the board of the hospital. He's the one who helped me get the quick appointment with Carrie's boss.

"What do you do?" she asked.

"Consulting, PR, that sort of thing."

"You must be good if you know him," she said.

I just smiled. If I told her much more, all I could do was bring her illusions down to earth, so I opted for mysterious.

"I'll have to Google you," she added playfully.

"So," she said to Chase. "If your ACL continues to heal well, you will be able to play as much as you want and be as mobile as you were before. But if you push it, if that ligament frays a little or if the infection returns, it's going to be a whole lot longer. You know how doctors always tell athletes, let pain be your guide?"

Chase nodded.

"You're going to have to be very, very disciplined. If it hurts – at all – here" – she traced a line on Chase's knee, "or here, or back here . . ."

Chase flinched a little, and Carrie nodded. "You simply have got to stop, ice, and take time off and let it heal longer. If you try to push through the pain with this, your future in your sport will be compromised."

She said these last three words very carefully.

"Do I make myself clear?"

Chase nodded.

"You'll have to keep up your quad and ham lifts to keep your strength balanced, or that kneecap will just keep popping out. You don't want me to have to put a screw in it, right?"

Chase winced.

"Ex-act-ly. Ten-pound weights, every single day, you know the drill, for as long as you want to play soccer. And you don't go anywhere without the brace for a while."

The doctor sat back.

"I want to see you again in two weeks. I want you to keep a log of your workouts and I want to go over it with you. In fact, I want you to do it online and email it to me a week from today."

"But I can practice."

Carrie eyed her wryly.

"Based on what I've told you, I want you to tell me the answer to your question."

Chase wrinkled her mouth. "Light touches, no contact, stop if it hurts."

"OK. So," Carrie said, standing up, "are you just visiting in Boston or are you going to be here for a while?"

Chase just shrugged uncomfortably, so Carrie looked at me.

"We have a lot of decisions to make," I said. We both looked at Chase, who looked at her flip-flops.

Carrie nodded slowly. I'd explained to David Friedman in our first visit that Chase had lost her mother in Chicago recently and had come to stay with me. I sensed that Carrie knew this. She gave Chase an appraising look.

"Well, I know you're a stud – *Sports Illustrated*? Are you kidding me?"

She winked at me. Chase half smiled.

"When Dr. Friedman told me you were a famous soccer player, I thought, yeah, right, at fifteen. Then I Googled you. Wow. Very impressive."

Chase combed through her hair with her fingers.

"I used to be pretty serious about sports when I was your age, so I have a sense of how it feels when you're injured."

"Skating, right?" Chase asked.

"Where'd you ever learn about that – did *you* Google *me*?" Carrie asked, looking pleased. Chase glanced at me.

"Well, I'm flattered. You know," Carrie said, hesitating a moment. "I've got a friend I'd like you to meet. She coaches a club team and a local high-school team, and I *know* she'd love to meet you. She might be able to give you some workouts, and she and I can talk about what you can and can't do. I have tremendous confidence in her."

She looked at me. "She's in Newton."

"What club?" Chase asked, eyeing Carrie cautiously.

"It's called Juventus. It's a big club; they've got their own clubhouse and everything. Jenna coaches your age group, U-16. They've won a lot of tournaments and they travel all over the place."

Chase didn't seem impressed.

"Her name is Jenna Eisenbech; she's great. She'd kill to get a player like you even just for some training over the summer."

Chase nodded politely.

"She played for the Renegades."

Chase's eyes flicked up, now attentive. I learned later that the Renegades was a professional team.

"Oh yeah," Carrie said. "Four-year starter at Boston College, three-time NEAC player of the year, first-team All-America, you name it."

She wrote down a name and number and gave it to Chase.

"Think about it!"

The following day, Chase slept as she often did, until noon, and then watched the soccer channel most of the afternoon. I came home for lunch and went back to my office, then came back a little after four as she was getting ready to go out for a run. When she didn't return by eight, my slowly unfolding anxiety turned into panic. After a while I'd gone out onto Beacon Street several times and walked around looking for her, hoping to find her on a bench on the Esplanade where she ran. At nine, I called the police. They took a description and told me I could come in and file a report, but were generally reassuring – summer, nice evening, teenage girl, not a high-crime area.

At ten, I called the police again, reluctant to leave the apartment for long. I also called the practitioner recommended by the school counselor in Chicago, mostly for someone intelligent to talk to: a woman named Kate, who practiced in Brookline. I left her a long voicemail message; by the time I got her on the phone, it was eleven o'clock. Responding to the panic in my voice, she told me to tape a note to the front door and go to the police station. I was in the hall putting up the note when Chase came thumping up the stairs.

She walked by me as if I wasn't there. I followed her into the apartment.

"Well?"

She looked at me a moment, then went over to the refrigerator.

"Well what?" she said, unscrewing the top of a Vitaminwater. She looked as if she'd run hard at some point but her T-shirt was now dry.

I started yelling, gathered myself, then told her with thinly suppressed wrath that what she'd done was wrong – that I'd called the police and was about to file a missing person report.

"You think it's OK for you to go out for a run and not show up for seven hours? What in your upbringing would ever let you think that was OK?"

I was standing close to her, obviously very angry.

"I met some people," she said.

"Did they live on Pluto?"

We went around and around like this for a while, getting nowhere. Then she turned abruptly, went into the bedroom, closed the door to the bathroom hard, and turned on the shower.

Tommy Boyan rule number one for parents: instead of arguing with a teenager, just stick your head in the microwave and set it for Cook Bacon. The results will be the same, but at least the cleanup will be easier.

The next day I got her out of bed at eleven and over cereal laid out some ground rules. Despite the rules, over the next two weeks the disappearances occurred with some regularity, though not as long as the first one. Our conversations afterward were just as abrupt and unsatisfying. When I told her we had to talk, and sat down facing her across my kitchen table, she sulked. I told her I was making an appointment for her to see Kate, the counselor recommended by the woman at her school in Evanston.

"Why?" was all she would say, to which I answered that she'd been through a lot and now seemed determined to put me through a lot, too.

"So maybe *you* should see her," she said.

"You didn't call Jenna?" Carrie Raynor asked at Chase's follow-up a few days later.

"Why not?"

Chase just shrugged.

I'd looked forward to this appointment ever since the night Chase disappeared for seven hours. Among the swirl of new people I'd met since flying to Chicago a month earlier, the young ortho seemed to connect with Chase more than anyone, certainly more than I did.

"Come on, girl. It's time to start putting things back together! I'll call her for you – OK? I'll tell her all about you; it'll be great!"

Before Chase could object, and it wasn't clear to me that she wanted to object, the doctor pulled out her cell phone and left a message for the coach. She seemed to understand intuitively that Chase needed work on a lot more than her damaged knee. Carrie glanced at her watch.

"Could you both hang out here for about twenty minutes? Then maybe Chase and I could run out for an iced tea?"

We waited; then the doctor came bustling out of the warren of hallways off the waiting room and left me alone with my phone. They were gone for nearly an hour. When they came back, Carrie gave me instructions where to find her friend Jenna, hugged Chase, and apologized to a woman and a young boy with his leg in a cast who were sitting in the waiting room.

As we were leaving, Carrie called to me. "Could you give me a call? In a day or two?"

From the way she glanced at Chase already out in the hall, I understood that this was between us.

Two hours later, Chase and I had taken the Green Line train from Children's a few stops up Huntington Avenue and were standing in a hot indoor arena at Northeastern University. Carrie's friend Jenna ran a summer soccer camp for inner-city kids on the university's basketball courts.

Jenna Eisenbech had a boyishly plain look about her: shoulder-length brown hair, thick eyebrows, lots of teeth, and a way of drilling her eyes into people when she listened that was disconcerting. No nonsense, this Jenna. Her attractiveness – slim, long legs; athlete's grace; her laugh; her brains; her smile – crept up on you over time. At first she was disconcerting.

Between our leaving Carrie's office and arriving at Northeastern, the doctor had obviously talked to the coach.

"So," Jenna said, ignoring me after a quick handshake. "You're the Bicycle Girl."

Chase's face took on a sour look.

"Hey, a little fame can't hurt. Carrie says your knee's coming along. What do you say?"

Chase tightened. She wasn't good with strangers. She finally drew out an "OK" seemingly from some private depth, like a deep-sea diver.

"Just OK? So what do you want to do?"

"Play."

"Good. We'll take it really easy. Besides, I won't have room on the roster until August anyway. We're going to Score at the Shore in North Carolina in July – you been there?"

Chase had not.

"I'll probably take at least three subs, so I don't think I could guest you, but it's possible. Forward is not my biggest weakness right now. You always play up top?"

They continued this sort of jargony talk long enough for Jenna to unwrap Chase a little, until she asked about her immediate plans.

"If you're just here for the summer and want touches, I'd be glad to let you train with us for a few weeks. But most of my team is pretty scattered right now and I'm starting high-school tryouts in August."

She looked at me. "You have a timeline yet?"

"Day to day."

"Well, that's cool."

She looked Chase over again.

"You got a weight room?"

When Chase shook her head, Jenna looked at me again. "You got a car?"

This led us to Newton the next afternoon, where Jenna worked at the larger Newton high school as a health teacher and head soccer coach for the girls' varsity. The school building was open all summer; Jenna managed to secure access to the school's elaborate training equipment and practice fields for her club players as well as her high-school team. She was getting out of her Toyota in the faculty parking lot when we drove up.

"Wow," she said, arms open, taking in my car when we wheeled to a stop in front of her. "That's impressive."

I drove a 1959 Jaguar XK150, royal blue with burgundy leather interior, a classic I'd bought ages before with an unexpected windfall and had spent far too much money maintaining ever since. Living and working in Boston, I'd been able to keep the mileage and maintenance down; the car could be horribly unreliable when really needed. And it had its dings. But there was no doubt it was a beauty. I loved it: the deep-throated, earthy roar of the double-overhead cams. The long bonnet, the smell of the hides. The useless radio. The canvas top that leaked in buckets. Chase's long legs barely managed to fit in the shallow foot well. She'd ridden in the car on visits to Boston before her mother's death, and always enjoyed it. In the ride out to Newton, she'd closed her eyes like a cat. Meaning hard to read.

The weight room was empty, but by the time Jenna finished giving us a tour of the school, players had begun gathering out on the field behind the building. A young assistant had set up orange cones and a half dozen players were warming up when Jenna led us outside.

"You feel like a little work?" Jenna asked, and when Chase shrugged, Jenna told her to take a few laps and warm up easy. As Chase set off around the field, Jenna signaled the other girls to join her.

The assistant walked over, ignored me, and asked Jenna, "Is that her?"

Other players arrived; soon a dozen or more young women were running and then began sorting themselves into warm-up drills.

"So how's she doing?" Jenna asked me.

"I really don't know."

Chase was the tallest girl on the field, but there were a couple of girls who were close. Most of the girls looked more full-bodied, with the thick boyish musculature of many women athletes. Chase looked unnaturally thin.

"She eat?" the assistant asked, as if noting Chase's stature at the same moment.

"All the time. And I'm pretty sure she keeps it in."

"Well you never know that," Jenna said. Which made me feel like clunking her on the side of her head with a brick.

Chase could not help but look awkward in the elaborate knee brace that covered most of her leg. As they shifted to the middle of the field to do warm-ups with balls, I couldn't detect her favoring her left leg at all. She seemed to move effortlessly, and I could only hope she was being careful and not pushing herself. While some of the other girls kept possession of the ball longer in shooting drills, dribbling and moving around other players before kicking the ball toward the net, Chase just seemed to flick the ball into the goal each time she touched it. I had no way of evaluating her play. The two women said nothing.

"How's she look to you?" I asked Jenna.

"Good. She's being careful."

When Jenna sorted the players for a scrimmage, she told Chase to take a few more laps. Another girl – who also wore a knee brace – was told to join her. The two lapped the field complex slowly, the other girl chatting easily, Chase looking at the ground. Jenna left the scrimmage and had Chase and the other girl do running drills on the next field while she watched. I stood alone, a soccer field away, wondering if Jenna was letting Chase overdo it.

From the field, the girls went into the weight room. After looking through the door a few times to see what Jenna had Chase doing, I leaned against a wall nearby.

A few parents who had dropped off their girls in the parking lot earlier were now waiting like me in the lobby. They sat on the stairway that led up to a mezzanine. I smiled, they smiled; it seemed to stop there.

Then one of them called out to me. "How's the knee?"

I shrugged, like Chase. The three of them slowly began talking to me so I had to go over and mingle, which was fine. I do the mingle thing pretty easily.

We all had younger girls; the older ones drove themselves to practice. They were all Newton parents whose daughters played for the high school and assumed Chase played for Juventus. The two mothers – one of whom, named Ellen, was a dazzlingly beautiful brunette, with a prohibitive rock on her left hand – wanted to figure me out. The father, whose name was Dan, wanted to talk about his girl. All three of them were pretty friendly. Dan went on and on about his daughter and her club and how they were nearly as good as Juventus, and it got a little tiresome. The second mother, whose name was Lee, wanted to talk about injuries. Her daughter was the girl in the brace who ran with Chase. We sat on the steps gassing for nearly an hour, but the girls were still in the weight room. I'd glanced in once and Lee sympathized when I said I wondered about my daughter doing too much.

"She will, they all do," she said with the fatigue of experience.

Ellen wanted to find out more about my daughter. I sensed a kind of edginess there; her daughter had played forward for the freshman team the year before and hoped to make varsity. She asked where we lived, and when I said Boston but that we were looking around, the conversation changed. Ellen was a realtor; she fished a card from somewhere, joking about not wanting to encourage competition in a way that hinted at some genuine ambivalence. Now Dan and then Lee wanted to know more about us. I just said that things were up in the air for both of us. The "both" seemed to have meaning for the women, and they backed off in their questions. Dan kept pushing for Chase's soccer pedigree, but I just said she played out of state and started ducking their curiosity after that.

"She's tall, she should play basketball," Ellen said, which struck me as funny but I stayed polite.

As the girls began filtering into the hallway, Ellen seemed to decide in favor of seeing me as a possible client and told me to call her. I was then left in the hallway alone. Chase and Jenna stayed after the others, huddling in a corner on a mat. The knee brace was off, and Jenna was manipulating Chase's injured leg, much the way Carrie had done in her exam.

"Hungry?" I asked Chase as the three of us walked to the parking lot. Chase and Jenna both said yes at the same time. I followed Jenna's Toyota to a Subway not far from the school and the three of us were soon eating sandwiches on a little tin table. Chase had tried to order an Italian sub, but Jenna told her she should not eat that fat, and both of them ordered veggie subs. It became clear that Jenna was recruiting Chase not only for her club team but for the high school as well. And she was good at it. She knew what not to say to teenagers. She didn't push. She kept her questions simple, looked straight at Chase, and didn't talk until Chase looked straight back.

I could see that Chase was taken with Jenna in a way that was different from the way she dealt with the others, except Carrie Raynor. She didn't put her head down and shrug, and in a minor miracle of communication actually spoke in sentences. They talked about what Chase saw in her future: over the next year, college, even beyond. I learned that Chase deeply wanted to play Division I college soccer, and that she had no idea beyond soccer what she imagined for herself.

"I don't know what I want to do with my life," Chase said all of a sudden. "All I've ever thought about is soccer."

Jenna told her that was exactly right; she was where she should be in her thinking. She was too young to worry about life after soccer but not too young to have long-term goals in their sport and to begin seriously thinking about what colleges might work for her.

As we washed down the last of our sandwiches, Jenna said, "You should play for me. I know things are tough for you right now, but we can help each other."

Chase gave her little half smile. I could see she was pleased. I took my shot.

"She's not going to play for anyone if she's out late all the time and I don't know where she is."

Chase rolled her eyes and sighed loudly in protest. Jenna sized up both of us, as if recalibrating the relationship, then looked squarely at Chase again.

"Your dad's the boss," she said with conviction.

I could have jumped across the table and kissed her. Instead, I fingered Ellen's card in my pocket, admittedly with enormous ambivalence. I'd spent most of my life in Boston.

That evening after dinner, while Chase watched a movie on MTV, I was standing out on my two-foot-wide balcony when the buzzer for the downstairs door sounded. It was Carrie Raynor. She breezed into my apartment, looked around the living room and said, "This is so nice!"

The living room was most of the apartment – open through the kitchen, the alcove, out to the balcony. All told it was pretty small, but it gave a better first impression. There were bookcases covering two of the walls and very old beams in the ceiling, and after I bought it I'd had a row of windows changed into a very large picture window that looked out toward the river. She looked around and seemed genuinely impressed.

"Very cool," she said.

Chase got up from the couch and Carrie greeted her warmly. "I just came by to see how you liked Jenna," she said, then talked briefly with Chase about the coach.

I offered Carrie a beer, which she accepted. After a while, the two of us stepped out onto the little balcony.

"So I checked you out," she said. "I read one of your stories online."

I may have looked a little puzzled, so she said, "In *Ploughshares*? 'Asleep in Warm Water.' I loved it!"

"Oh, thanks." I almost said ancient history, but I was not about to diminish the impression this woman seemed to be forming of me. Truth was, I'd written stories a very long time ago for a few of the small fries, and turned out a few articles a year as a contributor to the *Boston Globe*, but I'd never been able to make a go of it as a writer since I had to eat more than once a month.

I shifted the conversation to Chase because I was curious to know what she wanted to tell me without Chase around. She said Chase was deeply grieving for Taylor and needed counseling, that this should be a non-negotiable. She had recommendations for a therapist but would also check out Kate, the woman I'd already called, who sounded reasonable to me. She laughed when I suggested almost seriously that she be Chase's counselor. She said she'd lined up appointments for Carrie with Kate every two weeks and would catch up with me from time to time if that was OK. She was obviously taken with Chase. Carrie said Jenna would be great for Chase because the two of them were dedicated athletes who could speak each other's language. I'd already seen that. Then she delivered the message that she'd come to talk about and the advice stung me.

"You keep trying to figure out what Chase wants, Tommy," she said. "You need to make clear to her what you want. She's confused, she's a kid. You're her father. She needs to know you want her. If you do, it's time to step up."

4.

If I walked down our short dead-end street to what's left of the town forest, I could stand on the commuter-train platform and look out over the eleventh hole fairway of the golf course. From there I could watch her circling, stepping lightly in the first cut of rough as she sped through her laps. The first few mornings after we moved to the suburbs, I set my alarm at five fifteen so I could be out there when she first turned off of Brook Lane onto the course.

I don't really know why I felt compelled to watch her. At that hour in the summer it was dark, but the August heat would quickly burn off the eddies of mist lingering above the wet grass. I could see her most of the way around the loop she liked to follow at the edge of the fairways, on the holes that were out of view of the clubhouse. After a few days, I no longer needed to set the alarm; I could hear her moving through the kitchen and out the back door. I worried about her being out there. The town newspaper regularly reported on rabid raccoons, and coyotes apparently had become a common sight; though I never saw one, a neighbor closer to the golf course claimed his terrier had been eaten by them. I'd lived all my life in cities. Somehow it had seemed safer in the city, where she loped along the Esplanade and I only had to worry about nutcases.

When she came into view, emerging from the mist like some primordial creature, she moved quickly, in silence, workmanlike, looking down at the ground a few feet ahead of her dew-soaked Nikes, unaware of my watching from a distance. If she knew, she'd be more angry with me than usual. But there was nothing I intended to do about that. In actuality, I only went out there a few times to watch. I more or less grew used to the idea, and despite the promise of diseased predators, the golf course after all seemed pretty civilized. At least I knew where she was.

Carrie had OK'd the morning runs but continued to monitor Chase's activity throughout the summer. Jenna, another of the new women suddenly in my life, thought the extra workouts were wonderful and wished the rest of her players did the same.

Soccer turned out to be a very big deal for girls in Newton. It was a big deal among high-school boys as well, and the boys had football. The girls had field hockey, but soccer was the "A" sport. Soccer was well organized throughout the state for players from a very early age, so the parents were often as deeply engaged in the sport as their children. It was routine to see parents lined up thick along the edge of soccer fields every Saturday morning as kids not much older than tots roared across the grass, swarming after the ball. Sometimes I'd get to a field to wait for Chase to finish practice and watched games on the other fields. I couldn't quite believe some of the things I saw. Parents shrieking at little kids to "Mark up! Mark up!" Fathers running along the sidelines as their eight-year-olds broke away with the ball toward the goal, shrieking, "Shoot! Shoot!" It was also not unusual for teenage refs to be screamed at by some parents. This was an incredible thing to witness, very like a mugging: a girl Chase's age in a yellow shirt blows a whistle, and suddenly grown men are screaming at one another and calling the girl blind because she saw a collision between a pair of ten-year-olds differently than their fathers did. The older the players, and the higher the level of competition, the more hostile the sidelines could become, but this made some sense to me: there was something at stake for the high-school players, who all hoped for rides to colleges.

It wasn't just the intensity of the game. It was the way the parents all seemed to care, so deeply, how their child performed. It all seemed to me to be a mush of issues: equity, parental pride, public success, and possible embarrassment. Out on those fields their kids were performing in front of everyone; it wasn't like the privacy of a classroom, where only the kids saw what was going on. I couldn't relate to all this intensity. It didn't seem cruel or stupid. It was something new in my experience, how being a parent could sometimes express itself: to care so very much about something that seemed inherently unimportant, a game. From thinking at first, "these people are all whacko," I began to understand that there were entire fields of passion and engagement that had been absent from my life. I felt left out.

The selection process for the high-school girls' soccer teams in Newton was so competitive, and the scrutiny on the coaches so intense, the schools actually brought in independent evaluators to score the candidates each year and report the scores and the criteria to the public. It sounded so extreme it was comical, until I found myself in the middle of it. The extremes were not limited to the field. In the same way that some parents would change residences or spend small fortunes to send their children to high schools that would improve their college chances, the parents of some athletes would do the same to help their child earn a soccer uniform. As ridiculous as this sounded to me when I first heard it, I had to admit that in a way I'd done something similar with Chase. I'd made a decision where to live based on a soccer coach. And I was getting up at five in the morning to watch my daughter run around a golf course.

But there was another consideration at work here, too. After spending a fair amount of the summer mingling with parents from the club and the high-school teams, I began to feel myself lucky to have an athlete as a child, one who focused at least some of her energy on healthy pursuits. The anecdotes about other children, and the bad habits and affiliations they got themselves into, were more disturbing than the thought of hungry coyotes.

Despite her general reticence, I could see that Chase liked our new home, a three-bedroom I'd rented because my condo in Boston wasn't selling. The house was built on spec and hadn't sold either; it was so new the windows still had their little stickers. I knew Chase liked the golf course and her private mornings out there stirring the night mists. Maybe she liked the newness of the house or maybe, as Carrie told me, she liked that I stepped up and told her what we were going to do.

Which was exactly what I'd done, not long after we started making the daily schlep out to Newton for workouts with Jenna. On our way back to Boston one evening, I pulled over on Commonwealth Avenue near Boston College and just said, "It's time we made some decisions. I'm looking for a house for us in Newton. I want you to live with me. I know we don't know each other very well yet but you're my daughter and you impress the hell out of me. What do you say?"

She shrugged as she watched a pair of runners glide down the grassy strip in the middle of the street.

"I'm not sure what that shrug means. It's pretty much a yes or no question, Chase. We can talk about it. I'd love to talk about it. But it comes down to a decision for both of us and I've made mine. Do you want to live with me or not?"

"What's Gramma going to say?"

"She wants what's best for you. I think you probably know what's best for you as well as anyone."

"OK."

"OK what?"

"OK, I'll live with you."

"Chase." I used Jenna's approach, waiting for her to look at me. "I don't want to be an asshole here by pushing you too hard. OK sounds like you'll go along with it. If that's all you feel, then that's the way it is and I'll accept that. But is it what you want?"

"Yes," she said, growing quickly annoyed. "What else do you want me to say?"

"I guess that's it."

And that was it. It had to be. No loving gush, no fond embrace, just a testy exchange in a leaky old Jaguar during rush hour on the edge of Boston. I guess I did want more from her, more affirmation, or gratitude, or certainty, or some sign that this was truly what she wanted rather than what she accepted as a kind of default. I was relieved to have things decided. And yet I felt this welter of sadness. Chase had given me all she had to give. The exchange made me painfully aware of how much she was hurting, and how little affection there was between us that I could use to comfort her.

Near the end of August, my brother Fergie worked with Maris's attorney and the Chicago lawyer I knew from Boston College to wrap up the issue of Chase's custody. Fergie thought it was going to be a *pro forma* decision, since Chase was my daughter and Taylor had specifically written in her will that she wanted me and not Maris to have custody in the event of her death. But nothing was going to be simple with Maris. Her lawyer had filed some motion with the Chicago court to delay the decision again. Fergie went out to Chicago himself to deal with it, deciding it was better at that point for Chase and me not to be there.

A social worker and an officer of the court then came to visit us in Massachusetts just as we were in the process of moving from my apartment to Newton. Both homes were in complete chaos. The court officer wanted to see a copy of the lease on the Newton house, and the social worker spent some time with Chase while she unpacked her clothes in the new place. A few days later, my friend in Chicago called to say that Maris was trying a few other legal moves and was not going to let this go without a fight. Among other little gems of family romance, her lawyers raised the question of whether Chase was in fact my daughter. The judge declined to pursue this challenge since there was simply no reason to give it any credence. Despite Maris's last-ditch efforts, the judge ruled in my favor and custody was awarded to me without stipulation.

When my lawyer called and read me the brief decision of the court, I got this sudden choking feeling in my throat. It hit me so suddenly it was as if the ground had momentarily disappeared under my feet. Maybe a part of it was the speed with which the whole thing had come about: a death, a phone call, a move for both Chase and me into a totally new lifestyle. Maybe part of it was the recognition that this was going to cost time, money, a huge amount of energy, and a lot of emotional capital. The main thing I felt, though, was a sense of surprise and even pride – that this big, gangly, surly girl whom I didn't know very well was mine, my daughter. When she came home from a nearby field where she'd begun to work on her kicking, I said to her, "The judge issued the final custody orders this morning."

She stopped going through the refrigerator. "I'm staying here, right?"

"Of course."

She took a clutch of Vitaminwaters and an ice bag and went up to her bathroom without another word.

For Newton girls who were soccer players, the fourth week in August was charmingly referred to as Hell Week. This was when all the aspirants for the soccer team spent six days doing double workouts to determine who would make the varsity and junior varsity teams and who would be forever cast into shame and oblivion. While the hell distinction supposedly referred to the rigor of the workouts in the hot summer weather, in fact, it described what the parents went through to try and lobby their daughters onto the team.

Jenna scheduled a parent meeting for eleven in the morning when the first session was done. She'd told me beforehand that this was her way of trying to control us; otherwise, so many parents would hang around throughout the week that it would distract the tryouts. At the meeting, Jenna, her assistants, and the JV coaches all introduced themselves, and then Jenna explained the selection process, introduced the independent evaluators, and talked about what she expected of players for the coming season. She sounded direct, blunt. She said all decisions about players, position, and playing time were ultimately hers. She told people to stop sending her emails. She cited some numbers about the emails she'd received from prospective parents. It was pretty humorous, but a lot of people weren't smiling. We sat at picnic tables spread out on the shady porch of a large gazebo where the snack bar operated, though Jenna had already told us the snack bar would be closed for the week. We knew from home mailings that athletes would be responsible for bringing their own drinks and that there would be a lunch break of an hour only on Monday, after which they would picnic at the gazebo without the parents. Jenna sounded friendly but no-nonsense. She invited questions, saying, "This is your chance."

From the questions, I got another dose of the soccer craziness in my new town. Only a minority of the parents actually asked them, but whenever a question was raised about decisions or judgments, a lot of heads at those picnic tables started nodding.

"What if my daughter learned a different style of play than you're looking for. Will you give her a chance to learn your system?"

Nods.

"You've talked about commitment. Will girls who have decided to focus only on soccer be given more consideration than those who play other sports?"

More nods.

"How can you tell from watching a few drills and scrimmages how a player will hold up through a whole season?"

"Is it true that the daughters of town coaches have the inside track?"

Many nods.

Questions about injured players got the heads going like boppy toys. Several parents had daughters with recent injuries: how did the coaches plan on adjusting tryouts for them? Jenna's answer to this was not universally satisfying. She simply said she had seen most of the players during town or club soccer and knew what they could do. If there was any doubt, she'd keep roster seats open on JV for injured players on the borderline and could move players up to varsity if they were ready. This generated a whole spate of questions: When did she see this girl or that one play? Did some club teams (hint, hint, meaning Juventus) have an advantage?

"What about a new player from out of town who's been injured?" a mother asked, and heads turned to me. With a few exceptions, I'd never seen most of these people in my life, so how did they know who I was?

"There's only one of those that I'm aware of," Jenna said.

"Are you keeping a roster spot for her?" someone else asked.

"Yes."

This was so end-of-discussion blunt that people clearly didn't like it.

"I guess I don't understand that," one of the fathers said.

I'd been surprised at how many fathers were at the meeting. Most of the people I'd met in Newton had only one spouse working, invariably the father. Yet here we were, men with jobs, sitting in the heat on an August Monday worried about our daughters making a team. I admit I felt this sag of relief when Jenna flatly said she was holding a spot for Chase. I sort of assumed it; but amid all the questions that morning I began to wonder. After all, none of us had ever seen Chase play. All she did throughout the summer was light touches and running drills, not even a scrimmage. Carrie had said emphatically: no cuts, meaning no running with sudden changes in direction. Yet somehow the word had spread among the parents that a new unknown girl with injuries was getting a lot of attention from the coach.

"So you're holding a spot for someone you've never even seen play?" someone asked.

Jenna closed her eyes a moment, as if deliberating something. "Chase Ellis has played on four national age-group teams and is one of the premier youth soccer players in America."

People were taken aback. Apparently the word had not spread that Chase was a blue-chipper. All eyes quickly turned back to me, followed by whispers and wide-eyed looks at one another. "National team" had magic to them. I felt this sudden rush of some indefinable sentiment; more than just pride, it was as if I'd made those national teams myself. It felt exactly like one of those rare and fleeting moments in my own youth when I won an event at a track meet: a warm sense of prowess as if I'd actually done something important, that all eyes were on me and that I'd earned the envy of others. People continued to turn and smile at me after the meeting continued. It felt good. Who doesn't want to be famous for something?

As parents moved to the parking lot after the meeting, the buzz about Chase was on. People wanted to know where she had played, where we were from, what her injury was, and how she made the national team. I was surrounded by a phalanx of moms and dads chirping with excitement. If ever a player got a free pass from parents at a soccer tryout, it was my daughter. How did they transmogrify from stranger suspicion into groupie grope so quickly? I could imagine the Google hits on Chase Ellis over the next hour while people took their daughters home for a quick lunch. And I was right. When I dropped Chase off at the field for the afternoon session, parents got out of their cars and stood around the Jag.

"I can't believe it," one mother exclaimed. "She's the Bicycle Girl!"

Two days later, while tryouts were still under way, the weekly edition of the *Newton Times* appeared in our driveway. Chase was front page, below the fold: it was her famous upside-down picture with a tickler to the sports section announcing "U.S. Team Player Joins Tigers." The photo caption read, "'Bicycle Girl' Chase Ellis to lead H.S. Girls' Soccer." Chase and her accomplishments were the lead for a story about the promising season ahead for the high-school team. Jenna was quoted cautioning people not to expect a lot right away from Chase because of her injury, but went on to say how excited she was to be coaching a player "with her incredible talent." A few of the players were quoted saying how excited they were to have her on the team and how well the team was expecting to do. A sidebar listed Chase's soccer accomplishments, along with a photo of her taken at tryouts in which she towered over the players pictured near her.

A shorter story with the famous photo appeared in the *Boston Globe* the following Saturday. Jenna was quoted in much the same way, and Carrie Raynor was in the story saying, "She should be back to form in no time."

And Chase was quoted saying, "I just want to play."

Saturday afternoon, on the last day of tryouts, parents showed up at the gazebo: to pick up their daughters, to lobby the coaches, or just to look at the point boards. The point boards, large posters tacked to a wall, included a list of all the girls' names in tryouts; there were more than a hundred fifty players, with their scores posted in each of a dozen different categories. The scores were awarded by the independent evaluators. No one hovered around the boards; people glanced at them, covertly, and the girls seemed to ignore them. The points ranged from a maximum of one fifty on down. While it was not cut and dried, players who scored a hundred or more made the team, those from a hundred down to eighty were JV, those below eighty were dog shit, kicked to the curb. Jenna and the other coaches were locked in a series of arguments with one parent after another protesting the points awarded their daughters. There were a lot of glum faces leaving the gazebo. It didn't matter; the team was picked. The season started at practice the following Tuesday.

Even though Chase had only been able to participate in some of the drills and none of the scrimmages, she'd amassed nearly a hundred points. It was made clear the first day that Chase was on the team; there was no reason to pad her score. This seemed odd to me, but no one seemed to notice. Maybe it was the power of reputation, or even celebrity. Or maybe, as I suspected, it had something to do with all these points and judgments being incredibly subjective, and if someone had confidence in a player for any reason, they gave her big numbers.

As cars slowly left the parking lot, I joined a small group gathered on one of the side fields: Chase, in her ugly leg brace and looking sweaty; Jenna, with her hands on her hips looking tired; Kim, Jenna's assistant coach; a young woman named Samantha, the physical therapist who had been working on Chase's knee throughout the summer; and Carrie Raynor, who came out to the field to watch the last hour of tryouts and now wanted to evaluate Chase herself. After this, Carrie would be coming to dinner at our house. From across the field, several die-hard soccer parents lingered to watch the evaluation. I stood apart from everyone, on the sideline nearby.

Kim put orange cones on the field, and then in consultation with Carrie, led Chase through a series of drills: mostly cutting, left and right, around the cones, first without a ball and then with one. Jenna, still in her cleats. then faced off against Chase while Kim moved off to the side; the objective was for Chase to attack Jenna and work with Kim to put the ball between two cones a few feet apart. I felt like I was at the NFL Combine: so much attention by so many pros on one young athlete. Talk about excess.

Jenna took it to Chase. Both of them were thin, though Chase was a head taller and had those broad shoulders that made her look intimidating. But Jenna was buff from years of body work and seemed to have lost none of the quickness that had once earned her an All-America nod. Jenna pushed Chase hard off the ball, intercepted passes, stole the ball, and tapped it through Chase's legs. She pressured Chase to the sideline, pushed her with her side and back, and forced Chase to battle back or lose possession.

"Don't kill her!" Carrie anxiously coaxed, but Jenna continued to work her hard. Chase looked awkward, at times inept, always a half step too slow. She seemed to tire quickly, sometimes coughing. A few times Kim blocked out Jenna so Chase could get past the coach, but Jenna in a flash would be quickly back on her. A few times Chase made a nice touch, getting the ball deftly past Jenna as Kim looped behind the coach.

And then something more: one time, after Kim sent the ball to Chase and Jenna attacked, Chase suddenly moved with elusive fluidity. She faked to one side, stutter-stepped like a hoop player, and then with her injured leg somehow flipped the ball over Jenna's head. She spun her body across the coach's outstretched leg in time to catch the ball high in the air on her cleat and touch it back to Kim precisely on the woman's foot. Even I could tell this was a stunner.

"Whoa," Kim said, stopping to look at the girl. "You've been holding back!"

Jenna playfully pushed Chase's shoulders from behind with both hands. Chase half smiled.

Carrie yelled, "That's enough. Jesus, you guys!"

Kim produced a six-pack of Vitaminwater from a cooler and the women sat on the field drinking while I lurked nearby fiddling with the soccer ball. Carrie knelt down and helped Chase take off her brace and cleats. As Chase ripped the Velcro on her shin guards, Kim gagged and beat the smell away with her hand, drawing a laugh.

Carrie had Chase lean back while she moved her leg back and forth, twisting Chase's knee from several angles, sometimes hard, then digging her thumb into the soft areas around and behind the knee.

A few times Chase winced, though she tried to stifle them.

"It should hurt, baby," Carrie said, pulling a loose strand of Chase's hair behind her ear.

Carrie sat back, finished her exam and said, "Ice." Kim produced a bag and covered Chase's knee with it.

"So what do we think?" Jenna asked. "Chase?"

Chase, who had had a persistent head cold throughout the summer, started to say "OK," but went into a sneezing jag, then blew her nose on her shirt.

"Sam?" Jenna asked the physical therapist.

"Good balance, excellent lateral movement, good flex. Excellent quad strength." Samantha took a turn examining Chase's knee then looked at Carrie.

"Maybe a little swelling back around the bursa and on the inside?"

"Right," Carrie said. "There's a fair amount of atrophy still in the quads despite the work she's been doing. And a little tenderness here and there that we want to keep an eye on. What'd you think, Jenna?"

"Her condition's not great, which makes sense, but that's when injuries happen. She hasn't had a lot of touches in a long time but her skills are unbelievable. Her speed off the ball when she uses it is fantastic."

"Yeah," Kim said, "we can run her up and down the field like a crazy person and use her as a decoy."

This drew a laugh from Chase, a rarity.

Jenna looked at Chase. "You feel a little tentative in the fifty-fifties?"

"Yeah."

"What's in your head then?"

Kim answered for her. "David Perry in his yellow Mustang?"

Chase wrinkled her mouth. "I hate the brace. When I move to the left, I feel like I'm going to fall over it like it's a wall or something."

"OK," Jenna said. "What else?"

Chase wiped her nose on her shirt again. "This damn cold. I feel like I can hardly breathe."

"Allergies," Carrie said. The others nodded.

"What else?" Jenna asked again.

A reddish-colored dog frolicked onto the field nearby, then turned and ran off after a crow that was picking at the ground.

"I'm playing like shit," Chase said.

"OK, why do you say that?" Jenna pushed.

"I can't do anything."

"It's going to take a while."

"What if I don't get it back?"

Carrie tenderly put her arm around Chase's waist. "It's coming, baby. It takes time."

The women all nodded.

"So?" Jenna said, looking at Carrie. "What's the verdict?"

"Let's see how she does in full practice. No game minutes yet, obviously."

Chase sighed.

"There's no hurry. Maybe a little scrimmaging next week. Let's take this a step at a time."

"It's been a year," Chase, the center of this extraordinary scene, said mournfully.

"So another two weeks won't make any difference," Jenna said.

Kim pushed Chase back on the grass. "You're just a big old smelly slowpoke and who needs your sorry ass anyway!"

Chase's dour look disappeared for a moment.

I'm not really sure how Carrie's joining us for dinner came about. I don't exactly remember asking her, and I'm sure Chase didn't; she still acted like a houseguest. I felt a little like a houseguest myself in our cookie-cutter colonial. Carrie was a decidedly attractive woman who looked like she was still an undergraduate but had to be over thirty. I don't know the med-school numbers. So is it possible that a great-looking Boston doctor from Harvard might be interested in a nearly forty-year-old single parent who did PR work and obviously didn't make banks doing it? It occurred to me that she'd built this idea of me that was a bit inflated: the Boston apartment with the river view (that I'd bought when those things were dirt cheap), the literary-journal stories (good luck to her finding more than a few of those masterpieces), and the connections with the Boston muckamucks that I developed through my work but were not really personal at all.

I'm not saying I didn't have assets. I wasn't bad to look at. Nearly six feet; thin but not gaunt, bit of a workout freak, blond-red sort of curly hair high on my forehead, very Irish face, not killer but something there that women liked. I knew this because all my life I'd never really had trouble getting the girl I wanted if I had a little time with her. The real secret of my love life: make them laugh. Friendly, get them laughing, but don't be too much of a joker, then make a small move but let them know it's coming so they don't bash me on the head with a brick. I've done pretty well with that formula. Long-term relationships? Crappola. So what about perky Dr. Raynor? Well she did laugh a lot – at all the right moments. I had to figure the game was afoot.

I'm not sure how it worked out that I'd cook dinner. Until Chase moved in with me, I never cooked. I made coffee. I microwaved when absolutely necessary. Mostly I ordered takeout, and if they delivered, I was a customer. I lived in the city; no one who lives in the city has to cook. I lived by that credo, even though I knew it was total bullshit.

The suddenly escalating number of women in my life all seemed to be in agreement that I needed to feed my daughter better. Cooking in my tiny Boston apartment was a joke. I needed to do a three-point turn to change direction in the kitchen. But in Newton, where all life converged in the supermarket, I knew I had to start working the spatula. I remembered Carrie saying something about liking fish and living on salad. Hey, I could make salad, just chop and toss. I had plenty of leafy stuff in the fridge, all guilt purchases. And fish: well, I had a broiler; they swam, so just drown them in butter. Problem was, I had to work that Saturday, couldn't get out to tryouts until late when they were just about done, so I bought the fish the day before. Big mistake.

After we finished with Chase's evaluation at the field, Carrie, who had driven out to Newton in her Lexus, went gaga when she saw the Jag. Probably why I kept it all these years.

"Oh, my God. It's so cool!"

She jumped into the driver's seat, waved to Chase to jump in, and announced that I'd drive her car and she'd follow me. It was a muggy afternoon, over ninety all day; she was wearing black shorts down at her hipbone and a sleeveless emerald green top that stopped about an inch above the shorts. Her black hair was swept up above her long neck. I was not going to protest. She wiggled the gear shift and looked at me curiously.

"What's this thing?"

Before I could panic, she laughed. So she was into gotchas. But it made Chase laugh, second time in one day, practically a world record. She hit the starter button and Chase clicked on the crummy radio, producing static and classic rock in equal measures. Chase changed the channel.

When we clumped into our kitchen with the Jag after-run behind us, Carrie looked quickly at the place and said, "Do you miss your apartment on the river?"

I glanced at Chase and said not at all, an absolute lie.

Unfortunately, the smell of rotting fish would have totaled a grizzly. I'd put it in the freezer overnight thinking it would keep better, then left it on the counter in the morning because it felt like a shingle of slate.

"I just bought it yesterday," I complained, about to drop it in the waste basket. "How could it turn so fast?"

"No!" Carrie yelled, and stopped me from dropping it. "You think it's going to smell any better in there?"

As I wrapped it in newspaper that should have been read, I asked again. "Seriously, how could it turn bad like that, it was just off the boat yesterday morning?"

"Things turn quickly," Carrie said philosophically, finding this all very funny.

When I came back in from the garage, where I kept the garbage barrels, Carrie was already pulling things from the fridge and told me to wash my hands before I touched anything. "I think they need sand-blasting."

Chase perched herself on a stool at the ugly granite counter and was tearing apart pieces of wilted lettuce.

"Don't you want to shower, honey?" I said. An even bigger mistake than the fish. She shook her head in disgust and wordlessly stormed out of the room.

"I guess I didn't need to say that."

"No."

"I'm not too good at this."

"You're doing fine, Daddy-O."

We picked through the various bags of plastic from the veggie drawer, salvaging enough various kinds of lettuce to provide a platform for a salad.

"No, I'm not," I said, sounding a little whiny.

Carrie knew the bones of our family history: early marriage, early divorce, limited contact over the years, and a loving, wonderful, and competent mother who died in her sleep without warning. She said some things that were very reassuring, about me, Chase, and our short stay together so far, but I couldn't help but feel she was being polite more than actually commenting seriously on my limited parenting skills. There was no doubt that they were limited, and not just in the kitchen department.

I heard the shower start in Chase's bathroom upstairs. I told Carrie a little about Chase's penchant for disappearing, wandering off and connecting with strangers in Boston and then refusing to talk to me about it. I seemed to have no limit-setting skills and only managed to widen the gaps between us by taking her on and yelling when she failed to call or came in later than she'd agreed. I told Carrie the most I seemed to be able to get out of Chase was a shrug or a monosyllabic grunt from a face that had the look of constant disapproval.

"She just needs time, Tommy. Her mother was her whole life and she died suddenly. That's going to take a long time to work out."

Carrie and I had talked several times over the summer about Chase's visits to Kate, the therapist. My efforts with Kate to learn more about Chase had been politely rebuffed by the therapist in the interest of patient confidentiality, which I could sort of understand but also considered an utter pain in the ass.

"I heard Chase talk more on the field this afternoon than the entire summer combined," I said to Carrie. "We seem to have nothing to say to each other."

"Teenagers are tough," Carrie said. It occurred to me as I looked at the young doctor that it hadn't been all that long since she'd been one.

We talked for a while, mostly me venting and she offering encouragement. We both realized at the same time that the shower had been off for a while. Carrie went upstairs to check out Chase's room and draw her back downstairs. For a moment, as Carrie climbed the stairs, I imagined Chase having disappeared on the two of us, taking off for wherever it was she liked to go when she went out on her own. But Carrie did not come down right away, and I could hear across our carpetless floors the low murmur of conversation, mostly Carrie's voice punctuated by occasional silences or short responses from my daughter.

I drained a can of tuna fish that didn't smell much better than the haddock into a bowl and then added it to the salad and started chopping carrots and peppers. I also began making chocolate chip cookies, using the recipe on the back of the bag of semisweet chips. Women love chocolate, right? I was trying hard to decode the upstairs conversation and didn't realize right away that I had dumped the flower and sugar and butter into the bowl I'd used to drain the tuna. I was pretty sure I'd thrown out the juice.

A crash upstairs that sounded like furniture flying sent me running upstairs. On the way, I heard Chase's bathroom door slam hard and then slam a second time. A desk chair was upended on the floor and a few of Chase's things that usually sat on her desk were scattered across the floor. Chase was in the bathroom. A large picture of a young Taylor smiling like a fashion model hung alone on a wall above the desk.

Carrie was standing near the bed, looking stunned. We just looked at each other a moment. She held her hands at her sides palm-up, a gesture of confusion.

"She couldn't find an earring."

Chase did not come back downstairs for more than an hour. During that time, Carrie and I ate salad, along with grilled cheese sandwiches she'd made delicious by using gruyere cheese and adding oregano. I'd finished the cookies and they cooled on paper towels. Chase appeared, wearing plaid flannel pajama pants and a Northwestern sweatshirt despite the heat, and acted embarrassed.

"Sorry," she said to Carrie.

"Find the earring?"

"No."

"I hate when that happens."

Carrie made two grilled cheese sandwiches for Chase, who devoured them along with a pub glass full of skim milk and a shovelful of carrots and sliced peppers. The conversation centered mostly on Carrie as she responded to a string of my questions about her background. She'd gone to Harvard undergraduate as well as the med school. She was from San Diego: she desperately missed the good California weather during the New England winters, but loved the competition and challenges of the Boston medical scene.

"I love it here for that," she said. "I know I'm at the cutting edge."

"Where every surgeon wants to be."

"Oh, right. Hah!" She waved her fork like a sword at Chase's knee. "Look out, girl, or I'll fillet that kneecap!"

"No fish jokes, please," I said.

Early evening slipped into darkness as the three of us sat on stools at the kitchen counter. The conversation was almost entirely between Carrie and me. She made several runs at drawing Chase into the conversation, with very little success. Chase leaned back in her stool against the wall, arms crossed, picking at carrots or cheese dried on her plate. Carrie had a contagious laugh, throwing her head back and letting her shoulders bounce in pleasure. She asked about me, which was a lot less entertaining since I knew it all, but our talk began to feel like the exploratory give-and-take playfulness that can happen on a first date. Except for the six-foot teenager bundled in her sweatshirt who sat scowling next to us.

I kept reminding myself that Carrie should be here for Chase, and that I should find some excuse and let the two of them visit and enjoy one another. I was sure my presence was putting a damper on Chase, as it always seemed to do. But the truth was, I hadn't been with a good-looking woman for a while and I enjoyed her company. Once or twice my cell phone rang in the den but I let it go, I knew they were just calls from pushy clients.

Carrie noticed Chase's sneezing and runny nose. A pile of once-used tissues had accumulated in the trash barrel nearby.

"I want you to see an allergist in my building," she said confidently. "Did that start when you moved?" Chase shook her head, affirmative. "It probably has something to do with New England foliage," the doctor said. "This sort of thing happens to people a lot when they move." She looked at me. "You want me to set up a screening for her?"

"By all means." I started clearing the dishes.

"Are we going to eat the cookies?" Chase asked.

"The cookies!" Carrie said, and jumped up to get plates.

After biting into their first cookies, Chase and Carrie both stopped chewing and looked at one another. Chase let the cookie bite fall from her mouth onto a plate. Then Carrie did the same.

"What did you do?" Carrie demanded. She took a second one, bit it, and spit it out.

I took a bite of mine. "They taste like . . ."

"Stop!" I said, interrupting her. "I said no fish jokes."

Carrie hooted with unrepentant laughter.

Chase tossed her cookie like a Frisbee into the sink. "Pathetic," she said.

5.

I was not used to life in the burbs. In the first few days after we moved from Boston, I felt like I'd descended into the Great SUV Burying Ground. It seemed as if everything was a cliché of the American suburbs: moms shopping at supermarkets with their kids riding in baskets; all-white faces in loud pastels on the golf course; police who smiled and ate doughnuts; lawn sprinklers starting their daily hiss before dawn on street after street. I felt like the kid in the movie who fell through the TV into Pleasantville. There were almost no black people; the only groups of minorities showed up on the set-back streets with truckfuls of lawn mowers. Our house was one of four nearly identical buildings developed on a cul-de-sac near the edge of the town forest. Ours was the only rental; the developer who leased it to me believed I intended to buy the place when my condo sold, though he hadn't been able to persuade me to sign anything guaranteeing this.

I grew up in Dorchester, a neighborhood of Boston that at least to me at the time had the feel of a small town. We knew our neighbors, meaning we all knew who came home drunk at night, who beat his wife, whose cat pissed on the Sullivans' screen porch. Dorchester was OK for a kid and better for a teenager growing up, mostly because you could get out of it easily: hop on the Red Line, or when necessary, take a bus, zip, you're on your way in a few minutes to terrific ports of call: Quincy Market, Harvard Square, Back Bay, or the Wonderland dog track. In the suburbs, high schools are the center of social life for kids; in the city they're an interruption of it.

My parents were Melville Avenue Irish, with no lace in the windows, but all things considered, our family did well by Dorchester standards. Both my parents worked: my mother for a gajillion years at the Registry of Motor Vehicles near the Boston Garden, while my father managed and owned a piece of a bar in the South End called Drago's Bar and Sociable, one of the great watering holes of Western civilization; still is. My older sister, Trish, married a chef at one of those trendy waterfront restaurants, divorced him, then remarried him, then separated, then got back together, the ziplock-bag approach to marriage. My older brother, Fergie (OK, Fergus, a horrible name. In his cups, my father liked Yeats, but Fergie changed it to Ferguson when he was at UMass and no one called him any of that), is a lawyer and small-time pol, at one time the city's sheriff and now a member of the Boston City Council: Fergie Boyan, elected at-large every few years, probably thanks to his TV commercials selling his ambulance-chaser services. My younger sister, Anna, is a social worker at a very respected homeless shelter in the South End – a pretty, heart-of-gold depressive who has absorbed too much of her work and never goes home at the end of the day. We all stayed in Boston and see each other on holidays or if anything is wrong and often there is, and we routinely connect on the phone.

None of my family liked Taylor. They thought her a pole-up-the-ass WASP, a looker from New Canaan, Connecticut, which might as well have been Bel Air or Cannes or some other exotic domain they saw in movies but didn't believe in. We married young, just out of college. I went to Boston College, she to Harvard. We met in college somehow when I was working as a ward heeler in the early days of the Ray Flynn mayoral administration. The wedding was in the divinity school chapel at Harvard. My family came, and except for Fergie, who got soaked, and Anna, who kept trying to get spots out of Taylor's dress, the bride's friends and my friends mostly ignored each other. It rained. On the whole marriage, to tell the bitter truth of it.

Chase unexpectedly started her journey into life right around the time we were married, a honeymoon baby. We were both twenty-three when Chase was born. My family, especially my mother, would have died to help with the baby. We kind of hunkered down into an expensive apartment a few blocks from Harvard Square and Taylor dropped Chase off every day at a day care center next door to the building where we were married. Maris would drive up from New Canaan in her black diesel Benzo, take Chase for the day, and have dinner with Taylor at some restaurant, quickly passing to say hello to me as she reluctantly dropped off the baby. Taylor entered graduate school at Harvard when she was pregnant.

That was our relationship until Taylor met a lizard who worked as a postdoc at Harvard. When he left to take an instructor's job at the University of Chicago, she went with him, taking Chase. Fergie got me a lawyer and we all went at it, but Maris outgunned us. Taylor started to make a case for my being a slugger, which was never true, and a drunk, which was no more true for me than any other college kid in Boston, including Taylor. She got custody, broke up with the postdoc, then married another pole-up-the-ass named Dale Ellis, who turned out to be a real slugger, as well as a Hall of Fame lush. That divorce came through a few years later. None of Taylor's relationships lasted any longer than ours. Why did she change Chase's name to Ellis and never change it back to Boyan or McKinley after Slugger split? Now here's a peek into the character of my ex: because the Ellises were big money, that's why; they owned whole swaths of suburban Chicago. Which was another reason I didn't like the suburbs.

With good reason, since life in the burbs was less than excellent once I found myself out there with my suddenly full-grown daughter. We had to drive ev-e-ry-where. Not the sort of demand expected in the design of an old Jag. There were a lot of places where we could order takeout, but all of them were as bland as dirt. No Indian curries. No real Mexican. The only way to get something to eat with any taste was to drive into Boston or make it at home, and good luck with that. No Anna's Taqueria, my staple in the city. Newton described itself as a city, which of course was a joke. Boston is a small city. Newton is a town; forget about the structure of government. Any place with one Starbucks is a town in my lexicon.

For work, I had to take the commuter train into Boston, which was a total pain in the ass. I had great difficulty regulating myself by train schedule and missed my ride so often it became an embarrassment for me in my office. I grew up taking public trains, so what was the difference? The commuter train didn't come every two minutes and hardly stopped anywhere. Standing on the platform should have been a chance for some kind of social life, but even though people were highly routinized, taking the same train every day and even standing in the same places on the platform, they didn't talk to each other. They didn't make the obvious connections. It was more or less the same way they all seemed to disconnect with each other from their homes. Neighbors waved and at most would chat at the ends of their yards; no one got in each other's business. The kids played in playgroups or on teams and were driven everywhere instead of just spilling out onto the street to find out what was up.

There was virtually no diversity. Everyone was white, except the people who cleaned up property. One or two black families, a few Asians, were spread so thin around the neighborhoods that it was hard not to notice them. I grew up in a white enclave in Dorchester, no doubt about it, and there was probably as much racism on my street as anywhere in America. But for most city kids I knew, those of my own generation anyway, people of color were part of the variety and charm of life. At least that had been my experience, thanks to my mother and sisters and brother. In the condo where I lived for ten years, Beacon Street was an integrated neighborhood. And once you've lived that way, you miss it, you feel the thinness, the cheat of homogeneity. You miss those different faces, accents, cultural extras. I didn't feel like I could ever accept the absence of that. Maybe it was just a function of time, but I didn't want to ever get to the point where a white world was OK with me. I knew people far more politically sensitive than me who did make that adjustment, nominally, for their kids. Yet I couldn't help but feel that something else was going on there, something a little ugly. Maybe I'm whining again.

OK, there were some good things in the burbs. The house space. Chase could be in one room listening to music and I could be in another on my cell and we didn't hear each other. We had twice as many toilets as asses to put on them, always a good arithmetic. There was a predictable rhythm to things in the burbs, which sounds horrible but wasn't; people came and went at roughly the same times, the house lights went on, the lights went off, things quieted to an eerie stillness at night that turned out, surprise surprise, to be comforting. I never slept so well, one of the reasons I kept missing the damn train.

And sports. The town was sports crazy. Yes, Boston is infamous for sports lunacy. Go Sox. But it was different in the burbs. People actually played the sports they only watched in the city. Fields were everywhere. There was Little League and Pop Warner and more hoop than you'd ever find in your life in the Back Bay. Adult leagues abounded. There were dodge ball teams and volleyball tournaments, summer track for kids of all ages, road races, cross-country races, field day races, swim teams at the town pools, crowded tennis courts, and even serious bowlers. You could find this stuff in Boston, but you couldn't escape it in Newton.

More than anything, by a long shot, there was soccer. Town leagues, travel teams, club teams, indoor leagues, Futsal leagues, all ages, both genders: soccer was dominant. Soccer and all its attendant demands created social requirements and opportunities for a lot of families. A huge amount of people's discretionary time went into soccer. The people I got to know through Chase's teams became my social life outside the city. They were all a little soccer-crazed, with some serious blind spots about their daughters' playing abilities, and there was a subtext of competition among all of them that started with soccer but spilled over into other things as well, like who drove what and where whose kids went to college. But I started to get into it. It was seductive. I always liked competing. I liked games. And I loved the idea that my daughter was the best. Even if she wasn't, which of course was because of her injuries.

The high-school soccer season extended from the end of August until the middle of November, after which Chase's club, Juventus, would become active, with a series of tournaments, practices, and indoor demands. The high-school team was different from the club: more about social life, more rah-rah, more anchored in the fabric of high school and town. The club team, where the girls came from all over the state, was year-round, much more focused on the sport and at a higher skill level. It was good timing that Chase's reentry into active play was the high-school team. Jenna might have been even more cautious with Chase if her knee was green-lighted in the middle of club play.

With all the soccer activity, I hadn't given much thought to the high school itself. I did my homework before we moved; people who knew a lot more about schools than I did said our local high school was first-rate: good teachers, good facility, active parent groups, good numbers on the tests. I knew enough about education to understand that those all-important numbers were more a reflection of community economics than of anything schools did; but good numbers were good numbers and we all wanted them. Besides, I believed in public school. It never occurred to me that Chase might not have the same outlook.

At the end of the school day, Chase always had practice and managed to get rides home from a senior who drove to school and lived nearby. She'd usually be up in her room when I got home, making the short drive from the closest commuter station. She'd already hit the fridge and consumed all available junk, like ice cream and cookies and brownies; then she'd hunker down in her room. I'd go up to her door and knock, to let her know I was home.

"What," she'd say flatly.

If I made dinner, she either wouldn't eat it, or, if it was pasta or takeout, she'd take it into the family room off the kitchen and eat in front of the TV. I didn't think that was so great, but I was tired too, so I did the same. We watched the soccer channel mostly, sometimes *Seinfeld* or *Friends*. She knew all the episodes, but I only knew this through the very occasional comment she'd make, more to herself than to me, about what would happen next. I'd never been a big sitcom watcher. I felt this weight on me all the time, as if there were things I should have been doing with Chase that I knew I wasn't doing, like sitting down to meals with her at a table. We had this utterly useless dining room with nothing in it and a table in the kitchen where I stacked the newspapers.

I guess that was the real difference for me between life in the city and in the burbs. I was happy in the city; things were easy, predictable, entirely under my control, even the occasional Boston political *Gunfight at the O.K. Corral*. I could deal with that. But living amid so much grass and highway and middle-class standoffishness with a moody, unhappy teenager who glared at me every time I asked her if she wanted something to eat? Forget about it. Not what I bargained for. But there it was.

The school year started for Chase at the same time the high-school soccer season got under way. I dropped her off at school every morning before racing to the commuter station. I'd gone with her the first day, a half-day orientation for freshmen and new students, but left her there at her insistence once we walked in the door. I guess the discomfort of being new was outweighed by the anguish of being seen with a parent. The most I could get out of her when I asked how things were going was a shrug. I decided this wasn't good enough and tried pushing. She tended to be a little more responsive when I asked her non-personal questions, so I tried that approach. Were the lockers clean? She didn't have a locker. Did bells ring to end classes? No. Did most students take buses to get there? No, they drove or got rides. When this obviously anguishing grilling shifted ever so slightly to more evaluative questions, it started to feel like I was hauling freight. I tried the *Dragnet* approach, sticking to the facts. Did she want a locker? No. (Asking *why not*, too pushy, almost killed the dialogue.) Was her schedule the same every week? No, week A, week B. Did she think she was going to enjoy any of her classes? Shrug. End of conversation.

I found these nearly fruitless little exchanges maddening. But I had all these women in my life, or more to the point, Chase's life, who kept giving me advice. The one piece of wisdom I'd been able to squeeze out of Kate, Chase's therapist, had been to persist, that it was important for me not to just let her disappear into her shell but to try and engage her as much as she would let me. Easy for you to say, honey.

Samantha, Chase's physical therapist, said with enthusiasm that Chase's knee was making great progress; she was a workhorse, she'd be playing again soon. When I told her that Chase virtually refused to talk to me and spent all her time in her room, she said she did the same thing as a teenager. Didn't I? In fact, I didn't. I had two sisters and a brother to fight with constantly over space, food, TV, and who was it that used my hockey stick to stir paint. But Samantha, like everyone else directly connected to Chase's athletics, was thrilled to have a connection with her and just kept using that horrid cliché "all good"; what an imagination that suggested.

Carrie told me over the phone after the start of school much the same thing, and reminded me that Chase was missing her mother and that I was virtually new in her life so it would take time.

"I know a lot of people with teenage kids," Carrie said, "and they don't get any more out of them than you do."

This was supposed to be encouraging: raising teenagers may be horrible but at least it's horrible for everyone? Sort of like dying of nuclear fallout. Oh, good, we're all turning into rat shit; now I feel much better.

Before the first day of classes, Chase and I met with a guidance counselor, who received her transcript from the Chicago private school. Chase had excellent grades and the school had a good reputation. The counselor, who seemed a little ditzy, put her into a full load of Honors courses, which at this school was the name for the ball busters that had a higher GPA point value and allegedly had more pull with college admissions. She chose French as her foreign language, and based on her records, they put her in WL-3, which meant she was credited with two years of French from Chicago. This made sense: Taylor had been fluent in French; I remembered when Taylor used to drop Chase off in Boston on her way to Connecticut for those rare father's visits; their goodbye exchanges were in French. I couldn't speak a word of it, but their little conversations sounded French to me.

Generally, I stayed out of Chase's room, but one day shortly after school started we had to carry a new chair together up to her room. It was a heavy blue upholstered thing we bought at Crate & Barrel, expensive, but I could see she liked it from the way she sat in it at the store, so I splurged. The house had spare rental furniture, but unlike the house, it was not new; it had a kind of greasy yard sale feel to it and Chase silently turned up her nose. Up in her room, her clothes were all over the floor and a lot of the boxes from Chicago were still unpacked. On one shelf she'd put trophies, and on another were more pictures of Taylor: several studio portraits taken over the years and a lot of candids that Chase had stuck into a cork bulletin board she bought at Walgreen's. There was also an article about a book Taylor had published on some math problem.

"Oh," I said. "She wrote a book?"

Chase looked at me like I had the brain of a gnat. "She wrote lots of them."

This turned out to be an exaggeration, thank you, Google, but at the time I just nodded, impressed and wanting to change the subject. There was a color snapshot of Taylor looking very young laughing at the beach. "She looks really happy there," I offered.

"How would you know?"

"Well, I took the picture."

She looked at the photograph for a long three-count.

"Really," she said, not entirely suppressing her surprise.

"It was on Nantucket. We went there for our first anniversary."

"Well, I guess I'll never go to Nantucket then," she snapped and slammed into her bathroom. But at the last moment, before she banged the door shut, she looked back at me, eyes blazing, just for a second. I had no idea how to read that look. There was desperation in it; but it seemed mostly like desperation to get away from me as fast as possible. I turned back to the Nantucket shot as if it might have an answer, which of course it didn't. So I shook my head and left the room, shutting the door a little harder than necessary. I guess it was the language of the tribe.

Jenna Eisenbech became a different person on the sidelines of a game. Before the high-school season started, she seemed a little intense, but self-possessed and unflappable. With a game under way, she embodied too many of the clichés of sideline coaches. She was composed and unobtrusive until her team fell behind, and then she began to unravel. She paced; she screamed; she pulled players off the field with no apparent explanation, and sometimes chewed them out roundly, once even taking the girl by the jersey and getting in her face. Some of the parents complained, but from the safe distance of the opposite field, where we all stood or sat during the games. One parent defending her wondered why people allowed men to coach that way, but when a woman did it everyone began complaining.

Jenna had been the varsity's assistant coach the year before and was credited with the team's greatly improved season. Her record with the club team was beyond reproach. While club soccer operates in the rarefied atmosphere of soccer enthusiasts, high-school teams are more visible since they are more anchored in a single community. This may have been why Jenna started showing signs of stress. The team did not open the season well at all. An early *Boston Globe* pick to win the highly competitive Division I state title, the Tigers fell behind, with three losses in the first three games.

It wasn't just that they were losing; it was the way they were losing. In at least two of the games, parents on the sidelines all said Newton was the stronger team, controlling play and dominating possession. Soccer is a low-scoring game; a soccer goal is probably the rarest of points in sport, which means that underdogs have more chance to turn a game into a surprise victory. It can upend people's expectations. In the third game of the season, Newton played well but had several heartbreaking near misses, including two shots that banged off the crossbar. The game ended 1–0. The other team scored in the last two minutes when a swarm of players all hacked at the ball after a corner kick and a player knocked it from the hands of the keeper.

The Newton parents' reactions to the goal were extreme. Some complained of offsides – an impossible rule for me to decode. Most people screamed at the ref: the keeper had possession and it should have been the keeper's ball. To me this looked right. The Newton keeper had the ball in her hands and suddenly a foot knocked it away. We were standing very near the group of parents from the other school, who were yelling too, though they saw the play entirely differently and wanted a call against a Newton defender, who pushed the striker hard after a kick. When the ref let the goal stand, the other parents hooted while the Newton stands shook with stamping feet, catcalls, boos, and furious protests. After the game, the three refs fled quickly to their cars.

Jenna yelled at the ref herself, but not with the same outrage that she leveled at her players after the game. While the exhausted girls sat and drank water, Jenna yelled and used Kim, her assistant, to show the right way that things should have been done.

Chase threw her gym bag and backpack into the foot well of the Jag and stepped over the door into the seat of the convertible. From her scowl I knew to keep my mouth shut. She flicked on the radio and we rode home without a word. I could see that it was difficult for her to watch three games from the bench. She had been practicing with increasing intensity since the start of school, and had scrimmaged two days before their latest loss.

I wanted to sound sympathetic about the loss, so I broke the silence.

"Looked to me like your keeper had the ball."

"They're ridiculous! They don't know how to clear; they just stand there like stumps! It's pathetic," she shouted, punching her fists down into her seat.

I was too cowed to ask who she was talking about.

Later that evening, as Chase watched *Seinfeld* over a barely touched cheese omelet while I tried to figure out how to empty a vacuum cleaner, Carrie unexpectedly pulled into the driveway. It was the second time she'd stopped by since the night of the tuna cookies. She brought a fat bag of Fresh City veggie wraps and sat in the family room eating with Chase, clicking off the TV. Carrie had come to tell us she'd arranged an appointment with the allergist she'd talked about for the coming Saturday. While Carrie talked, Chase slowly consumed her wrap and then the one Carrie brought for me. I tried to stay away and act like I wasn't listening, but the empty dining room was like an amplifier for every sound from the kitchen area. After eavesdropping for about five minutes, I felt like a total boob. I went out in the garage to pour oil into my oil guzzler and after a while came back in to make decaf.

Chase shouldered her backpack with all her school books in it and clumped upstairs to her room. Carrie sat and sipped the coffee, the one thing I made that tasted edible.

"Do you have a problem with her playing?" she asked.

"Huh?"

Carrie laughed. "You look so goofy!"

She explained that Jenna had called her and wanted to know if Chase could play. Carrie apparently told the coach she'd already told Chase it was up to her at this point. I hadn't known that.

"So," I said, trying not to look goofy again. "What does that mean?"

"I guess it means she's a little hesitant about playing. She's experiencing the absolutely normal reaction of most athletes after a serious injury. They desperately want to play and are scared to death of it."

The front door banged, and we both watched Chase through a side window jog off toward the golf course. When she returned more than forty minutes later, Carrie and I were still sitting at the kitchen counter. Soaking wet, Chase, came into the kitchen, got ice cream out of the fridge, and started scooping. Carrie wanted some, too. This time I knew to keep my mouth shut about taking a shower. We sat there for some time, Carrie talking about growing up as a figure skater in San Diego.

"It never got colder than seventy and I chose a winter sport – go figure!"

"Need any help with your homework?" Carrie asked as Chase moved to leave.

"Uh, well, I guess not."

"OK, but let me know if you do, OK?"

It sounded to me like Chase wasn't sure what she wanted, but Carrie didn't move.

It was getting late and there was a proposal sitting unfinished in my laptop that I needed to email a client before the next day, but we were still gassing in the kitchen. Carrie liked to talk. I had to keep telling myself this was an over-thirty medical specialist at one of the world's great pediatric institutions. She seemed a little like another teenager, the antidote to the surly one. I wasn't complaining. Not about Carrie anyway.

The next game was away, in Braintree, another *Globe* top preseason pick, and one that had made the state semifinals the year before. The game was practically a slugfest. The Newton parents who showed up in droves kept complaining that the ref had lost control, though the one thing he surely couldn't control was the partisan fury from both sides of the crowd. The word on the Newton side was out: if I had a nickel for every parent who asked me if Chase was going to play I could have bought diamond earplugs.

About ten minutes into the second half, with still no score on either side, Chase moved to the midfield line waiting to sub in for the first time.

"Now we see," one of the fathers said a little cynically, making me wish I had those earplugs.

I'd never seen Chase in a game before. The only thing I could see distinctive about her was her height, but this was not much greater than several of the other girls. She was put at right forward. I'd learned recently that this was the top scoring threat. She looked stick-thin, and to me a little awkward, moving up and down the sideline in steps and jerks, watching the ball, and trying once or twice to make runs though the ball didn't come her way. It was hard not to notice the nearly full-length brace on her left leg. She was on the opposite side of the field from the sideline crowds. When she did get the ball, she flicked it away quickly, once or twice holding it briefly and then sending it back to the midfield. There was absolutely nothing distinctive about her play as far as I could tell; she might as well have been invisible. She was subbed out after just eight minutes. I know because for some stupid reason I timed it.

After this, several parents asked me, "Is she OK?"

I would just say, "She's playing," which would usually elicit some sort of upbeat response.

With about fifteen minutes left in the game, Braintree scored. Newton parents complained about the defense breaking down, at least those parents did who weren't sitting or standing near the parents of defenders. Jenna was reamed out in absentia by a whole cluster of parents in the bleachers for her substitutions and the formation she was using.

"The girls aren't getting it!" one mother complained.

Chase was subbed back in with about five minutes to go, and once again moved up and down the sidelines following play but getting only a few brief touches. Across the field, Jenna was growing more agitated. When a ball was knocked out of the end of the field by a defender, a Newton midfielder set up to take the corner kick. Jenna ran along the sideline waving and screamed across the field. She wanted Chase to take it. I could hear a few grumbles among the parents wondering about this decision.

Chase ran quickly across the field, and waited a moment while the Newton players shifted around the goal. The ref waved at her. She stepped into the ball with her right leg and launched it hard. It zoomed out high over the players like a rocket and unexpectedly arced inward just past the keeper, then banged off the far post into the goal. Tie game.

It was as if world peace had been declared or we all just won *American Idol*. Everyone from Newton launched themselves into the air, me higher than anyone. Across the field, Jenna pumped her fist. Newton players swarmed Chase, who stood with her arms at her sides and the half smile on her face. The team then ran back to the midfield, mindful there was still time for a win on the clock. But three chirps of the whistle ended the game soon afterward. People were still elated.

"She bent it!" they yelled. "She bent it!"

"That's what I'm talking about!" the cynical father yelled.

I felt like my whole body had been lifted up by invisible hands. I had to turn away from people congratulating me because tears were welling up in my eyes. Wow, I thought, wow, she really is something different, to pull it out like that. I'd loved sports all my life. That kick was the kind of thing that champions did. I laughed to think of all the clichés about digging deep and what happened when the best got going – they all suddenly seemed utterly true.

"The season starts now," someone said as we crossed the parking lot, the elation charging the parents as we moved to our cars. It was just one kick, but that didn't matter. Hollywood had come to Newton and we were all believers. Anything could happen.

Carrie came bustling into the waiting room where I sat as Chase was seeing the allergist. I'd decided for some reason to let her go in by herself. I felt a little foolish tagging along with this full-sized person with shoulders like a linebacker. Carrie half hugged me with one arm then walked back into the exam area. After another twenty minutes, Chase and Carrie came out with the allergist in tow, who ordered a series of routine tests. Carrie hugged Chase, made the "I'll call you" sign to me with her finger and thumb, and jogged off down the hospital corridor.

She didn't call. She came out to Newton late that afternoon after finishing her round of appointments. I was supposed to go to a Red Sox playoff game with a crowd of people invited to the Bank of America lux box. Frankly, I preferred the idea of spending Saturday evening with a hot young doctor to a platoon of forty-something guys, but I didn't know if she planned to stay. Whatever was going on between me and Carrie, if there was anything going at all besides her genuine concern for Chase, it was vague and unsaid, and I was being too much of a wuss to do anything about it. Not my usual way; but I was feeling a little like my whole life had been turned upside down, which it had, so I wasn't reading things too well.

"She says she's not sleeping," Carrie said as I pulled a couple of Sam Adams Lights from the fridge. I silently wondered if I could keep the chitchat about Chase going until midnight.

"Is she?"

"How in God's name would I know; she wouldn't tell me if the garage was on fire."

"That's what she told David this morning."

"That the garage is on fire?"

"No, goofy!" She slapped my hand. "That she doesn't sleep."

"She'll have an excuse tonight; she's at a sleepover."

Chase had in fact gone out with her team for a sleepover, a psyche, as they called pregame parties, to help them get ready for their next game on Monday. Chase had brooded about not knowing what clothes to pack before I took her. She had piles of them, boxes of them, racks of them, but only wore gray jeans with holes or plaid pajama bottoms and the same sweatshirt. I have no idea what she decided to take, but it fit in a CVS bag that couldn't hold a bottle of tonic.

Carrie talked about allergies and stress and the ways that sudden changes can affect people, especially teens. She went on at some length, enjoying her own knowledge. Like most guys alone with a pretty woman, I acted like the universe hung on her sentences, though to tell the truth Carrie could get a little boring; she sounded like a medical text. I wanted to know what was possible here. It was Saturday evening and she was on her third Sam Adams in my kitchen. There was the fact that she was my daughter's doctor and things were stinko between me and Chase, so I didn't need to gum them up worse by making a move on the person she seemed to like best. But it was my Saturday night, too.

I needed to break out of this set piece of the two of us in the kitchen talking about Chase. I asked her if she wanted to take a walk. She did. We walked on the golf course, took pretend swings, banged into each other as we walked, sat on a tee bench. She talked more about San Diego and ice skating. I got really bored and finally made a move, and then I knew why she kept coming to our house, and we went back to it.

The next few weeks I felt like I was living from soccer game to soccer game. The excitement of the team winning after such a slow start was contagious, not only for the regulars who showed up on the parent sidelines but among everyone I saw around town. Chase was a genuine local celebrity, and in an oddball yet admittedly delightful way, I was sort of one, too. I got to meet a lot of people in Newton that fall. It truly was a gas. It started to feel a little like living in the city, where people in your neighborhood knew you and dropped by with beer and chips when the Sox were on the tube. Well, not quite; but it wasn't as chilly as it seemed at first.

Jenna steadily increased Chase's minutes on the field and it made an unmistakable difference. Chase had awkward moments, when it looked like her balance was wacky and her left leg wouldn't hold. But those moments didn't last, and as the season continued, there were fewer of them. She made mistakes, too – putting a ball behind a teammate, missing a header, or flubbing a kick. But who didn't?

There were also times on the field when Chase simply dominated, moments when her game was so much better than the others that there could be no doubt that this was a superior athlete. And she was unselfish. She'd sometimes look for a pass when she had a shot, and sometimes the team would pay for this. The shots she took were fired by a cannon. A few of her shots were spectacular. Against Framingham, with the score tied in the second half, Chase dropped back near the Newton goal to block a shot and took off down the sidelines in full sail, outstripping not only the defenders but her own trailing team; she went coast to coast, as they say in hoops, drew out the keeper, threw in a double-deke, and walked the ball into the net. We watched on the sidelines, screaming harder as she hurtled down the field, and when she cruised through the defense so easily it was as if we were all witness to something truly important. There were times when it seemed she could score at will. At those times, I understood what Taylor's colleagues had told me in Chicago about her going nuts over Chase's soccer.

Carrie began adjusting her schedule so she could come to some of the home games. I had a sense of how difficult this was for her. When the final whistle blew, she'd jog over to the team side and grab the ice bags, making Chase ice her leg, from below her knee up to her hip. Jenna would wait to start the postgame team meetings until Chase's brace was off, her ice packs were set, her leg elevated and comfortable. It was like the ladies of the court could not relax until the tsarina was ready for her tea.

Chase was hardly a prima donna; her natural shyness prevented that. On the field, though, she could be abrupt, and impatient with the mistakes of her teammates. In the first days of the new school year, Jenna had talked to me a little after practice about Chase's toughness on the other players. Jenna said Chase simply had no tolerance for bad play; in frustration with her slowly returning abilities, she could snap at teammates viciously. Her teammates had distanced themselves from her off the field. Jenna was concerned that Chase's attitude was affecting the team's chemistry, because the other girls were sensitive to her impatience. But now that the team was winning, the connections between her and some of the girls seemed to be improving, though only on the field. Led by Kim, the assistant coach, a few of the girls learned that the best way to connect with Chase was to tease her; she was comfortable with the kind of low-grade insults that are usually more characteristic of male athletes. She rarely teased back, but the banter did seem to relax her.

After Chase executed a bicycle shot one afternoon in practice, Kim shook her head and said, "That was freaky." The team picked up on it and soon Chase's team nickname became Freaky. It was hard to read how she felt about people using it. Maybe it was who used it. When Kim called her Freaky, Chase would flash her half smile. But when teammates used it, there may have been an edge to it, as if maybe there was something freakish about her, and the nuance was not lost on Chase. When one of the fathers said, "Great game, Freaky" after another win, Chase glared at him in a way I thought she saved just for me. Oh good, I thought, so I'm not the only one she thinks is an asshole.

As the season unfolded through the fall, Chase's relationships with her teammates did not seem to improve. None of them ever came over to the house, and often it was Kim or Jenna who brought her home from practice instead of one of the girls with cars. Jenna had begun to make Chase skip practice occasionally, or hold back in more aggressive drills, because her knee had started to flare up a little, especially after games, but then sometimes after practice as well. Chase didn't complain, and Jenna needed her in the games. Carrie looked at it several times on the sidelines after a game, but thought it was residual swelling and that ice afterward should handle it. Carrie loved watching her play almost as much as I did; the thought of her being benched when she could obviously play so superbly seemed unnecessary. When Jenna pulled her from a practice and told her to get the ice bag, Chase would walk off the field looking as if her world had been turned upside down.

Sooner than we expected, a delivery van showed up one afternoon at our house with the last boxes of belongings from Illinois. The two movers carried them into the dining room and put them on the floor. Maris had taken great care to pack things and labeled the boxes carefully. We had the movers take most of the crates up to Chase's room, but a few of them were marked "Soccer Things" and seemed likely candidates for the basement. Chase flipped the boxes open one at a time, seeming to know what was in them, and started upstairs.

"Do you want them upstairs?" I called after her. "Or should I put them in the basement?"

"I don't care," she said.

It was boxes of mostly used soccer equipment: old cleats, T-shirts, parts of uniforms, and balls, along with a few pieces of new equipment that had not been taken out of the plastic wrapping – gloves, socks, nylon winter underwear, that sort of thing. I looked to see if she might be able to use some of it and save me money but all of it looked too small for her now. There were also a few crates filled with shoeboxes that held videos, none of them commercial, all marked with tape and dated in Taylor's small, neat printing and sorted by season. There were what looked like training logs, too. They seemed to cover a lot of years. I left all the stuff in the dining room for about a week, and when Chase ignored them completely, I took the boxes into the basement and forgot about them.

"You don't have a cat, do you?"

"Only in the garage."

"In the – oh, right! – Hah! But you don't, right? Or a dog? I would know if you did I guess."

"You would know, Carrie. No floor life. The coyotes on the golf course eat them."

"Get out of here. You drag me out where there are coyotes?"

"And the deer and the antelope play."

She laughed into the phone. "Don't mess with me, mister. I'm a working girl. Her allergies are probably not the problem; she's got the usual list: cats, dogs, dust, leaf mold."

"Leaf mold; oh, my God, not *leaf mold!*"

"Cool it, Goofy. I want her to see someone about not sleeping."

"She's already seeing a therapist."

"Not that!" She started off on a long explanation of chronic fatigue syndrome. I listened more or less; it sounded like something a Harvard-educated orthopedist would love to dig into but it didn't quite sound to me like Chase.

"You want her to see another doctor."

"Are you kidding me, Tommy?" She sounded suddenly annoyed. "She told me she was getting maybe three hours of sleep a night. I tried to get her to keep track of her sleep in her workout log but she hasn't done it, yet I know she's worried about it. It's awful! All that stress she puts on her body and not sleeping? She's overtired; this is serious. Or it could be serious," she said, modifying her tone a little, shifting from date type to doctor type. She started another lecture, the endpoint of which when it came was that she would take Chase back to Children's for another appointment.

"Should she be playing soccer?" I asked.

"I don't think we want to take it away from her, at least not yet, but we've got to get a handle on her sleeping or it could be a problem. This guy I want her to see is very good."

She explained he was a neurologist by training but had another specialty in sleep disorders. A brain guy. Carrie wanted Chase to see a brain guy. She then asked another stream of questions, only a few of which I could answer.

"Carrie," I said, growing impatient. "You would know better than me. She talks to you."

She was silent a moment. "Not really."

"Her grandmother's coming up tomorrow; maybe she talks to her."

"Yah think?"

"No, actually, I don't think. But she is coming. I think she's going to come to the game."

"I thought she hated soccer."

"I think she hates it less than the idea of spending the afternoon alone with me."

"Well, good luck with that. I got work to do."

"Later, my pet."

Her voice dropped playfully. "Did you just call me your pet?"

"That's where this conversation started, didn't it?"

I expected Maris to come in with guns blazing, turning up her nose at everything. I forgot she lived in a suburb, too. Newton looked a lot better to her than Boston or Harvard Square, or for that matter, the last place I had lived with her daughter. Her aspiration had been to time her arrival for late afternoon when Chase was out of school, but she had reluctantly agreed to come to Chase's game, so she had to come earlier and check into her hotel. I'd offered to meet her there, just off of Route 128, but she declined, as I expected. She used her Benzo's navigation and found her way to our house.

I met her out in the driveway. We skipped the French double-cheek greeting that we'd done when we had first seen each other in Chicago last May. Since then, the only way I really wanted to greet her was to beat her to death with a dead-weight lawyer. I'm a Boston guy, and I respect the towny motto: forgive and forget, but always remember. I remembered the way Maris and her lawyers dealt with me during my divorce. I remembered her promoting the slugger business when she knew as well as Taylor that I never touched her daughter once in anger. And I especially remembered recent history, all her custody maneuverings. But Chase had asked me twice in the morning if Gramma was coming, and I had to slip behind the thin veneer of civility. Which was exactly what Maris was doing, though far more easily than I could.

"That's your car?" She looked askance at the Jag.

"A classic."

"Aren't we all."

She made a polite show of looking at the car. "Seems like a teenager's car," she said dismissively.

"Yeah, you're right. Chase loves it."

In the house she declined my offer of coffee-tea and asked for a drink. I'd made a pot of Starbucks when she called from her car but poured her a stiff glass of Chardonnay. While I fixed myself coffee, she swirled the wine and walked around the family room.

"How is she?"

I told her. OK, I wasn't precisely honest. I left out the part about Chase seeing a counselor and a physical therapist and now a brain doctor. And the part about how she didn't talk to me and slammed out of the house on the least provocation, and disappeared and wore the same clothes all the time and had no friends that ever came over to the house. I did tell her, however, about the leaf mold.

Maris wanted to know who the allergist was. I told her a little – a very little – about Carrie: mostly her credentials, her diligence, and that she might be at the game today.

"Well, house calls," she said, as if this was expected, but I could see Carrie's credentials impressed her.

During our marriage, Taylor had complained to me often about her mother and fretted over the usual daughter anxiety that she might one day turn out like her. As Maris and I sat in opposite chairs in my sterile family room, she reminded me of Taylor in subtle ways, like little ghosts. Her precise way of looking at things. Her seriousness, even when making light of something. Her way of communicating that little things were important and should not be overlooked. Physically, Taylor had taken after her father: the height, the athletic background. Maris was thin, not tall, and though fair like Taylor and Chase, she didn't have the McKinley quality of being physically imposing. There was an elegance about her, like a good piece of cutlery. And yet, as is often the case with elegance, it was in her manner of withholding, of keeping things back, of understatement. Of things understood with the slightest nod and no words spoken. And in her simple, understated, and very expensive clothes. As we talked, briefly and politely, mostly small talk about Newton and selling condos and how to pick a health club for a teenager, she was working to be civil. Maybe she realized I'd won the custody fight, and she needed to be careful with me to keep the connection with her granddaughter. Or maybe she was just biding her time and hoping to find dirt under the rug. I thought about an old Tommy Boyan rule of social discourse: people feel about you the way you feel about them. I had decided not to pick a fight during this visit, and I felt like she was doing the same. We were like two teams facing each other and relying on our defenders.

She did raise one complaint. Why hadn't I replaced Chase's cell phone? Maris was not able to reach her on the phone so easily nowadays.

"I did replace it."

"When?"

"One day after she lost it. It was insured. Kids lose them all the time."

"Oh. Well, perhaps I misunderstood."

Bang. Ol' cool-as-a-cuke Maris took that shot between the eyes without even blinking. So Chase didn't want to talk to her any more than to me. Why did I not feel a tad bad to learn that? And why did I not tell her that Chase was in effect doing the same thing to just about everyone? Forgive and forget, but always remember.

The plan was that Maris would come to the game with me, drive back to the house so Chase could shower, and then take Chase out to dinner. I told her there was a good new Japanese restaurant in town where a lot of the teenagers liked to go and watch the chefs. Maris nodded coolly, what a sport. She would do what had to be done. We drove to the game in her car. She simply handed me the keys as we walked down the driveway.

The teams were warming up on the field when we walked down the gallery sidelines. I introduced a few of the parents I'd gotten to know to Chase's grandmother. Ellen, the pretty realtor whose daughter was a midfielder, looked Maris over, smelled money, and attached herself, while others gushed about what a wonderful player Chase was. Maris gamely took a seat on the bottom row of the bleachers and looked as if she hadn't missed a game.

Chase saw her, came loping over to the sidelines, and lifted Maris off the bench with a hug.

"Gramma," she said, and held the hug long enough to tell all of us that Gramma was important.

Maris looked at the brace on Chase's left leg. Her face flashed with concern, but she only said, "I'm sure that's annoying."

"I hate it."

"I'm sure it'll be off soon," then she looked at me quickly, "won't it?"

I nodded. "She's ahead of schedule," I lied.

One of the parents pointed out a TV crew setting up on the sidelines and said they were there because of Chase. Maris looked puzzled. It obviously made no sense to her; why would television care about a game because of her grandchild?

"Where is she?" Maris asked when the game started. Sitting next to her, Ellen explained that the coach had been increasing Chase's minutes but that she was still not starting.

"Our not-so-secret weapon."

Early in the game, one of Newton's defenders was back-tackled and had to be helped off the field. Maris's face tightened but she said nothing about it, instead asking Ellen questions about the rules and the play. Chase was subbed in after ten minutes, her earliest appearance in a game yet. With good reason. The Dedham side was undefeated so far in the season and had already beaten Newton earlier, 3–0. With the opponent's goalposts to our right, Chase in at right forward was directly in front of us. Several times early she glanced at Maris. When Ellen said something about how Maris must have enjoyed watching her granddaughter develop as a player over the years, Maris did not explain that this was the first of Chase's games she'd seen.

Halfway through the first period, with no score yet on either side, Chase took the ball at midfield from a long keeper punt, quickly cut through the Dedham defenders, and fired a low shot past the keeper to break the ice. Maris seemed jolted by the explosive reaction around her.

"Oh, my, God," she laughed, her hand over her mouth.

"A goal's a big deal," I said.

"I guess so!"

Just before the end of the half, Chase scored again, this one on an incredible header just inside the box off a high cross. The reaction was just as explosive.

"Oh, my God," she said again, though this time it was the header that surprised her. "Doesn't that hurt her?"

During the short break for halftime, a woman in a windbreaker who had been watching the game came over to our seats.

"Hi, Tommy," she said, holding out her hand. "She's doing great."

I introduced Maris to her; she was the head coach of the Harvard women's soccer team. It was the second time she'd come to a game. The NCAA recruitment rules enjoined her from initiating contact, but we'd been introduced by Carrie, sort of a semi-innocent social contact, so as I understood it the connection was acceptable. The coach told Maris that she'd seen Chase play over a year before at a tournament in Las Vegas.

The second half was similar to the first. Dedham scored early, drawing within one goal, and Jenna quickly subbed in Chase. Chase set up a goal with a precise pass from deep in the corner to an attacking midfielder, who pounded home the shot. Minutes later Chase attacked, breaking through the midfield and firing a long shot into the upper corner of the net. The Newton fans were jubilant. Maris stood and clapped with gusto as Jenna quickly subbed Chase out. From across the field, we watched the ice bags appear; with a three-goal lead, Chase was done for the day.

"I am so impressed," Maris said, hugging Chase as the players with their gear crossed the field after the game. She whispered something to Chase; Chase stiffened. As they walked arm in arm toward the car, Chase's eyes were tearing up. She'd obviously said something like, your mother would be proud. Well, it was true.

Maris climbed in the back of the car with Chase and put her arm around her, reaching up awkwardly to cover the shoulder span.

"That was wonderful," Maris said. From the car we saw the TV crew interviewing Jenna. "They should've talked to you!" Maris said. "You did all the shots!"

"Coach talks to them," Chase said flatly.

"Well that doesn't seem fair."

When we got home, Chase surprised me. I didn't expect her to complain openly about our life in Newton, since she seemed such a stoic, the classic athlete who quietly takes the pain. But I didn't expect her to show Maris around the house as if she'd just bought it. The forty-inch TV with every cable channel. The takeout numbers we kept on the fridge. Her room: the new chair, she even made Maris sit in it. Her bathroom with the makeup lights around the mirror. The white plastic stack baskets I'd bought for her clothes since she refused to put them in drawers. (Turns out she'd straightened things up the night before her grandmother came.)

"Now that's clever," Maris said gamely.

I left when they got to the growing shrine of Taylor pictures and clippings.

"She misses her mother," Maris said downstairs while Chase showered.

"Of course she does," I said, trying not to sound as if she'd baited me.

Maris was driving back to New Canaan in the morning, though she was touched by Chase telling her she should stay with us and that we had a nice guest room. I couldn't quite imagine Maris sleeping in a rented bed. She stopped by the next morning to say goodbye while we raced around getting ready to drive to school and the train. She brought bagels and hot chocolate for Chase and coffee for me, which we really didn't have time to eat. While Chase was upstairs pulling soccer gear from the dryer, Maris handed me an envelope. I thought for a moment she was giving me a check and didn't know how to react.

"You don't need to read it now," she said in a way that told me I was not permitted to read it now.

"It's a letter, from Taylor. To you." She looked at the envelope. "It was with her papers. It's about Chase."

"Oh." The envelope looked flattened by time. "When did she write it?"

"Some years ago, I believe. It was with her papers," she said again.

I had the feeling that this was her story and she was sticking to it. We heard Chase upstairs.

"I'd put it away," she said. I must've looked puzzled. "I think it's just about custody issues."

She looked at me pointedly. "I don't imagine it would be appropriate for Chase to see it. I'm sure you understand."

"It's about custody?"

"I think you should put it away."

"You were sitting on this during the hearings?"

"I didn't have to give it to you," she said.

"Right," I said.

After Maris pulled out of the driveway, I dropped Chase off at the high school and pulled the letter from my pocket while I was waiting for the train. The envelope said simply, Tom Boyan. It was not Taylor's handwriting, and she'd never called me Tom in her life. I was pretty sure the envelope was addressed by Maris. Which of course meant she'd read my letter and had held on to it for months, ever since Taylor's death.

When I read the letter, I knew why Maris had been reluctant to give it to me. I also knew why she'd been so insistent on my not showing it to Chase. As I rode on the train into Boston, I thought about how Chase would react if she read it. One day of course she would have to read it. Maybe it would be good for some things to come out into the open. Undoubtedly, it would be difficult for all of us. But to give her the letter now, with her mother's death still recent, whatever good might come out of her knowing the truth, it would be too cruel to consider. To tell the truth, in realizing this I surprised myself. My first thought was for Chase. My decision was to do what was best for her, not for me or anyone else. It's what parents do.

6.

Early in October the Newton High School open house was scheduled for two hours on a Wednesday evening. I looked forward to it. I knew a lot of people from soccer who would be there.

"See you tomorrow night, Tommy?" "Absolutely, Ellen" – and I knew people there would want to talk because Chase was getting so much attention. I was looking forward to meeting some of Chase's teachers, since she never said anything to me about school. My sister Anna had scolded me over the phone the afternoon of the event.

"For God's sake: don't just talk about soccer, Tommy. You're getting a little boring on the subject to tell the truth. You need to meet her teachers, put a face to their names. Ask questions, you know."

The line of cars bumping their way into the school parking lot was long and slow. I worried about the Jag overheating. With the top down, I was cold. The rattly British heater blew tepid air into the chilly evening, but walkers waved to me as they passed and I liked that. Chase was at home, huddled up on her bed with a spread of papers and books. There would be no students at the open house, except a few show horses and suckups who worked as ushers.

Everyone gathered in the school assembly area to hear the principal and a few others talk about the school's mission, a lot of edu-babble pap that was like every other school: high standards, all children, rigorous teaching and learning, curriculum that is coherent, the whole child. Like I expected incoherence? Or children sawed off at the hip? The head of the science department got up and droned on about the new state science graduation tests that were kicking in and how the school was doing science across the curriculum this year. What. A. Geek.

Then a student with some personality got up and explained the evening, with an overhead schedule behind him. We had copies of our kids' schedules and would zip through a day of classes, each period lasting ten minutes, with five minutes to crush in the hallway.

The place was packed. We all wore name tags. I wanted people to know who my kid was but our names were different. So I wrote "Tommy Boyan," and underneath it, "Chase Ellis's dad." As I did it I thought, this is like being a groupie. I quickly got used to giving the explanation for why our names were different, whittling it down almost to a sound byte.

"Divorce; it's her mother's name, but now we're a single-parent family."

People would just look and say, "Oh, I'm sorry," and I would say, "Yeah me, too, especially for Chase." Very heartfelt. Tommy Boyan, man of heart.

There was a festive quality to the event, especially in the halls as people mingled their way around the slightly confusing building. Anna had been right to zing me ahead of time about the soccer talk. It was so tempting. And unavoidable. Again and again people reacted:

She's great! We saw her play, wow! I saw her in the paper! What a game! I walked around with Lee, a woman I'd met at soccer practice over the summer, and her husband; their daughter shared a lot of classes with Chase. Their daughter was also returning from a knee injury, but was not yet playing. Lee kept saying how amazed she was that Chase had returned to form so quickly. I wanted to say that maybe she still has a way to go, but that would have been too boastful, even for me.

I expected the teachers to be equally impressed, at least about soccer. And a few were, commenting on how great it was for the school to have her on the team, or admiring her commitment. When I first walked in the room, her French teacher said something in a heavy southern accent that she meant to be funny, something about hurting her neck when she looked up at Chase to talk. But the tone with the teachers was different. They looked at me differently, not all, but most of them. The French teacher buttonholed me at the end of the miniclass as I moved to the door. She wanted my email address. As she dutifully wrote it out in a planning book, I asked why. She looked around at the parents milling around us and said, "We may need to adjust Chase's schedule. Let's talk."

Her English teacher was a young, athletic-looking man whom the parents had said was considered hot by their daughters. When he saw my name tag as people filed into his room, he asked me to call him, and also asked for my email. The look on his face told me it was not for soccer chitchat.

By the time Chase's math teacher did much the same, I'd gotten the message. I figured math would be Chase's best subject, so I waited after the short lecture for the room to clear. As parents began filing into the room for the next class, I said, "Chase is having some trouble, I gather." The math teacher simply but firmly said yes.

"Her mother was a math professor," I whined.

The woman just nodded patiently and then recommended I call Chase's guidance counselor. That was the slightly ditzy young woman Chase and I had met with before the start of the school year who had set her schedule. The math teacher thought it might be time to bring in several of her teachers for a conference. It was not just the recommendation that troubled me. It was the way she spoke – the grave look on her face – like she was a doctor and suddenly I was being set up to learn my child was terminal. OK, I was overreacting. I'd grown fond of having people look at me as if I was the father of a god. All I could think as I left the room was that it had hardly been a month, how could things sour in school so quickly. She hadn't even taken midterms.

I skipped the last class on Chase's schedule and asked where to find the health classrooms. I had to bump my way through two hallways and a crowded stairwell, but I found the cluster of rooms not far from the gyms. I'd been down there before, over the summer. Jenna taught health and was about to start her last miniclass, so I listened and waited from the hall. When her class was over, she saw me at the door. She must have seen the panicky look on my face, though I was trying to be cool.

She listened with the head-cocked intensity I'd grown used to over the past four months. When she'd heard enough, like a coach, she trimly cut me off.

"It's too early for them to know that," she said. "There's an alarmist in every teacher. I wouldn't get all wound up over this; Chase is a smart girl."

I felt instantly better, but needed more reassurance.

"How do you know that? I mean you don't have her in class or anything. Maybe she's a soccer idiot savant."

Jenna laughed, and looked at me playfully. "She takes after her mother, right?"

"I'm serious. I mean maybe she has a learning disability or something."

"Then it will come out. Just," she held a hand up, looking around at the few parents still around the halls, "just don't get too caught up in the whole teacher conference thing. They'll have her in special-ed classes before we know it just to cover their own asses. I've seen her transcript from Evanston. She's going through a lot right now; she just hasn't kicked it into gear yet on the schoolwork."

"So what do I do?"

"Have you talked to her dean?" I shook my head. "Well, that's it then. Call her dean tomorrow morning: Chris Winberg. She's great! Really. I absolutely trust her. That's exactly what you should do."

"I will," I nodded. "OK. I feel better."

"You should. Don't worry. Chase has been through a lot, but she's a rock. Don't go getting her all upset about what her teachers say about her. She's probably worried about it already, and it'll just freeze her up. She's going to be fine. More than that. She's going to excel." She gave me a friendly pat on the shoulder. "Be positive, Tommy. You're good at that."

"That's how we roll," I said. And I did feel better. For about three minutes.

Before my meeting with Dean Winberg took place, something happened on the soccer field that may have diminished Jenna's certainty that all was rosy. It was not such a big deal, really. The parents along the sidelines, me included, at first thought Chase was jobbed, and let the ref know it in no uncertain terms. It was only after the game that we put together what had actually happened, but we were still caught up in the emotion of the game and had no intention of being reasonable.

Newton was not playing as well as we'd seen them do before. The game was at Weymouth: the home team had strong, slow, hard-hitting players who banged our girls relentlessly and closed tightly around the net. Chase was dropped several times during the game, not unusual for players at this level, and quite common for forwards. As usual, she slowly got up and worked her way back into play. Jenna would sub her out as soon as she could after these hits to be sure of no reinjury; it was so commonplace I didn't worry. But Newton was not getting through. Once Chase made a gorgeous kick – I'd learned it was called a through-ball – but the other Newton forward mistimed it and was called offsides. Newton players, along with parents, objected, including Chase, who glared at the ref. The game went on, the ref ignoring everyone. (Moral of story: never, ever become a ref.) Jenna kept yelling at the players from across the field and pushing the air down with both hands, a signal to ease back on their roughness.

"Play your game!" we heard her yell; she wanted them to stick with their finesse possession game, not get drawn into a smashmouth.

There was still no score, and as the clock ran down, the game got rougher still. Chase was tackled in the box on a near breakaway, but drew no whistle. From the side we screamed at the ref, "PK! PK!" demanding a penalty kick or a yellow card, to no avail. A Newton midfielder was grabbed by the shirt and hip-checked to the ground by another defender. When Weymouth attacked, our girls fought back in kind, and did draw whistles. The Newton parents were beside themselves.

"Let's go, Chase!" one of the fathers screamed. "Take over!"

By my clock, the forty-minute second half was over and we were into stop-time when Chase took a midfielder's pass twenty yards from the goal, juked to the left, and fired a hard left-footed missile that whizzed past the Weymouth keeper's outstretched fingers. Sideline pandemonium.

Then the ref blew the whistle and we thought the game was over. Double the pandemonium. But no. He was calling the shot back. His arm went up; offsides was the call. Newton parents screamed, "She had possession! She had possession!"

I screamed with the rest of them, even though I couldn't for the life of me figure out how offsides worked. We looked at the linesman, who should have made the call. The linesman had not called it. But it stuck. The ball went to the Weymouth keeper for a goalie kick, the score still double ought.

As the keeper moved to kick the ball, Chase stood and glared again at the ref, who ignored her; she held the look as the ball moved into play. Then she turned, raced back up the field, and ran down the Weymouth midfielder, who had possession. She stole the ball, tore back up the field, and launched a kick from virtually the same place she'd taken the shot that was called back. Again, the keeper was not quick enough. This one counted.

After a brief celebration, the Newton girls jogged to the midfield slowly, while the Weymouth side raced into place to try to tie it up. Chase stood where she'd taken the shot, and as the ref jogged by her, she said something to him. From the sidelines we couldn't hear it. We were told later she'd said, "Fuck you."

The ref immediately pulled a red card from his chest pocket and held it up, stopping play. Chase walked off the field. Newton fans booed.

Some of the Newton girls held out their hands in disbelief, "What! What!" But that was it. The red card meant Chase was suspended from the next Newton game as well as the remainder of this one. Play resumed, and in a moment the ref blew the three whistle blasts ending the game.

The players and coaches on the opposite sideline had heard what she said. There could be no doubt about the call. The soccer rules were clear the world over on swearing at the ref: a red card was automatic.

As Kim drew the team together on the hill near the field after the game, Jenna stood with Chase off to one side. Word had drifted over to the bleacher side on why she'd drawn a red.

"That was weird," someone said behind me. Chase knew the rules. It looked so cold-blooded; it seemed she'd drawn the suspension intentionally.

"What were you thinking?" I asked her on the way home.

Each of her answers was preceded by a brief silence, as if she might not have to answer if she waited.

"The ref sucked."

"Don't they all suck?"

"Yeah, they all suck."

"So what are we talking here – you going to draw a red card all the time?"

It was a stupid thing to say.

"Yeah, maybe I am."

"Won't be too good for the team."

"Then fuck them, too."

We finished the ride home in silence.

I met with the Newton dean a few days after Chase's red-card game. Chris Winberg was about my age, a warm and friendly woman who led me into an office filled with plants and family photos. She made me a cup of tea. We cut through the Mr. Boyan, Dean Winberg pretense and got to Chris and Tommy with ease; it was like that.

She'd done her homework for the meeting, and as I sipped my tea, she quickly got down to specifics. She had Chase's transcript and had called the dean at Chase's private school in Chicago. She'd also made the rounds of Chase's Newton teachers and brought examples of her work to show me.

"She's at the wrong level of classes here, Tommy," she said, after sharing some of Chase's assignments. "I'd like to move her out of Honors right away."

"She's not smart?"

She laughed and shook her head.

"She's not prepared, that's all. She was working at a different level in Chicago."

"I thought private schools were supposed to be hotsy-totsy."

"I'm sure they are hotsy-totsy, in a lot of ways." What a diplomat.

"But this is really about curriculum, not ability. If we move her back to regular classes, she can build a stronger foundation."

She was using diplomacy on me now, but I wanted to believe her.

"What does this mean for college and that sort of thing?"

"Not much," she shrugged. "A lot of colleges don't even look at GPAs recalibrated for Honors points."

She explained what that meant, but it seemed a little edu-babbly.

"The point is, she's more prepared for regular classes this year and we can reconsider Honors again for her junior year. As far as college is concerned, it's better that she do well in regular courses than poorly in Honors."

That made sense to me. I pushed her back to why Chase was unable to handle Honors.

"Her mother was a math professor, an academic superstar. I just don't get how Chase could have this shitbum foundation."

"It's not shitbum," she laughed. "But," she looked out the window a moment, "from talking to her last dean, I more or less got the feeling that they expected a lot more of her in sports than in the classroom."

"*Aha.*"

"Exactly."

"But aren't we doing that now, by moving her back?"

"I think it's more about putting her where she can succeed. Plus," she sat back from the table and looked at me thoughtfully, "your daughter has been through an unbelievable amount of stress in the last few months, wouldn't you say?"

"Absolutely," I said, for some reason feeling a sudden rush of guilt.

"I had a long talk with Jenna Eisenbech yesterday."

She looked at me and waited. I couldn't read if she thought Jenna was a good thing or a bad thing. It then occurred to me she might be trying to read me the same way.

"Jenna told me that Chase was the one who first discovered her mother was dead."

I nodded.

"And she's seeing a therapist now, I understand?"

We both nodded some more, a regular pair of boppy toys.

"So, Tommy."

She started counting off issues with her fingers.

"She's an only child, in a very close relationship with her mother. She finds her mother dead one day, and a few weeks later she's been moved to Boston. She's living with her father, who's had," she hesitated, "limited contact with her for several years."

I nodded, the guilt now feeling like a basketball of pus in my chest.

"She's then moved again, to Newton, a new home, new coach, new team, and a completely different curriculum in her classes. And," she stopped me before I could jump in and gush with agreement, "she's suddenly under a lot of pressure on the soccer field too, right? And I understand she's just coming off a major injury?"

"Yeah, they shoot horses for it."

She laughed again, good-naturedly. We both sipped some more tea.

"That's one hell of a load for anyone to deal with. But a fifteen-year-old girl? I think we need to lower the flame here a little, don't you?"

I nodded some more.

"How's she doing at home?"

"I don't know. She doesn't talk to me. She always seems pissed-off."

This didn't seem to trouble the dean. She asked some more questions: Was Chase eating? Like a horse, but too much junk. Other medical problems? I told her about Carrie, the allergist, and the sleep guy. Medications? I told her the sleep guy wanted her to take some medication to help her relax but Chase wouldn't take it. Friends? I hadn't seen any yet.

"Would you mind if I called her therapist?" she asked.

I fished out a card from my wallet and read her the number.

"Have you talked to Chase?" I asked.

"Not yet," she said, smiling, as if I'd just scored a point in a friendly game, though no games are ever completely friendly. "But I will. Count on it."

She said she would talk to Chase about the proposed schedule changes, and about the possibility of a tutor for several of her classes, just to help her make up the ground she'd lost in the first six weeks. She also said she would ask Chase how she feels she's getting along in Newton.

"That'd be great," I said.

I wanted to tell her about Chase's red card and her anger after the game, but she glanced at her watch and so I didn't push it. I also wanted to ask her who would pay for the tutor, but I didn't want to add money problems to the growing load of crap in the wheelbarrow I was now towing around behind me.

The no-friends business started to chew at me. All my life, it was my friends who got me through things. If it wasn't for friends, I'd be unemployed and broke. I cashiered regularly on all my high-school and college buddies, to say nothing of family and neighborhood. But that was the Boston way: who you know, how you get things done in a city where everything is personal.

I felt like I had to do something. But Chase was so private about her room, her things, her attentions. I couldn't just waltz into the house with a bunch of teenagers in tow, Surprise! I had a kind of goofy idea; I had to talk to Jenna about it.

The big subject among the parents on the soccer team, after the hours we spent at games and fundraisers gassing about the games themselves, was college. Especially among the parents of juniors and seniors, for obvious reasons. But the conversational pot could be stirred with any high-school parent by asking a college question. Families were worried about college, talking to their kids about college, schlepping in their SUVs to local colleges, and talking to their banks about the college poorhouse.

So I talked to Jenna about a little team outing. For the girls and parents. A night of soccer and spaghetti sort of gig, at Boston College, my brother's and my alma mater. OK, BC was not exotic to anyone living in Newton; it was just down the street, but that was the appeal here. It was a way to get the girls together nearby but with a little special thrown in. Jenna loved the idea, though she didn't see how it would affect Chase's friend issues.

My job involved doing a little work with people at BC, including the president's office. Like most colleges, the school had a slew of programs and connections with their neighboring city of Boston, and over the years I'd been involved in helping to put a lot of them together. It was Public Relations 101: some client, a business type or a city pol, needs something to buff up his do-gooder résumé or constituency services, so we create a little school-based program in Boston, a partnership to bring public and private together. Good for the company, good for the pol, and good for the university, especially if it pulled down a little corporate or public dough. It's what I do.

The players and parents met early one Friday evening in late October in the soccer field parking lot and carpooled the short drive to the campus. All the players and nearly all the parents showed up. Chase rode with Kim and a few teammates; I went on ahead with Jenna in her car. At the college, they were led through the athletic complex and into the stadium used for soccer. That night the BC women were hosting the University of North Carolina, one of America's premier collegiate soccer powers. The parents sat in reserved seats; the girls were down on the field, close to the action. UNC won 5–2, but BC gave them a fight; it was a pretty good game.

Afterward, the parents and coaches were steered into a very spiffy reception room in the administration building adjacent to the president's office. We had drinks and chatted with the athletic director and the school's vice president for looking good, a guy named Jimmy Donovan, a buddy of mine from the dawn of man.

"Tommy Ballgame!" he greeted me, using my overworked nickname, and welcomed his guests with one arm around me. The girls were taken into the locker rooms to mingle with the players of both teams. They then joined the adults for a pasta dinner set up in a bigger room nearby, along with some of the BC players, including their captains and coaches.

I'd arranged for a couple of speakers, thinking I needed a program to hold the thing together. Jimmy played host, introducing the BC athletic director, who talked about high-school athletes making the jump to college. He was very careful not to promote BC (hardly necessary at that point). I told him five minutes max before the dinner; he talked for nearly fifteen, but the parents ate it up. One of the BC captains then talked briefly about being a student-athlete in college. She was really good; we all ate her up.

Then my brother got up. He did a version of a routine I'd heard him do before, about how hard it is to plan for the future because life is so unexpected. His basic message was, Don't just dream: do it now. He spoke for nearly fifteen minutes too long. I thought I'd told him beforehand, but it didn't matter. Fergie was a comedian all his life and no one could work a room like he could. He'd be mayor of Boston if his wife didn't keep an iron grip on his throat like the Boston Strangler. He got people laughing, especially the girls, who loved his nearly X-rated irreverence. It was a good thing he waited until the spaghetti was done or everyone would've been spitting tomato sauce.

After that, we all mucked around for a while; the college president came in to meet people, and Fergie and I did our gluey thing so the evening didn't sag once the food was gone. Fergie was careful not to make a big deal out of Chase. He knew instinctively that she probably got too much attention for her own good among her teammates, and he knew my agenda for the evening. I produced a Nerf soccer ball and managed to get Fergie and the college president to go at it with some of the girls, which was a total hoot, since every guy, including a priest, thinks he's an athlete.

On the way back afterward, I felt proud of myself for pulling it off. Jenna was a little starry-eyed about the gig; she thought everyone had a great time, including Chase, and I could see that. Chase loved it when Fergie tried to wrestle with her to keep the ball away; she laughed repeatedly with my big bear of a brother grabbing her by the waist.

"So, Jenna," I said a little tentatively. "You think something like that can help loosen things up a little between Chase and her teammates?"

"It's always great for teams to have fun together."

"You ducked the question."

"No, I didn't!"

"Yeah, you did."

She thought a moment as she drove, then spoke carefully.

"Chase's problems with her teammates are not going to be solved by a fun night at college."

"I thought it might help."

"Oh, I'm sure it did." She glanced over at me. "I didn't mean . . ."

She started to apologize, but I waved it off. I felt a little disappointed, to tell the truth, Jenna was suddenly being a bit of a downer.

"I just figured people might start to like her if they felt she had a fun family."

"Well, they like you, Tommy, but I don't think that's what you had in mind, was it?"

Another Friday night, this one in late October. (Why does the shit always seem to hit the fan on the weekends? Check the emergency rooms, the police blotters. People really screw up on the weekends. Maybe we should all stay bored and work-blitzed.)

The high-school soccer season was nearly over and the state tournament was soon to begin. Newton had to play a makeup game in Framingham the following Saturday afternoon. Chase left the house early in the evening for another one of the team "psyche" parties they held before every game. These parties consisted of the girls sitting around in pajama pants eating pizza and pumping each other up for the game, followed by a late romp around town tossing rolls of toilet paper all over the houses of the varsity boys' players. While the girls were tooling around with their TP, the boys' team was doing the same thing to the houses of the girls. Sometimes they connected. Maybe they shared their rolls.

"Call if you need a ride," I said as she left.

"I won't," she said.

"I want you home by midnight."

To this she nodded ever so slightly, a major concession for Chase.

I expected my evening to be a lot less entertaining than decorating the neighbors with TP. Carrie had a dinner party at a colleague's home in Brookline and she wanted me to come, she said, because otherwise the evening might be a little dull.

"So, are you punishing me or them?"

"Both! I want us to liven things up, Dummy."

I loved when she called me Dummy or Goofy, sort of the nickname equivalent to spit in the eye. But she was a looker. And smart. And she could shift gears between goofy and insightful without missing a beat, and I liked that.

We rolled down a long driveway in the Jag to a house tucked into a private forest on the edge of Brookline. Carrie said it once belonged to one of the Lowells. It looked like a fair chunk of the Lowell population could fit in it. The entry hall felt like the lobby of the Boston Public Library, lots of tiles and echoes.

Dinner was one of those semi-stiff affairs where people are put in their seats by the hostess, even though this one pretended for about eleven seconds that she didn't care.

"Oh, well, maybe boy-girl?"

There were eight couples, including me and Carrie; the other men and a few of the women were doctors, most of them surgeons. Carrie introduced me as a writer and political consultant, which sounded good and seemed to be the way she saw me, but it definitely gave a false picture of the grunty and low-level work I spent most of my life doing. This, however, was hardly the place to correct the impression.

"So," I said as we sat down after drinks to eat. "A lot of you guys put your hands where the sun don't shine?"

This engendered a lively round of yuck about surgery, which actually got pretty funny.

"I just hope you all washed your hands," I said.

"Tommy works with politicians," Carrie offered, "so he has to wash his hands a lot."

Now we were into politics, and naturally I had stories to tell. In my experience, the more outrageous you are willing to be with people who feel a little awkward or reserved, the more genuine the laughs will get, because laughing is like gas: you basically want to let it out. Carrie kept encouraging the gluey thing, so before the conversation died in the men's room at City Hall, I shifted the talk to soccer. As I expected, most of the couples had kids who played the game at one level or another, so the table got fully involved. When I finally let it slip that my daughter played for Newton, and they figured out that she was the one they'd read about somewhere, I really began to enjoy myself. Having a child who is a star at something, especially sports, is like a drug: it fills in all the holes in the rest of your life and makes you feel like you've accomplished something, even if all you've done is to make your kid a semi-basket case. I didn't think I'd done this with Chase; if she was in the basket it wasn't my doing. But the chance to brag was increasingly tough to resist.

The doctors turned out to be regular sports.

"She's in the *Globe* all the time," one of them said. "You must be incredibly proud of her."

"Yeah, definitely, especially in those family moments when she comes home after school and tries to put her assignment notebook down the garbage disposal."

This drew out the teenagers-are-horrible stories and we all got into that hot topic.

We moved back into the living room the size of a bowling alley and had decaf and more drinks. One of the guests – a brain surgeon I wouldn't let cut into my brain if I had the Hope Diamond in it – was complaining about malpractice insurance. The doctors were all members of a lobbying group that was unable to get movement on legislation at the State House to support lower malpractice insurance rates. I didn't say anything, but they all sounded like they didn't know squat about local politics, which was probably healthy. I must've had a provocative smile on my face – I really didn't want to say anything – because our host turned to me and said, "Tommy, you're a political consultant. What would you do?"

I was stuck. I didn't want to sound like a total dummy, so I said their doctors' membership group had lobbyists who were probably working on the issue.

"That's just it," the brain surgeon said. "They haven't been able to get it out of the subcommittee for years! I just don't get it." Everyone commiserated.

So I shot my mouth off. Maybe I wanted to impress Carrie after she made me sound like I should be on CNN. I said anyone who wanted to move a piece of legislation shouldn't diddle around with members of a subcommittee; they needed to work behind the scenes with the Speaker of the House and the President of the Senate and nail down their support. Then it would get to the floor. But the brain surgeon wouldn't let it go. He said the legislators didn't want to touch the package because it included a cap on medical damages.

"Everyone wants to be able to sue their doctor for millions," he said.

I said it had to be packaged as a way to save insurance costs for everyone, since everyone hates insurance. We got into a sticky little argument about how to do that. I kept shooting my mouth off and drinking more wine. The whole time Carrie kept staring at me, as if I was speaking in tongues and she was worried about my own brain needing a little chop-chop.

My cell phone started vibrating so I slipped through a set of French doors into a library to check on it. It was Jenna, which seemed odd to me, so I answered.

She asked if I knew where Chase was.

"She's at the psyche," I said. Coaches didn't go to the pregame gigs.

"No, she's not," she said.

Apparently the team captain had called Jenna a little while before. Chase did show up, but after a few minutes she went out to the street and got into a red pickup truck. She didn't come back, and no one recognized the truck. After a few hours and Chase not answering her cell or her home phone, the captain thought it felt a little weird and decided to call Jenna. She didn't want the girls or Chase to know she'd done it.

"Maybe she just went home," I said. "She doesn't always answer phones."

"I'm at your house now," Jenna said. "I don't think there's anyone here. She has a curfew, right?"

"Midnight." I glanced at my watch; it was already one o'clock. "So I should come home, right?"

"I think so."

Carrie looked a little wounded when I said I had to leave. I told the guests my teenager was riding around in a truck after curfew; people smiled and heads nodded.

"Go, Tommy," the hostess said and gave me a kiss, surprising me a little. As I got my coat, I offered to take a cab and leave the Jag if Carrie wanted to stay, but she insisted on coming with me.

On the way home, I followed Jenna's suggestion and drove past the high-school student parking lot – a hangout, of all places – and the soccer field parking lot. No sign of Chase or pickup trucks. When we pulled into our driveway, we saw Jenna leaning against her Toyota. The three of us went into the house. There was no sign that Chase had been home: no lights, no open food on the counters, no music shaking the plaster. Carrie kept saying she was probably out with a boyfriend and figured I'd be home late and was stretching it. I said I didn't think she had a boyfriend, and since she was fifteen, I didn't think in any case she should be out after one thirty with him. Jenna agreed. I wasn't actually worried; I felt like I had to do something and mostly felt a little clueless about what the right parent moves should be.

Jenna made a few calls and then we were stumped; all we could do was wait. When I reminded them that this was something Chase had pulled before, they seemed to hear it for the first time. On a long-shot hunch, I thought of looking at the golf course, since Chase spent so much time out there running at all hours. Maybe she was out there running now. Carrie stayed back to cover the phone and make coffee while Jenna and I walked down the street to the cart path.

We could hear the muffled music of a radio somewhere, followed it, and soon saw the truck at the end of a cart path behind the eleventh tee. The truck must have driven over part of the course to get to where it was parked.

Jenna seemed to recognize the truck. We walked across the fairway, but when we were about fifty yards from the pickup, Jenna touched my hand to stop me.

"Chase!" she bellowed. "Chase Ellis! Come out here right now!"

Jenna yelled a few more times, and after about a forty count, the passenger door opened. It was Chase. She took us in and started walking across the grass in the direction of the house while angling away from us. She had a slow stomping way of walking that told me she was angry. Not as angry as Jenna seemed, however; the young coach cut down the angle and stopped her with a look. I followed Jenna a little slowly. Jenna was leaning in to Chase's ear and nearly whispering. I could hear the sharp edge in her voice. I'd seen her do that to players in practice but it was a lot more intimidating out there in the dark with the raccoons and coyotes. Chase mumbled something about none of her business and stormed away without a look before I got to them.

Jenna went over to the driver's side of the truck and started yelling into the open window. The driver with a shaved head who didn't look like a teenager sat quietly, ignoring Jenna.

"Who's this?" I asked.

Jenna said his name was Kevin Lassiter; he had graduated "a few years ago." To the driver she said, "This is Chase's father." The cab smelled strongly of beer, and there were opened cans in the console between the seats. She told Kevin to get home and that she'd be calling his father and possibly the police. When Kevin's eyes flicked at her a little contemptuously, she added, "She's fifteen, Kevin."

"We weren't doing anything."

"Giving alcohol to a minor is a misdemeanor, and you know that as well as anyone."

Kevin started the truck motor and we stepped away as he shifted into gear and backed out onto the rough.

"I guess she wasn't running," I said.

"He's definitely not someone we want her spending time with," Jenna said. Her jaw was clenched as we walked back across the fairway.

Carrie met us at the door, her face scrunched up in concern.

"I think she may have been drinking," Jenna said, reluctantly.

"I have no idea what to do now," I said.

As had often been the case in my life, I was surrounded by women willing to do my thinking for me and I didn't mind.

"I'll talk to her," Jenna said, and went upstairs.

I told Carrie about the bullet-headed prick in the car.

"Well, I'm glad that's all there is to it," she said. "I know you've got to bear down on her for it, but just remember the kinds of things all of us did in high school."

She laughed in a charming way and I wanted to feel a little better about all of it.

Jenna and Chase began shouting upstairs – mostly Jenna – but Chase quick and hard in response.

"Should I go up?" I asked.

Carrie said she thought so. I started through the empty dining room, but Chase's bathroom door slammed in a way that told me she'd be in there for a while. Soon Jenna came downstairs and sank into one of the chairs at the kitchen table. She was shaking her head, silently distraught.

"I guess being a coach is a lot like being a parent," Carrie said after a moment.

Jenna looked at me. "You know I have to do something about this," she said.

I didn't know what she meant.

"A school adult catches a student-athlete drinking, even off campus, it's an automatic three-game suspension. It's MIAA state rules."

"Oh," Carrie said. "Of course."

"So, she misses tomorrow," I said.

Then I knew why she was upset.

"And the first two games of the State Cup."

Jenna nodded.

"Do you have to turn her in?"

"I could pretend I didn't see it, I guess. It's not like she was seen out in public intoxicated."

"Is she intoxicated?" I asked.

Jenna just slowly rocked her head; she was thinking about my first question.

"She's picked up at a team party by one of the major assholes in this town," she said. "She blows off not only your curfew but team curfew. She's drinking on a public golf course in a truck and is caught by her coach and her parent. I don't think we want to ignore this, Tommy."

"Busted," I said.

Jenna nodded. "Busted."

"My last question," I said. "Is this what she wanted to happen?"

7.

Throughout the fall, the coverage in the town paper and in the *Globe* had gathered steam as the team continued its success; the press and the wins had the predictable catalytic effect. The girls' soccer games became one of the best-attended sports in Newton, especially after the TV crews began showing up, maybe thanks in part to the undeniable fact that the high-school football season was a total stink bomb. In recent years, the girls' soccer team had either missed out on the State Cup playoffs or not made it past the first round, a qualifying game. This year, the expectations for the team were nearly boundless as the end of season approached. I was stopped often in the supermarket, at the field, or especially at Starbucks, and listened while people praised Chase and asked about her. In the days following the red-card game, I must've been buttonholed a dozen times by people telling me that Chase hadn't deserved it, or good for her for standing up for her team, or all refs are incompetent anyway so don't worry about it. Newton had managed a win in the game that Chase couldn't play because of her red-card penalty, so there was no love lost that time.

During the season, the *Globe* had routinely covered Newton games, and at the end of the season before the tournament, the team was ranked third in the state. Photos of Chase – current game shots, thank you – found their way into the town paper maybe half a dozen times. They even did an interview with her a couple of weeks after her red-card game. They asked questions like, "Who's your favorite singer?" ("Joan Jett," she said, which didn't surprise me since Jett was Taylor's favorite.) "What's your favorite subject in school and why?" ("English," she said, because the teacher is fun.) "What do you like to do most in your free time?" ("Run.") "Who's your biggest soccer fan?" ("My mother," which of course was true. And just stab me in the heart with a tuna fork, why don't you?)

What intrigued me most about the *Globe* interview, which when printed ran two bars wide down a full page in a Saturday sports section, was that in several of her answers she actually put more than one sentence together, something I'd not heard her do since Taylor died.

"What do you love most about soccer?"

"The games are always close and anything can happen. The team can't let down even if we dominate. And we always have to work together."

"What do you see for yourself in your immediate future?"

"I want to play soccer at the highest levels. I want to play Division I college and compete for a spot on the U.S. Nationals. I like the West Coast style of possession play in college, but most of all I want to play for a winning team."

"What about after your playing days are over?"

"My playing days will never be over. I'll still play from my wheelchair."

With all the hoopla about the team and Chase, her three-game suspension just before the tournament was like a bucket of ice on the community spine. Chase was benched, no reasons given, for the Saturday makeup game following her night on the golf course. People just assumed Jenna was resting her, since the Framingham team was depleted by injuries, and Newton won 2–0. It wasn't until a meeting after the game that teammates and parents were told. The athletic director came to the end-of-season parent gathering at the gazebo at which the schedule for the coming tournament games was given out. After a little business was dispensed with nervously, the AD announced that Chase Ellis had received a mandatory three-game suspension "for disciplinary reasons" and would miss the first two State Cup games.

Before the news about Chase, the spirit of the team and the parents had been excited, maybe even a little raucous as the meeting started. When the AD announced the suspension, the mood in the gazebo took El Nose Divo. It was like hearing that Lassie'd been shot. People were stunned. They gaped at each other, then gaped at me, while I studied the grass stains on my running shoes. Then they started demanding explanations.

The reaction of the players was notably different. First, they were surprised, naturally, they hadn't heard since Jenna had told no one but the AD; they gasped right along with the parents. But then looks were exchanged among themselves, and jaws tightened, and eyes narrowed. None of them looked at Chase, who was sitting on the end of one of the picnic benches, turned slightly away from the other girls at her table. They knew the rules. They were at the psyche. They must have quickly figured out what rules had been broken. One thing you can say about teenage girls: however catty and fickle and self-conscious they may be, they know everything.

The AD gave no explanation.

"The reasons for the suspension are between the coach, the player, the MIAA, and the player's parents. There will be no further discussion of the infraction."

To his credit, he toughed it out, despite a heated grilling.

When the meeting broke up, people slowly left the gazebo, led by the players, who seemed eager to get away from the adults so they could talk. Except Chase. She stayed at the picnic table. I went over and stood next to her, feeling that she might need a bodyguard, until Kim, the assistant coach, came over and slid onto the bench beside her. Kim was more popular among the athletes than Jenna, mostly because she was irreverent and not nearly as tough on them. Kim put her arm around Chase and talked close to her ear, so I stepped away, not wanting to look as if I was eavesdropping. After our scene in the kitchen earlier, I didn't really see any point to my talking with Chase anyway; I figured what the hell, let Kim take a turn. I watched people hanging around the parking lot talking, many of them looking over at the gazebo. At one point I'd caught Jenna's eye just after the announcement, but she was looking so grim-faced I just turned away.

After her shouting match with Jenna at two in the morning, we'd let Chase go to bed while Carrie, Jenna, and I drank coffee and talked. I told them I was clueless as a parent, something they already knew all too well, though they didn't say it. I'd set curfews for her before; sometimes she kept them, sometimes not. I never felt I had any real impact on what she did. I didn't feel as if she was a guest in the house, although in some ways I felt we were both guests in this little town of booster clubs and lawn sprinklers. I simply felt that I didn't have any leverage. There wasn't something she wanted that I could hold back from her if she didn't do what I said. How could I say, you're grounded, when she walked out of the house the moment I said it?

Carrie suggested we talk to Kate, the counselor: that I shouldn't just call, but make an appointment and get into the process myself.

"This isn't just about personal counseling anymore, Tommy," Carrie said. "It's about family counseling."

I knew she was right, but I felt embarrassed as she said it. Jenna just listened quietly, probably thinking about her State Cup being in deep trouble.

The next morning, before Chase came downstairs, I called and made an appointment with Kate: one for me, and at her suggestion, the following one with Chase and me. I told her about the night before, and the likely suspension from soccer. She said she thought the suspension would not be a good thing. I told her I wasn't very jolly about it myself but that it was not negotiable, and tried to engage her in a conversation about Chase, her defiance and obvious unhappiness. Kate listened but would only respond by saying that we needed to get into this in a session, not over the phone. I told her I thought Chase was in crisis or at least approaching one. She said she would call Chase herself later that day.

After Chase came downstairs and banged around in the refrigerator with all the warmth of a convicted felon, I told her that she and I needed to talk about last night. She glared for a second and continued banging. The peanut butter jar, the jelly jar. The silverware drawer, the dishwasher. I watched, leaning against the kitchen table while she slammed together a sandwich and started for the back door as she took a bite.

"Whoa," I said, stepping in front of the door. She looked at me with disdain and turned around, surely heading for the front door. I wasn't going to chase her.

"I made an appointment to talk to Kate."

She turned on me, jelly on her chin.

"That's none of your fucking business."

"You're my business."

"Bullshit."

"I'm your father."

"An accident of nature."

"No. The dream of two people who once loved each other and always loved you."

She threw the sandwich at me. When I blocked it at face level, it spattered purple jelly and Wonder Bread.

She was nearly into the dining room when I said, "You wanted that suspension. You did it on purpose."

"You are a total fucking asshole," she screamed at me, looking like she wanted something else to throw.

"You knew exactly what you were doing. Just like the red card. So what happened to still playing from your wheelchair?"

I didn't see her again until she turned up, quite unexpectedly as far as I was concerned, on the sidelines of the makeup game that afternoon. She was in uniform, even though Jenna had told her the night before that if she came to the field she should be in civvies because of the suspension.

When Kim finished talking quietly in her ear after the team meeting, Chase stood up and started for the parking lot. I walked beside her until she growled that she had a ride. I said I wanted her to ride home with me. She ignored me, and jogged off across the field, stopping to take off her cleats when she reached the parking lot. From there she looked around as if for an expected ride but couldn't complete the connection. She then turned around and ran back across the field, smoothly and without apparent effort, in stocking feet, carrying her cleats, with her team bag strung across her shoulder, then disappeared from view down a side street. I looked around the parking lot for a red pickup.

Newton survived the qualifying game against an undefeated team from Stoughton that went to penalty kicks, and was then eliminated from the tournament against Dedham, a team they had beaten earlier in the season. Dedham shut them out 3–0, as Newton's offense could not finish, despite a lot of chances in both halves. It was Chase's third and final suspension game. I didn't go to the games, and neither did Chase.

Chase's suspension was described in an article in the local weekly newspaper, with a big headline in the sports section and more detail than should have been included considering that Chase was a minor. "Unnamed sources" made it clear that Chase had been suspended for an alcohol violation, and unnamed team players were quoted as saying that she'd let the team down. Jenna was quoted saying simply, "There was a violation, we've dealt with it, and we're putting it in the past." From the tone of the unnamed source quotes, and the looks I got at Starbucks, putting it in the past was going to take us well into the future.

At a coaches' meeting held during the weeks of tournament play, Chase was chosen as a first-team All Star player, and was shortly thereafter named to the *Globe*'s All-Scholastic first team for Massachusetts. A head shot of her and a paragraph about her season and stats appeared along with those of the ten other players selected from across the state. In the paragraph it referred to her as "the Bicycle Girl."

Two weeks after the suspension, Chase played in the regional all-star game. I'd considered not letting her play – as a consequence for her continuing belligerence. Both Kate and Jenna thought that would be a mistake. Jenna thought since she'd earned it, and completed her suspension, she had every right to play if she wanted. Kate said that soccer meant a great deal to her, despite my argument to the contrary, and encouraged me to let her have the one thing that was giving her some sense of continuity. I felt that if soccer was the one thing she seemed to care about, maybe taking it away from her until she began meeting even the most minimal expectations for her behavior made sense. But I let them overrule me.

In the all-star game, Chase's side, including the best players from eastern Massachusetts, dominated the game, in large part because of Chase. She scored five goals, three of them unassisted. She played with tight-jawed relentlessness, sailing down the sideline with terrific speed, crashing defenses despite body check after body check. She even managed to convert an errant block by the opposing keeper into a goal with a spectacular bicycle shot, electrifying the crowd and igniting camera flashes throughout the night air. She barely acknowledged the congratulations from her all-star team. Carrie and I both noted that the two other Newton girls on the team did not join in celebrating with the others after Chase's goals. It was probably not lost on them that Chase had her best game of the season on a team where she was in effect playing for herself. Jenna would say later that she played better because she felt less pressure to carry her team the way she did throughout the regular season.

Ten minutes into the second half, with Chase's side up 5–1, Chase was taken down on a hip check by a defender as she attacked the net. This time she did not get up, and had to be helped off the field. It was her right knee. Carrie cried "Oh, no!" when Chase went down, jumped from the bleachers, and ran around the field to get to her. Play stopped briefly, and one of the players on the field told Carrie she thought she heard two pops. Carrie threw aside the plastic cold packs and demanded ice; looking at me she said, "Get my car."

Later that evening in the Children's Hospital emergency ward, Chase had an MRI. She and I then waited silently in an exam room until Carrie rejoined us. She came in smiling, gave Chase a hug, and told her not to worry: it wasn't too bad. There was swelling and bruising but no collateral tissue damage. It was a patellar subluxation, which meant her kneecap had slid out to the side, and then slid back in. Those were the two pops the field player had heard when Chase went down.

Carrie knelt down in front of Chase and smiled.

"The good news is the ACL held up wonderfully! The not-so-good news is that we're going to have to deal with your kneecap much more aggressively so it doesn't keep popping out on us in the future."

Chase had been crying off and on since leaving the field, first in pain, then in despair. But she rebuffed everyone's efforts to talk to her except Carrie.

"What's that mean?" she asked.

"Well," Carrie said. "Rest, then a lot more rehab to strengthen all the muscles around your knee. Maybe," she said, looking thoughtfully at me, "we rushed your return to play a little. This time we're going to be more careful."

Carrie seemed pretty upbeat, but Chase, disconsolate, wasn't buying it.

When Carrie left the room, Chase looked up at me, her face lined with exhaustion.

"I guess I answered your question," she said finally. I didn't know what she meant until she impatiently gestured at her seat. She was sitting in a wheelchair.

A reinjured knee meant Chase could not join the Juventus club team for a series of tournaments planned for the Thanksgiving and Christmas holidays. The one at the end of December was a special loss. Top clubs from all over the country went to Florida, where players had the opportunity to showcase their skills for college coaches from all fifty states. I knew from brief phone conversations I'd overheard between Chase and Jenna that the tournaments meant a lot to both of them. Jenna stopped by the house often, finding one reason or another to keep contact with Chase. Although Chase was supposed to be in the weight room after school, working on developing the muscles around her knee that would give stability to her kneecap, in fact she was coming home often directly from school and going to her room. She was obviously depressed. Missing the tournaments was certainly part of it. I felt bad for her, and for Jenna, too; but I also felt some relief that I would not have to shell out a couple of grand a pop to send Chase off in jets to expensive hotels and restaurants.

My money situation was getting worse. A lot of this had nothing to do with Chase. I was in a bit of a downtime even before she moved in with me. My work tended to come in streaks: one new client and a little job often resulted in a few more assignments and then sometimes a big job. I'd resisted going to work in a PR firm, because those places were cesspools. I'd been too independent all my life to start competing for partner status with post-teenage B-school grads who drove Porsches and made client connections with chums from Choate. When Chase moved in, I wasn't particularly busy but I had some outstanding receivables that were trickling in, so I managed the house rental and the move. I eventually collected most of those, which basically involved bird-dogging my friends for money, something I was never good at. But I hadn't generated much of anything new. And I hadn't been spending a lot of time in the city in the late afternoon to evening hours, which was a loss: these were the times when I could connect with potential clients at an assortment of bars and health clubs or run into them at event receptions. I felt the pull of home.

Which was a very good thing. One afternoon in November I left my office early in the afternoon with the intention of dropping off the Jag for service, another drain on my finances since I'd been using it much more than when I lived in the city. The Jag took sixteen quarts of oil, needed a new slave cylinder every two thousand miles, and went through tires like they were made out of cheese. In Boston during New England winters, I took cabs. In Newton I managed to find a service shop where the cranky owner seemed to know something about the madness of British motors. On the way there, I drove past the top of our street, and as I passed I glanced down at our house. The red pickup truck was parked out front. It was not quite two o'clock in the afternoon. Chase was supposed to be in school.

I confess there was a part of me somewhere in my lazy soul that wanted to just keep on going and act as if I hadn't seen anything. I didn't want another scene with Chase; our interactions since her suspension had been cold at best and sometimes volatile, me yelling or her yelling about stupid stuff around the house. I had no idea how to handle what could be a dicey scene in my own home, but I had to do it. I turned the Jag down our short street and wheeled into the driveway, gunning the engine to announce my arrival.

I'd made it eminently clear to Chase after her night in the pickup that seeing a twenty-year-old was absolutely off-limits. Jenna had been with me for this scene and it was good to have backup. But Chase and I had gone a few more rounds on it by ourselves the next day. These were mostly me trying to explain to her why it was unacceptable and her saying

"Whatever," the teenage expression that instantly provoked the parent strangler reflex. Her impeccable line of reasoning was that they hadn't done anything so what was the problem. I would counter by noting that abandoning her team, disappearing with a stranger, and getting drunk two hours after her curfew was not exactly *Barney and Friends.*

By the time I was on the stairs to our second floor, Chase was out of the bedroom on the landing, in soccer shorts and a T-shirt, looking nervous. Kevin got to the bedroom door about the same moment I did. I kept telling myself on the way into the house, he's just a kid, he's just a kid. I was afraid of overreacting. But standing there in my daughter's bedroom pulling his sweatshirt on with his belt unbuckled, he didn't look like any kid.

I just said, "Get out."

Up until then I was OK. Parental, the authority come home, take it one step at a time.

But then I followed him out of the house, and cut across the lawn to come up to the door of the truck just as he was getting in. I surprised him. I grabbed the door and pulled it open hard, spilling him onto the street. I looked around the street then grabbed him by the sweatshirt and slammed him back hard against the truck and then lifted him close to my face.

"I see you around Chase again, you little prick, you won't have to worry about the police; I'll fuck you up a lot worse than they will."

I pushed him back into the truck cab; he hit his head on the roof as he fell back in. And suddenly he looked like a stupid kid from the suburbs who'd gotten roughed up for the first time. I stepped away from the truck and he drove away, with his tires shrieking.

OK, it was stupid. But I grew up in Dorchester. We didn't call shrinks or counselors or discuss discipline with teenagers over scones and Starbucks; when someone hit us in any way, we hit them back in kind so our sisters didn't have to do it. Kevin was sneaking into my house when I was at work, he was messing with my fifteen-year-old daughter, and he needed to know who he was dealing with.

Chase came running across the lawn, screaming at me, "You fucking asshole, you stupid fucking ass," that sort of thing. From the way she looked, I expected her to start hitting me, but she stopped short at the edge of our lawn and swore at me. She was virtually out of control – surely she was out of mine.

"Get in the house," I said, but she'd already turned and headed back inside, slamming the door behind her. When I got inside, she was upstairs slamming the bathroom door and locking it. Five minutes later, as I was leaving messages for Jenna and feeling a little desperate, she slammed out the front door as she left wearing a sweatshirt and jeans. She wasn't supposed to be running on her injured knee, but as I watched her through the living room window, she began running up Brook Lane toward town.

The next morning she still had not returned. I sat on a stool in my kitchen talking to a Newton policeman. I'd spent most of the past eighteen hours on the phone with one person or another, and no one had any idea where she'd gone. An hour after she left, Jenna returned my call and I told her what had happened (leaving out my fond goodbye scene with the pickup prick). Jenna made a lot of calls, too, then came over to the house. Eventually we decided to call the police, even though the time I'd called the Boston police looking for her they'd offered little help. By morning the police had at least determined that Chase was not with Kevin Lassiter. The police in my kitchen asked me about him.

"He claims you knocked him around."

"Bullshit," I lied. "I told him he was a little prick and I didn't want him around my daughter, but I never touched him."

The Lassiters owned a landscaping company in the town; landscaping was big where there were so many lawns.

Jenna, still in the kitchen with me, cut in. "Dave, you know what a shithead that kid is. He'll say anything."

The policeman quietly seemed to agree with this assessment.

"He could also be lying about not seeing Chase last night," she added.

"I don't want him near my daughter," I said. In addition to being panicked about Chase on her longest disappearance jag yet, I'd been accused of roughing up a twenty-year-old with a lawn business behind him. It seemed that taking the offensive was the best strategy. I was glad Jenna knew the cop as well as she did.

"We can do a restraining order, but first I think we want to find her," he said.

During the night we'd already gone over all the possibilities we could imagine. Jenna had called Chase's high-school teammates. Though this seemed unlikely, given the tensions around Chase, especially after her suspension contributed to the team's elimination from the State Cup, we still called them, because the police kept asking. The parents we talked to were surprised, sympathetic. The girls were much the same, though Jenna had to caution a few of them not to turn this into a gossip thing, which of course was utterly inevitable. We called the homes of a few of the players from other towns on Jenna's club team who had worked out with Jenna over the summer, to no avail.

I made the call I'd dreaded at around ten o'clock at night, after she'd been gone for close to eighteen hours. Maris had not heard from her, and to her credit did not panic. I discouraged her from driving to Newton on the chance that Chase might call or show up somehow in Connecticut. Since the call, Maris had called back a half a dozen times, not just to express her disapproval of me but to make suggestions, a few of which were actually good. She gave us names and numbers of people in Chicago whom Chase might have called or contacted by computer, assuming she'd managed to get herself online; these people might have known something.

The police asked me the night before whether Chase was carrying anything when she left or if she had any money. She'd been empty-handed as she jogged off up our street, but I didn't know much about her money situation. I never needed to give her cash, even though I spent goo-gobs of it on one thing or another related to her. Although some of Taylor's financial issues were still tied up in probate, Maris had arranged to deposit a regular allowance in an account for her. As far as I could tell, Chase rarely spent any of the money, except to call Domino's for herself at odd hours and hand the driver a $20 bill of her own. While the police were in our kitchen, Maris called to let us know that Chase had in fact gotten cash since leaving the house, a maximum ATM withdrawal of $500.

"Where was the ATM?" the policeman asked.

Maris read an address off the bank website that surprised her, since it was in Boston.

"That's Back Bay Station," the policeman said. "That definitely changes things." He made a call on his cell phone, and used the expression "runner" to describe her. He didn't mean athletics.

Based on the information Jenna and I had piled on him for several hours, Dave the cop seemed to think that the most likely place she might go – if she wasn't just holed up in a Starbucks tossing back hot chocolates – was Chicago, where she knew the most people. From Back Bay she could have easily gotten on a train or headed for the airport or the bus station. The knowledge of the ATM kicked him into a much higher level of activity. He stayed calm, but I had the sense that he believed the next few hours were critical. We talked a little about runaways, or runners, as he called them.

When I mentioned she had a therapist, he took Kate's number. I had spoken to Kate twice the day before: once shortly after Chase left, and once when she'd called back in the evening. I was glad the police were going to call her. While Chase seemed to value keeping her twice-weekly appointments with the therapist, I found Kate far too guarded with me. Maybe a cop would help her to step out of her therapy mode and recognize that Chase could be in a more urgent kind of danger.

By early afternoon I was feeling like my kitchen was an investigation headquarters. I suppose in a way it was. Jenna left shortly after the police earlier in the morning, but returned when her health classes were done in the early afternoon, turning over her club practice to Kim. Several parents from the soccer team came over. Ellen, the pretty realtor who knew my addiction to coffee, brought a tray full of lattes and made herself at home at the kitchen counter, fielding calls from other parents who were following up with us. Carrie called throughout the day and said she'd bring dinner that night. Around lunchtime, Anna, my younger sister, pulled into the driveway in her Jeep. She hugged me and told me not to worry. Around Anna I worried just a little less about Chase because now I had to worry about Anna, too. To me she was the living incarnation of the idea of human vulnerability, all that was disturbing as well as all that was beautiful about it. In her unassuming way, she quietly took over the kitchen, feeding everyone who came into the room, including the police, with snacks she kept making and toasting in the oven. Anna knew how to take care of everyone but herself.

After the police left in the morning, I logged a call to Fergie. When he called back midmorning I told him what was going on, but unlike everyone else I told him about thumping the little shit Kevin around.

'Oh, you stupid ass,' he said.

"That's what Chase said."

"Well, she was right. What in the world got into you, Tommy?"

"I think it was seeing the little dickhead in her bedroom buckling his belt."

"Anyone see you thump him?"

"Only Chase."

"She did? Shit."

He insisted on details. I wasn't really worried about knocking the dickhead around; I couldn't imagine any parent in the world except Kevin's having a problem with it. But it did bother me, for all sorts of reasons, that Chase must have seen it. Based on what Jenna had told me, I guessed Kevin had a police record, and Fergie would track it down; he had legal connections out the kazoo, and everyone liked to do favors for the popular city pol.

I told him about the lawn business.

"Tommy, trust me," he said. "They try to fuck with you over an assault, we'll file against him for statutory rape."

I started to say I didn't know what the two were doing in her bedroom but he cut me off.

"It doesn't matter," he said. "We'll scare the shit out of them. They won't want to press a pair of pants."

He also said he'd make some calls to Chicago. He'd been the one to call our sister, most likely to get out to Newton, where her pathetic brother was bungling his family life.

In a way I was the one who figured out where Chase was. Most of us believed she was somewhere in Boston. I knew she'd made connections while staying in my Back Bay condo, but I had no idea who they might have been. Between the Newton and Boston police and Fergie using his clout as a city councilor, a lot of people armed with a picture of Chase were checking out places where teenagers might hang out. Connecticut seemed less likely, but I was relieved that this possibility kept Maris from hightailing it to Newton. We checked Chase's cell-phone records online, and with a little help from customer service, we learned she hadn't called or texted anyone since she left the house. This would be a startling thought to the parents of most teenagers, and an impossibility for the teenagers themselves, but that was Chase: she wasn't comfortable with gadgets and had the computer skills of a gerbil.

Chicago was still a possibility, though Chase's name had not turned up on any planes out of Logan or Providence, and she hadn't used the credit card Maris had given her during the summer. It was less easy to check on buses or trains out of Back Bay, but the police worked on it. There was a regular train to Chicago, the Lakeshore Limited, leaving Back Bay Station a few times a day and arriving at Union Station in Chicago about nineteen hours later. Prodded by Fergie, police in Chicago made efforts to look for her on the train from Boston and at the Chicago station, but these were probably fairly routine checks. The police and Fergie also called the Evanston police, who took a lot of names and promised to do some checking. Dave the cop and Fergie, working independently from one another, both asked their police contacts to drive by the house where Chase grew up, but there was no sign of anyone there and the house was locked. It had been on the market since the end of the summer, and while Maris told us there had been several open houses, there had been no compelling offers on the property yet. Maris told the police there was no way Chase could get in anyway; Chase had given her keys to her grandmother when we left for Boston in June.

It was then I remembered the way Chase had appeared and disappeared in her Evanston house at odd times without people noticing. She'd slipped in and out quietly through a basement door. When Dave was on the phone to one of the Evanston police that evening in our kitchen, I told him about the way she did this. They sent a duty car back out to the house, the third time police had been by the place. They used the same door, and found her on the second floor of the empty house, asleep in her old room.

A round of talk ensued to figure out what to do next. Everyone assumed I should go to Chicago, except me. It's not that I didn't want to go. I just had this gut-level bad feeling about seeing Chase again after she saw me push her sleazy friend into his truck. Plus, it was abundantly clear to me, and probably to everyone else, that Chase was running from me. So maybe the thing to do was to have an ambassador go out and bring her back, or at least get out there and figure out what the next move should be for her. It wasn't clear to me that by myself I could bring Chase back.

I even called Kate the Curt, who usually had very little to say to me, including throughout the one appointment we'd had together, where mostly she asked me questions and crisply deflected the ones I kept asking her. As to Chicago, Kate also thought I should go. She declined my offer for her to go instead. And no, Chase had not called her during the thirty-odd hours she'd been missing.

"It's your job, Tommy," Anna said.

I prevailed upon Jenna to go with me. If Carrie had been free to go that might have made more sense, but Carrie had to be in surgery the following morning and her schedule was always ridiculous. I could see Chase throwing a major balk at the idea of going anywhere with me. I had no idea how long we'd be in Chicago this time, but Jenna was willing to go and seemed to think it would not be difficult to persuade Chase to come back with us. We booked seats on the redeye and were heading to Logan airport within an hour after learning she was in Illinois.

I'm not sure what I expected in Chicago. As it turned out, it was mostly routine. Chase was at the police station when we got there, asleep in a staff lounge with a female officer watching the tube on the opposite couch. A sergeant in charge had arranged for Jenna and me to be picked up at O'Hare, an act of kindness that impressed me. When we got to the Evanston police station, he met us in the lobby and told us Chase was asleep and offered us a whole tray of Dunkin' Donuts. Police everywhere see a lot of parents whose teenagers have bolted on them for one reason or another, so this was nothing new. He said he'd spent some time last night talking to Chase and thought that her running away had more to do with her mother's death than an argument with her father. I didn't tell him about Kevin. He told us several of the Evanston police knew Chase from soccer: one was a part-time ref and others had kids who played on one team or another. I then realized that the ride from O'Hare, the coffee, the kind words, and the general good spin on the whole experience may have had at least something to do with the Bicycle Girl. I wondered how much Chase had let them see of herself.

While Jenna and I sat in the staff lounge, Chase woke up. The female officer got up and stood with the sergeant by the door, talking to one another, and giving us some but not total privacy.

"Hey, girl," Jenna said.

"Hi," Chase said to Jenna, looking at me from the side, nervously crumpling a tissue in her hand and wiping her nose with it; the cold or the allergies never seemed to go away.

Jenna was good; she knew to ask Chase safe questions, at least at first. Had she eaten? Had she been able to sleep for long? How was her knee feeling?

Chase answered her briefly, but in sentences. It seemed like she felt she was in trouble and was hoping to hold off the hard questions as long as she could.

"How'd you find me?" she asked Jenna.

"Your father figured it out," Jenna said, stretching the truth.

The police at the door listened briefly, then slipped out, leaving the three of us alone. I felt like I had to break the banality of this scene; sooner or later the conversation would have to escalate and I wanted to start the process while I had help available.

"Have you talked to anyone at home?" I asked.

She looked at me like she didn't know what to say.

"In Newton," I said. She shrugged. I waited.

"Kim." We waited a little more. "And Gramma. She wanted you

to call when you got here," she said. "And Carrie. She called like a hundred times."

Chase half smiled.

"She's worried about you."

"I know."

This was my time to make a move. I knew I was in the doghouse because of the Kevin thing and whatever else was behind Chase always battling me, but I had to do something.

"So what do you want to do, Chase?" I asked.

She rubbed the crumpled tissue up and down on the side of her mouth and shrugged.

"Tell me what you want and we'll try to make it happen. Tell us where you want to be. But if you come back to Newton, some things have to be different," I said, with as much kindness as I could get into my voice. Jenna on the couch next to me moved a little uncomfortably.

"Go back, I guess," she said, finally.

"You can't keep disappearing on me, and cutting school, and seeing some twenty-year-old guy with a police record."

"You went after him," she said, her voice suddenly full of accusation.

"I told him I didn't want him seeing you again."

She glared at me; I had to say something more.

"He started to come at me so I pushed him into the truck. That was all there was to it."

I could feel Jenna's eyes on me; this was all news to her. I could see Chase wasn't quite sure how to evaluate this, so I knew she hadn't actually seen me nearly dump the schmuck on the street. If she believed me, it would be an enormous load of anxiety off my shoulders. But whether she believed me about Kevin or not, her wordless anger toward me felt like a living presence in the room.

"We weren't doing anything," Chase said, not very convincingly.

"Yes, you were," Jenna said, and repeated the same list I'd given her: running away, cuts, seeing someone she knew was unacceptable for a fifteen-year-old.

Chase just wiped her nose with the tissue and looked guiltily at her knees.

"Can you expect your father – or any of us – to put up with stuff like that? You think because you're a soccer star you can get away with this nonsense?"

Chase looked at Jenna through tightened eyes.

"No," she said, as if she'd never expected to hear such a thing.

"Well, that's the way you've been acting. Like some absurd prima donna."

Jenna didn't stop there, dredging up the suspension, the red card, her criticism of her teammates on the field. She hit her pretty hard.

"I think you're a good kid and a great player, but you give everyone attitude, all the time. It's got to stop. The attitude has got to stop."

Go, Jenna, I thought. Chase started to say something and then stopped herself.

It occurred to me then that her circumstances were not exactly conducive to candor. She was sitting in a police station, with two police hovering outside the door, with her coach and her father bearing down on her, and her soccer career – the only thing that seemed to motivate her – on hold because of a repeat injury that could take more months of painful rehab. The only connection she'd made with someone even close to her own age away from the soccer field was with a twenty-year-old beer-guzzling lawn trimmer with a police record. No wonder she kept quiet. I wished I knew what it was she almost said, but I also knew from recent experience that asking her would not produce any answers.

A few hours later, the three of us flew back to Boston with nothing resolved. I felt like I was returning with a sedated tiger who could wake up again at any moment.

8.

At Carrie's prodding, I went back to see Kate, Chase's counselor, armed with Carrie's encouragement, to push for answers rather than just fielding more questions. I would have arranged for a different counselor for Chase at this point, one who was a little more forthcoming, but everyone seemed to think this a dumb idea. What I thought of Kate was not as important as what Chase felt, and Chase had never balked at an appointment.

I parked in the driveway of her big Tudor house on Fisher Hill in Brookline and walked around to the office wing of the house. Her husband practiced there as well, so there was a regular little jam of cars looping in and out of their driveway, though they'd arranged the layout so that people coming didn't have to bang into people going, always a good idea in the mental health racket.

Kate was a small woman, with dark hair and thin glasses, about thirty years old, very big eyes, sort of a plain, pinched face, and a bone-chilling seriousness that made me wonder why Chase seemed to like keeping their sessions. Maybe it was just me. This was our second appointment; neither of us had been able to persuade Chase to make it a three-way.

Shrinkology was not my thing; I once had to go to a court-mandated counselor after a whimsical Boston judge suddenly became annoyed at me in a courtroom over a series of speeding tickets. I went three times, sat in a cushy chair facing a cushy guy with a beard who looked like Hollywood central casting had sent up a Freud type for a razor blade commercial. I understood absolutely the need that my daughter's behavior expressed for professional intervention; but it just didn't surprise me that after six months little bug-eyed Kate didn't seem to be getting anywhere. Or at least nowhere that I could see.

In our first conversation I mostly sat swiveling in the leather chair and answering her questions while trying to get her to fill me in on what was going on in the brain of Chase Ellis. This time I was determined to get more out of her. She knew what I was there for and started out the session by telling me that Chase repeatedly and strongly had pushed her not to discuss what they talked about with me.

I found this galling.

"You've got to give me more than that," I said. "When we say anything to one another it's all spitting and spatting. She's cutting school to screw around with a screw-up and she took a train to Chicago to get away from me. I mean, Kate, for Chrissake. If you don't want to break confidences, then just tell me what to do. I'm not an experienced parent. I'm not even sure I should have custody at this point."

I looked out the French doors of her study onto a small bleak garden that looked like the dead of winter.

"I just don't get her. She's like a sphinx with me. I really think she hates me. Why doesn't she want to live with her grandmother?"

"Is that what you want?"

"Of course not. I'm just trying to make sense of things here. Please don't interview me again."

Kate swiveled a little in her chair. Just a pair of swivelers, what a scene.

"I think it would help you to understand better what Chase has been through in the past few months."

She listed stuff I'd already heard from all sorts of women in my life: losing her mother, relocating, living with a father she didn't know, on and on.

I cut her off.

"I understand all that. Her life has been turned upside down. But what do I do? I can't bring her mother back. And I can't let her disappear with a scumbag in a pickup truck or jump on a train to Chicago when I try to discipline her. That's what I need. Tell me what to do."

"I'm not sure you do fully understand."

I could see I was going to get a lecture, so I swiveled a little more and looked glumly at the garden while she continued.

"Have you ever heard of PTSD? Post-traumatic stress disorder?"

"Yeah sure, I guess so."

"You know that it can be very serious and extremely debilitating?"

"Yeah, it's like shell shock. Soldiers can be zombies for years after combat. You mean like that?"

"I mean exactly like that, Tommy."

She leaned forward in her swivel, probably relishing the idea of a good gooey pathology.

"Chase has been through something that is even more complicated and potentially debilitating than a lot of shell shock victims."

"Oh, come on."

She ignored me.

"Children often can have very unpredictable reactions to death, especially the sudden death of a parent. Teenagers may see death the way adults do, but their reactions are often very different. They can sometimes react in extreme ways – and often display extreme behaviors that are very, very difficult to deal with."

"You mean becoming suicidal?"

'Most definitely. But that's just one expression of it. They may also start doing very dangerous things: drugs are especially common, or drinking and driving, or driving wildly, or other kinds of extreme physical risks. If they have the means or opportunity, they may suddenly get into skydiving or jumping motorcycles, or other dangerous things. They become unusually impulsive. They may be drawn to the very things that should terrify them. They become counter-phobic. Counter-phobic behavior is very common for grieving teenagers. Do you understand the idea of counter-phobia?"

"Well, yeah, I guess so."

"Chase has all the classic symptoms. Trouble sleeping. Extreme mood swings. Explosive anger following long periods of sullen silence. Isolation. Asocial behavior. Always on the edge – either wired and intense, or just the opposite, seeming numb and unfeeling."

"You just perfectly described her for the last six months."

She nodded. "There's often some constant nagging little illnesses or chronic physical problems that won't go away."

"She's had a cold for months. We thought it was allergies."

She nodded again. "I suspect the way she's been playing her sport also fits this pattern – throwing herself into the games with abandon despite the risk of re-injury – which actually has happened to her. Or hypochondria: complaining often about headaches or menstrual cramps."

"I haven't heard any of those."

The look on her face told me she had.

"But grief is a very subtle and difficult form of post-trauma syndrome. It goes deeper than the emotional struggle to cope with a sudden shock, because it gets tied up with the genuine feelings of love and loss for a loved one. Chase's relationship with her mother was very intense, as complicated as mother-daughter relationships can be. There were things," she pulled back a little here, "that we're working on in our sessions. Suffice it to say, Chase's discovery of her mother's sudden death has had a crushing impact on her. It's not unusual for teenagers in Chase's circumstance to become obsessed with the person they've lost."

I told her about the growing shrine to Taylor in Chase's room, the photos, letters, and clippings that had been steadily increasing in numbers on the walls of her room.

"I hadn't known about that," she said. "But that sort of thing is expected. It's also not unexpected," she said, shifting in her chair slightly, "for Chase to have brought a boy to her room for what may have been unprotected sex."

I got a sick feeling in my stomach. "She had sex with that slimeball?"

"I'm not saying that – we're still sorting it out," she said. "But I've been in contact about it with the dean at her school."

"Chris Winberg?"

She nodded. "You gave us permission to speak. Schools have experience and resources in dealing with issues like this. Dean Winberg is being very helpful with Chase."

"I can't believe this," I said, shaking my head. "So what should I do?"

"Well, for starters, you've already been doing a lot of what needs to be done. You've seen to it that she's kept every appointment here. You made the connection between her dean and me. You've brought her coach – whom Chase respects – into her everyday life, not just on the field. You've gotten excellent medical care for her. You've kept her grandmother in the loop. You had her courses in school changed to reduce the academic stress."

"I didn't do all that; the dean did the school stuff."

"I understand, but the point is, the right decisions are being made for her and Chase has excellent resources at her disposal. Now it's just going to take time. And no," she said, anticipating my question, "no one can say how long it will be before things normalize for her. Unfortunately, as a single parent, you're going to take the brunt of her downturns."

"Downturns," I said with a laugh. "So what do I tell her when it's time for bed and she bolts for the door and God knows where?"

She laughed amicably enough.

"I wish I had the answer to that, I'd get rich helping parents set limits for teenagers. You just have to tell her exactly how you feel about what she's doing. If you can, you need to separate the behavior from her as a person. You know what I mean?"

"Don't tell her she's a screw-up, tell her what she's doing is going to screw her up."

"Right."

"I don't think I've ever told her she's screwed something up. I've gotten angry when she's disappeared, and I get on her about not being a slob, but mostly she's so secretive I don't really know what she's up to."

"You need to talk to her and tell her how you feel."

She looked at me as if waiting for me to say that this wasn't easy for me.

"Even if you don't think she's listening. I think she hears you even if she acts like she doesn't."

"Now you surprise me." I looked out the window at the garden, the light was growing darker. "You said the way she plays soccer is a part of her grieving: throwing herself around with abandon, that sort of thing. Is soccer a good thing or a bad thing for her? I mean I know it's a good thing, but is it too much?"

"I think soccer is holding her together. It's the thing she talks about the most. She worries about her performance, but I also think it gives her great satisfaction and a sense of accomplishment."

I felt relieved. I'd been worrying about this lately, the way Chase played, and the pressure that Jenna, the other players, and the school put on her to carry the team.

Kate followed my eyes out to the blighted garden.

"There may also be issues here with you," she said carefully. My attention snapped back to her face. "Which is why I think it's very important for the three of us to meet together. And it may take some time to peel back some of these issues."

"What issues?"

She paused for a moment. Then she said, "There are issues in your relationship with your ex-wife that we need to explore with Chase." I had the feeling this was all she was going to say on this little gem of intelligence.

"Ancient history."

"Not necessarily."

"I haven't been involved with Taylor for over a decade."

"In Chase's experience, you're very much involved with her mother."

"Now you've lost me."

"Let's take this a step at a time, Tommy. If you can understand what Chase is going through, and how her unpredictability fits a predictable pattern, if you will, that's a big step. And if we can get the three of us together to work on some things, I believe Chase will make a lot of progress. I'm very confident of that. She's a very strong young woman."

I could see from her looking at the clock behind my head that we were running out of time.

"No child-care tips for the witless beginner?"

She smiled sympathetically, then thought of something.

"I have one very strong suggestion."

"Shoot."

"I would not, under any circumstances, do anything physically rough in anger with anyone around Chase."

She looked intently at me to be sure I understood.

"You mean like pushing a scuzzball into a truck."

"That's exactly what I mean."

I immediately got defensive and started to explain, fully prepared to lie my head off. But she waved it away.

"If I came upon one of my daughters the way you did, I'm sure I'd want to smash the creep with a baseball bat." I started to like Kate the Curt right there. "But it is particularly important for you not to do things like that."

We looked at each other for a long moment.

"I never touched Taylor in anger in all the years we knew each other," I said.

"It would be very ill-advised for you to go crashing home this afternoon to tell her that," she said. "In a contest of your word against her mother's, you will not win. Let's work on it together with Chase. I think I can help."

I felt accused of something and couldn't defend myself. A welter of intense feeling rose in my throat, as if I was going to cry. Being a guy, I knew how to kill that off quick enough: some victory.

"OK."

"OK," she agreed.

Chase loved *Harry Potter*. Taylor had read her all the books as they were published, and then Chase read and re-read them herself. She owned all the movie DVDs and would often play them in her room, reciting the dialogue to *Sorcerer's Stone* while doing her rehab exercises. After she moved in with me, I bought a paperback copy of the series to catch up with her. Once, while the soccer team was waiting to get on the team bus after an away game and parents were standing around chitchatting, I scored some points with my distant daughter. A small gray rat jumped out of a dumpster near the high school and scurried across the parking lot. The girls jumped back, even though they were thirty feet away.

"Peter Pettigrew!" I cried, "Get him!"

Nearly everyone laughed, especially Chase, who then started talking to the nearest player nonstop about the third book, a stream of talk the likes of which I'd never seen from her.

The new *Harry Potter* movie was opening in a few weeks. Chase tried to buy tickets for herself online but theaters in the Newton area were soldout, except for a few midnight showings a week or so away on school nights. I suggested she wait a day before buying them, that maybe I knew someone and could get her in sooner. She looked a little worried but said she'd wait.

The next morning I was on the cell as soon as I hit the commuter train platform. Someone would know someone, I just had to dig. I was a perk grifter, who better to grift for than my daughter? By the time I got to Back Bay Station, I'd gotten lucky. One of the city's big investment firms had bought up an entire opening-night show at Copley Place for clients and their children. I knew the managing partner and talked to his secretary. I got six tickets. When I went to pick them up an hour later, I chatted up the secretary and got four more tickets. Turns out she had three young daughters, and all of them loved soccer.

Chase was utterly delighted; she laughed and clapped her hands like a little girl, then in a flash her mood turned around completely. She looked suddenly anxious, pensive, almost sullen. I silently guessed the reason: she didn't know who to invite or how to pick some and not others. I asked her who on the team liked *Harry Potter* the most. She reeled off names, including Kim, the assistant coach.

As I called Kim, I said to Chase, "Let me be the asshole here."

Before the opening, we all met at the commuter station and rode into Back Bay on the train. The investment house had put out a spread at the theater, particularly appealing to much younger children, which meant Chase and her teammates loved it all – lots of finger food, free promotional posters, and a new line of Harry Potter toy samples. Chase was like an eight-year-old, wide-eyed, wanting to touch everything. During the movie, she talked almost nonstop to Kim, who was sitting next to her, despite people in front turning to shush her. At one point, Kim leaned over to me and shook her head, laughing, and said, "Who knew?"

As we filed out of our seats, Chase described in detail scene after scene in the book that the movie had skipped or glossed over. It was not frustration but homage.

"Tommy!" The secretary, whom I'd only seen from across the

theater, now came rushing across the lobby, with a whole team of parents and preteen girls in tow. The little girls were whispering as they gathered around Chase. One of them had recognized her and they all started looking at her like the way Chase had looked at Dumbledore. One of the youngest girls actually asked for her autograph, which drew the attention of people nearby in the crowded lobby. Chase looked embarrassed and didn't know quite what to do.

"Show them your lightning scar, Freaky," Kim cracked.

The teammates laughed. Chase took the movie program held out to her and quickly signed her name while saying to one of the parents that she really wasn't famous.

"So what, it's cool," said a teammate, who then hip-checked her playfully. Chase was enjoying herself.

Like all holidays, Thanksgiving was a big deal in my family. Every year I went to my sister Trish's house, where her in-again-Finnegan husband took a busman's holiday from his restaurant and cooked turkey for all the Boyans. Everyone wanted Chase to come, persuaded that all she needed was a little Irish-American gush and gluttony to overcome all that WASPy tight ass.

But it was not to be. For years, Chase and Taylor flew to Connecticut to spend Thanksgiving at Maris's house with Chase's uncle Arlen's family. Since this was their tradition, and since everyone was trying to preserve continuity in Chase's upended life, this was the way it shook out for us. Naturally, they invited me, too, and thought I would come. But it seemed to me that it made more sense for Chase to spend some time away from me and Newton in a way that was meaningful for her rather than as the result of one of her sudden exits. Plus the idea of sitting down with Maris made me want to skip the turkey for the Tums.

Trish had one of those skinny little townhouses in the South End with the kitchen in the basement and the entire first floor a dining room. It always got pretty comical with everyone having to shuttle a gajillion dishes up and down the narrow stairway, especially since most of us were pretty looped by the time the bird landed. Her husband Dieter's German restaurant was normally more beef than bird or fish and more sausage than anything, which was fine with yours truly. What guy doesn't like sausage? Bacon, too: sausage and bacon. Which was how he made the stuffing. He broiled these turkey breasts that he crammed with the stuff, then coated them with some kind of spicy sauce, and if the rest of my family weren't all such pigs, I could have killed myself on that food.

Everyone turned out for the feed, except of course Chase. Fergie and his bitchy wife were there with their two boys home from college and their older daughter, with her ugly boyfriend; Trish's three daughters, college-age and going to school locally while working; my mother and father; my aunt and uncle, who had lived next to us when I was growing up but now came up from the Cape, along with their three grown-up kids, two of whom had their spouses with them and several extremely young children of their own, who thankfully ate by themselves in front of the DVD player; and Anna, alone of course; and me, also usually alone. Fergie sat at one end of the table, my father sat at the other; we kept the two of them apart as much as possible; Dieter and Trish barely sat anywhere, as they and my mother ran miles of laps on the stairway; and I sat in the middle of the table surrounded by college kids, in charge of controlling the consumption of wine. Twenty adults, one table, a shitload of bottles and turkey breasts, the grab was on.

Chase was the hot topic. I was OK with that. I knew I needed help. It took about twenty years to explain to my mother why she wasn't there and she still wasn't getting it. Why didn't they all just come up from Connecticut? That was my mother; anything beyond Gallivan Boulevard was a Third World country. But Mom wasn't the only one disappointed by Chase not being there.

The latest edition of *Sports Illustrated* had passed through everyone's hands within five minutes of their finally finding a parking space. Chase had once again made it into America's biggest sports mag. This time it was just a headshot, in the "Faces in the Crowd" section, where young athletes and amateurs who did something special were pictured, along with a few sentences about what they'd done. The little write-up described her record five goals in the state all-star game. The photo looked like a mug shot. Everyone kept grabbing the magazine and hogging it, each time reading aloud the five goals sentence and then asking again why she wasn't there with us for turkey.

"Too good for us now she's famous, Tommy?" my father said.

"She was famous a year ago, Pop," Anna said.

"And she was too good for us then, too."

It felt good to brag about her soccer season, and naturally I went on too long about soccer. A few of my nieces played soccer in high school; they seemed the most disappointed by Chase not coming. They followed the Newton games every week in the *Globe,* and one of them said she'd put a clipping with Chase's photo on her office bulletin board. This excited my mother, who produced from one of her countless shopping bags a similar clipping of her own. People liked having a sports star to brag about. One of my nieces, who went to UMass, gushed, "Oh yeah, Tommy. Everyone there got really excited when I said she was like my niece; it was Chase this and Chase that, they'd all heard of her, yah know?"

At the dinner table, the conversation stuck on Chase for a while, though this time it was not about soccer. I hadn't wanted to tell them all about our recent troubles, but it just sort of spilled over. To tell the truth, it felt good to get the poison out. I started kind of slow, just picking up on some general comment someone made about teenagers. But it didn't take a lot to open the floodgates. My brother and sisters both knew about the trip to Chicago, but no one else did. On hearing about it, my mother got so upset we almost had to administer oxygen, but the Burgundy worked well enough. When she heard her big strong granddaughter was getting counseling, she practically swallowed her tongue.

I didn't tell them a lot about the slimeball in the pickup, only that there had been a boy involved. My nieces had scoped that out anyway. The collegians ran through a round of anecdotes about troubles they'd had with their parents over sex and discipline, and it all got pretty raunchy, especially while my mother was taking plates to the basement. Anna wouldn't let people use Chase directly for comic material; as soon as someone joked about boys and sports or her size or some such, Anna turned a withering look on them, pointed her fork and said, "Enough."

But I wanted to know stuff and managed to shift the talk into a more serious gear. This was a whole table full of former reprobate teenagers and their parents, all of whom must have wrestled with the crap I was dealing with now. They had the huge advantage of growing up with their kids, while mine came back to me with a phone call. I figured there was wisdom here and I needed to tap it.

"Come on, you guys, I'm serious. I need help here. I'm totally clueless. What do I do when she totally ignores me and walks out of the house any time she pleases?"

"You stand in front of the door and knock her on her ass if she reaches for it."

"Bribery. Absolutely. It's the only thing that works."

"Just tell her she's grounded. Unplug the fucking TV."

"She always seemed so shy."

"No curfew, no soccer; case closed!"

"Where does she go? She meets her boyfriend on school nights?"

"Do you smell her breath when she comes in?"

"You want us to take care of the shithead for you, Tommy?"

"I don't get it. How can she be out screwing and boozing and be in *Sports Illustrated*?"

"Have you asked your priest?" That was my mother; shrieks of laughter followed that pearl.

They began to understand some of the problems when I told them about her having her own credit card and bank account.

"You gotta get control of that right now, Tommy. That's bullshit!"

Everyone quickly agreed that I needed to wrest control of the gravy train from Maris one way or another, that a fifteen-year-old with discipline issues should not have her own bank card, especially an apparently bottomless one.

"Ask her if I can borrow it," Dieter said.

We kicked around a lot of ways to set limits on a teenage girl, some of them funny though utterly impractical. Trish's girls were pretty savvy and had some helpful hints. They were the ones who said to get control of Chase's money and they asked a lot of questions about things she liked – clothes, food, TV, that sort of thing— – to try to find things to offer or take away. They especially wanted to know about Chase's friends.

"She doesn't have any."

"Oh, come on."

I shook my head. "Nada."

"Aside from the scumbag."

"Right."

This chilled the jokes for a little while. They insisted. What about her teammates?

But Fergie, who'd met the team, shook his head.

"She's on her own in that crew. But isn't it always hard for a star player to make real attachments on a team?" he asked.

The younger people at the table readily agreed. "Especially a girls' team," one of my nieces said. Heads nodded among the females.

"You have to find a friend for her, Tommy," Anna said, but people shot this idea down immediately. How could her father find her a friend? Take your pick: door number one, number two, or number three? I told them I'd tried several times to get Chase to invite her teammates over to our house. It had gotten so I wondered if she was in some way embarrassed. But after our evening with the team at BC, I knew it wasn't me that was holding her back.

No one came up with any reasonable strategy for drawing age-appropriate people into Chase's life; she had to do it herself. Then people talked about how shy Chase could be; one of my nieces told a story I hadn't heard before of Chase on a visit from Chicago as a ten-year-old refusing to get up from a playground bench to play with a group of kids.

"But they were all older," another niece remembered.

"She's still very shy," Anna said, someone who knew a thing or two about shyness.

"You're in a very tough situation with her," Fergie said. "You've got no history. Half the time the only reason our kids ever did what we told them by the time they were teenagers was because we'd raised them and at least a part of them still wanted to please us."

"Or at least not piss you off," one of his sons said.

"Well that, too, but I think the history works there more than anything."

Trish agreed. "You've just got to assume that she wants things not to be so stressful at home, and work things out with her so they can normalize a little. Do a behavioral contract."

That sounded like a horrendous idea, but I listened to her explain it anyway. We all knew I was feeling pretty desperate about the whole thing.

"Just bring her here, Tommy," Anna said. "We'll take care of her."

Maris drove Chase back from New Canaan earlier than expected, returning early Friday evening instead of at the end of the weekend. As Maris waited in the family room while I made coffee, Chase seemed interested in the food I'd brought back from Trish's. She took two slices of turkey breast, a plate of sausage stuffing, and a piece of Dieter's unbelievable apple pie then silently disappeared to her room.

Maris looked a little blitzed.

"How'd you like a Manhattan?" I asked.

Bingo. "But I have to drive," she said.

"Stay here. I'll spray Raid in the guestroom."

I made us a small pitcher of Manhattans. I wanted to use lighter fluid instead of vermouth in the hope of poisoning her but I had to get along with her somehow. Gramma was important to Chase. This was against every fiber in my nature but it had to be done. So I made the

Manhattans with enough kick in them to lift a soccer ball. Maris didn't seem to notice, eating the cherry with obvious relish. I sat in the chair opposite her. She evaded my question about why they were back early, saying something about Chase having homework.

She took a long sip, then said, "I think the reminders of Taylor were too much for her."

I told her a little of what Kate had told me about grief as a way of making her feel she'd made the right decision.

"I should talk to the woman myself," she said, a little too sarcastically.

I immediately got up and wrote down Kate's number for her. She didn't know if I was insulting or helping her. Upstairs, Chase was playing Joan Jett loudly on her stereo.

Maris asked politely, so I told her a little about my Thanksgiving, including some of the comments about limit setting. We kicked around the money thing a little, and she seemed to understand – against all my expectations – that Chase having seemingly unlimited money might not be a good thing right now. Maris and Taylor both grew up in families where money was a given; one of the prevailing tensions between my ex-wife and me had been my refusal to consider graduate school and a more serious career than ward heeling for a local pol.

I had the feeling that maybe forty-eight hours with Chase had included more for Maris than just reminders of Taylor.

"She can be stubborn," I said.

Maris nodded slightly after taking a refill on her Manhattan. "Like her mother." She said that Chase probably should have gone with me for Thanksgiving. I told her Fergie and Carolyn were expecting her as well as Chase for Christmas in Boston, which was not exactly true, but I knew bitchy old Carolyn would be fine with it; she was mostly just bitchy to her husband. Maris said she'd think about it. She didn't look like she'd think about it. And I didn't actually want her to think about it. But she clearly felt Chase in Boston for Christmas was the right way to go. No doubt poor Maris had gotten a good slug of teenage stubbornness. I wanted details, but I would've needed enough Manhattans to float her Benzo before I got much more out of her.

Later that night, while Maris was getting ready to sleep off the cocktails, I looked into Chase's room. As usual, her stuff was all over the place, mostly several generations of dirty clothes tossed willy-nilly. I wasn't ready for that battle. But several plates with leftover food on them were on the floor. The last thing I needed was roaches, though this was the suburbs and they'd probably starve.

"You need to take your plates down and put them in the sink," I said.

"Right," she shrugged, after seeing I wasn't just going to pass by her door.

"I want you to do it before you go to bed. And put them in the dishwasher, please."

She snorted dismissively. "You need to do that."

"You need to do it. I don't need to do it."

I almost said something about her being a slob, but remembered my talk with Kate.

"Everyone needs to work at taking care of things. I know it's annoying, but you can handle these little chores; you're not a sloppy person."

"How do you know what I am?"

"It's true. I could tell that from your clothes. But the way you arrange things like your trophies and pictures, you're an organizer. Look at the way you take care of your equipment."

And it was true. On her long window bench she'd stacked practice shorts, soccer socks, T-shirts, and sports bras.

She saw where I was looking, walked over to the bed and flipped her T-shirts onto the floor. Up until that moment, her acting out had been things she'd done on her own, or refusals to do what I asked, like putting dishes in the sink. But this was a direct in-your-face challenge. I was immobilized. I could either scream at her or insult her or walk away; that seemed the full range of my options.

"Chase!" Maris screamed from the hall, offended. I hadn't realized she'd come up behind me. "Why are you so defiant!"

"Just leave," Chase demanded of both of us, then did so herself, slamming her bathroom door, which she would have to share at some point that night with her grandmother.

"She would never, ever have acted this way if Taylor were here," Maris brooded.

In mid-December I met with Chris Winberg again one afternoon at the high school. I'd called her because we had discussed hiring a tutor for Chase the first time we met but we still didn't have one. Chase's schedule had been changed as promised, but her grades for the first marking period were awful: the Ds and C-minuses seemed pathetically inadequate for a person with such a competitive spirit and an academic family background. Even in my worst days at Catholic Memorial High School, I never brought home a report card like that. My father would have beaten me to death with his bar cloth.

Chris explained the tutoring situation: Chase had not only rejected the idea of a tutor, but even after Chris thought she had finally prevailed upon her, Chase began refusing the tutors on a case-by-case basis.

"I made the mistake of suggesting soccer players and other athletes for her," she explained.

"I finally figured out her objection."

Chris shook her head as if amazed at her lack of insight.

"These are people she competes with; the last thing she wants is to be taught French or algebra by a rival for playing time. Thank goodness for Jenna Eisenbech clueing me in on that notion."

We kicked around the idea of hiring a local college student. I even suggested one of my nieces, a junior at UMass, even though I wasn't sure she'd do it and the schlep out to the burbs would be a pain in the ass for her. Chris knew several other students, male and female, who could handle the work and would need the job, but that it might be easier for Chase to connect with someone outside the school.

I remembered some of our family conversation at Thanksgiving.

"You know, Chris. It would be outstanding if you could find someone her age. Maybe somebody different. But definitely not competition."

The savvy dean seemed to understand my thinking. She looked at her desk for a little while, rubbing her chin, then nodded at me slowly, still thinking things over.

"I may have an idea," she said slowly, then smiled warily. "How different?"

Megan Sullivan was different. Not just different from Chase. Or from Newton. More like, different from Earth. Metal detectors clattered up and down the Eastern Seaboard when she so much as moved a muscle. Not that her muscles were all that visible; she was pretty much a mushball of loose fat. She wasn't obese, not at all; she just had a lot of flesh, most of it showing, none of it looking like it had ever been threatened by exercise. She rang our doorbell early one evening in mid-December, and when I answered the door, she spilled into the front hall, laden with backpacks and wheezing from apparent exhaustion.

"I walked," she announced, sounding like she'd amazed herself.

"From where, Bolivia?"

"From the high school."

She made for the kitchen as if she lived there. The high school was less than a mile from our house. Chase had been upstairs but came down at the bell and eyed the young woman suspiciously from the stairway.

"You got any water?"

"Do you know a house that doesn't?"

She thought that was funny.

"Uh, bottled water?" she said.

"Who *are* you?"

"Oh, right." She explained, introducing herself. Ms. Winberg gave her our address and said we needed a tutor.

"You are Mr. Ellis, right?"

"No."

"Oh, God, don't tell me I went the wrong way."

She looked around the kitchen as if she indeed was in Bolivia. I explained that Chase had a different last name.

"Oh, OK. Mr. Boyan; got it."

"Call me Tommy."

"You mean like you're still stuck in childhood?"

I heard Chase snort from the foyer.

"Yes," I said. "I refuse to grow up and accept my Newton destiny."

"I can relate. So where's Golden Girl?" she said, though I suspected she knew full well that Chase was lurking nearby.

"I wouldn't call her that if you want to live," I said.

"Oh OK, that's cool."

"Is it?"

"Oh, I don't know. Don't confuse me."

She put her hand on the refrigerator, asked if I minded, then pulled it open and looked in. "I just want to take a little peek. Wow, junk food. Is that for you – or for the Girl Who Shall Not Be Named?"

It was hard not to like Megan Sullivan. She was slightly less than five and a half feet tall, wide in the hips, and her very Irish-looking face was pale and freckled. She was in the right place for freckles; Chase and I both had them. The metal on her was not only implanted but also dangling, from her neck and wrists: scores of bracelets up her arms, and necklaces heavy with ornaments, some of which looked like dogs' teeth. She wore black jeans and a black shirt and a black vest over it with a jumble of stitching on it. She didn't have a coat with her, but that was typical for a teenager, even though it was freezing outside. Her hair was streaked blond in places; whatever her natural coloring had been, it was suppressed long ago. The most striking thing about her other than her abruptness was how pretty her face was, despite the weight problem, the metal, and the makeup, most of it around her eyes. She had a large, freckled, rosy-cheeked prettiness that was startling; somehow it seemed out of place in the otherwise chubby jingling punk-goth package.

"I'm only taking this job if I get a ride in your car out of it," she said, pointing out the kitchen window. "I've seen it around town; it's one of my top-five favorites ever."

I asked her what the other four were. They were so completely undistinguished that I knew she was no motor-head.

"Those cars are crap," I said.

"So's the food in your fridge."

"You don't have the job yet," I said. "I'm not the one you'll be tutoring."

"I think you might need it. Food, by the way, is my life."

I almost said, I can see that, but I'd learned not to make weight jokes around a teenager. I asked her why the dean thought there might be a fit here. Since I hadn't heard Chase go back upstairs, I assumed she was still lurking near the front door.

"She said Supergirl needs some brushing up. I'm pretty good at that."

She explained: she'd worked as a tutor for the past four years, first in middle school and then last year at the high school. She was in Chase's class, a sophomore, though she could have passed for ten years older than Chase. She was an honor student, high honors she noted with some pride, all in accelerated courses. She wanted fourteen dollars an hour and a ride home, assuming she could get a ride there after school, depending upon the schedule she and my daughter worked out.

"Fourteen dollars an hour?"

"That's it: take it or leave it."

"Does that include time in my refrigerator?"

"Wow, Chase Ellis," she said, looking behind me. Chase was standing at the kitchen door.

"You look bigger than in the halls. I'm Megan. You were in my French class for about a week. *Bun joor Mayum-zull Eylisss.* Can you believe a Georgia cracker for a French teacher?" She laughed at the idea.

"I think you made the right move dishing off that babe."

Chase looked at Megan, wincing slightly with the discomfort she tried to hide whenever people commented in one way or another on her soccer renown.

"Hi," she finally said, her eyes scanning Megan quickly.

"I feel like I'm in the presence of a celebrity."

"That's nice," Chase said sarcastically.

I felt badly for Chase at that moment; I knew she was curious about the odd young woman, but even in her own home she didn't feel comfortable enough to respond with more than off-putting monosyllables.

"So what do we need to do to close this deal?" Megan asked, looking to me then back to Chase. "You need a tutor, right?"

"Why," Chase said, not a question.

"Because your grades suck?"

Chase's eyes narrowed.

"You don't have to like seriously learn anything from me," Megan said. "I can just help you figure out how to get the grades. That's my specialty – beat the system."

"Yeah, learning's such a waste," I said, "especially at fourteen an hour."

Megan smiled and asked Chase, "Why don't you let me show you a few things right now, and if that works for you, then we're like off to the races?"

"What subject?"

"You pick. I've got them all scoped out, don't worry."

She smiled her surprisingly pretty smile.

"I'm like the Chase Ellis of grade grubbers."

Chase shrugged.

Megan looked back at me. "If you let me cook here sometimes, I might lower the rate to twelve an hour, if you supply the food that is."

"You want to cook for us?"

She thought this was pretty funny.

"No. For me, God. We don't have much of a kitchen at home," she said, looking at the ugly granite counters,

"And food is your life," Chase said dryly.

I'd been hoping Christmas with the Boyans would produce a Scrooge-like epiphany in my surly, sad-eyed daughter. I think she had a good time. I know she had a good time, actually. My family knew how to do holidays, even if they put it on a little bit thick and washed it down with too much of the happy sauce. The clan gathered every year at Fergie's big Colonial on the West Roxbury Parkway. Fergie did pretty well in his law practice and it showed in his house. His wife, Carolyn, only worked as a volunteer at the Holy Name, along with her full-time job of keeping the short leash on her garrulous hubby. To her credit, she put an enormous amount of work into the holidays or any gathering of the family at her house, and since what was left of her side of the family had long ago moved its life to Florida, the holidays were all about the Boyans.

Christmas was her masterpiece. The tree stood in the grand hallway, extending two floors up; they had to decorate the top half of it from the big stairway. Evergreens and candy canes festooned the hall, the living and dining rooms. Johnny Mathis vied with Nat King Cole for supremacy on Fergie's sound system. All of us loved the holiday, as Fergie once said, both getting and receiving.

The plan called for Chase and me to drive into Westie for Christmas Eve and stay at Fergie's overnight, where there was room for all the cousins and their kids, although people had to double up here and there. Christmas Eve Day before we left, Chase mostly stayed in her room; she had been given the green light to run again on her injured knee, but lately had not been hitting the golf course with the same regularity as before. I'd told her in the morning that we were leaving at four, and then didn't see her again, though I kept sneaking to the foot of the stairs and listening for floorboards squeaking to make sure she was up there. At nearly four, I tapped on her door; she was slow turning the music down. I said it was time to go. The house was pin-drop quiet for about two full minutes before she finally opened the door. She was wearing jeans and the old sweatshirt that said Northwestern on it. From her expression she looked like I was taking her for a root canal.

Maris had declined to come to Boston, which was fine with me; we were getting along better than ever so why push it: forgive and forget, but. Then the inimitable Carolyn somehow managed to find a rare gem of charm in her coarse little bag of a personality. She persuaded Arlen and his flock of prep schoolers, and then prevailed on Maris to make the drive to Boston and arranged with a neighbor who went to Ireland each year for the holidays to loan them his house two doors down on West Roxbury Parkway. Fergie told me she won over the McKinleys by simply saying they all needed as a family to rally around Chase. "And that," said John, "is that."

Chase had never been to a Boyan do, and while she'd met most of my family at one time or another on her brief visits to Boston, the meetings were usually just one or two Boyans at a time and never longer than a downtown lunch. It was obvious to me from the moment we got to my brother's that Fergie had coached the clan about Chase beforehand. I fully expected them to descend on her like coyotes on a neighbor's cat, but they didn't. They held back, a little. It was a little too obvious, actually. All my nephews and nieces casually said hi, maybe threw in a routine hug, but then stared at her covertly and talked hurriedly among themselves if she left the room. It was somewhere between the rock star and the leper treatment. Fergie sort of half hugged her and made a teasing joke; Carolyn kissed at her cheek then went back to work being bossy; and only my mom and Anna let it fly, both giving her long hugs that Chase took in about as comfortably as a six-year-old boy.

Maris and company arrived shortly after we did and got a cool greeting from everyone, which made it a unique holiday for us to say the least. Seeing Maris in the middle of my family for the first time since my wedding brought back some very painful memories for me. I could see it had the same effect on my family, especially my mother. I'm sure Maris knew this, yet she was elegant, no denying it. Fergie, Anna, my mother, and even my sarcastic sister Trish were heartfelt about the loss of her daughter, and the Boyans absorbed the McKinleys into their boozy comedy of errors much the way they absorbed the booze. Arlen and his three children seemed genuinely charmed.

Dieter, Carolyn, and my mother all competed for two days to see who could put the most food on various tables. Not even my father, who turned up his nose at most food not made by my mother, would deny Dieter always won the quality toss. But leave it to my mom for sheer bulk. Food and alcohol was how we celebrated. Everyone drank, whiskeys of all sorts especially Fergie's wildly expensive unblended, and bottles of red wine. Beer for Fergie's sons, joined with enthusiasm to everyone's surprise by Arlen, and even sugary sparkling Burgundy in wine glasses for Chase and Arlen's kids, all of them younger than Chase. Maris looked on in shock when my dad poured Chase a glass for Christmas Eve dinner.

"She'd better start learning soon or they'll drown her in college," he said, and no one argued with him.

Jack Boyan was born in Kilkenny and was a man who knew a

thing or two about drinking.

How could Chase not have enjoyed herself – all that gassy Boston Irish charm released by fatty food and a flood of drinks? The dining room was packed to the walls for every meal, all leaves were in the table, and all we did was cram it down. Late Christmas Eve most people walked down the parkway to the Holy Name for Midnight Mass. Maris and Arlen's slick wife, Claire, a lawyer, went with my family, while Arlen and I stayed with Chase and his kids, who went to bed early. I sat in Fergie's study listening to my brother's extensive collection of Motown. I'd knocked myself out earlier dancing with Claire and Trish's daughters to Smokey Robinson. Arlen sat in the living room with Chase. Chase looked a little hammered, to tell the truth, not so much from the Burgundy; more from the Boyan excesses. She hadn't said much all evening, but people let her unfold at her own pace. There had been very little soccer talk, which for some reason actually seemed to put her more at ease.

Anna had left for several hours in the afternoon to help staff the kitchen at her homeless shelter, but she returned before the end of Mass after the usual cell phone threats, mostly from me. Throughout what remained of the night, Chase sat in the living room on the couch between two of Trish's daughters, who made fun of everyone, including Chase; she just sagged into the cushions looking buzzed. Fergie and I did our recitation of "The Eve of St. Nicholas," with the props and skit, and then sang our raunchy duet of "Oh Holy Night," with my mother screaming her annual objections.

Christmas morning was more of the same cornball stuff. My mother and Trish made mountains of popovers that everyone slathered with butter and jelly while we crowded onto the floor around the tree to open presents. Our family wasn't big on spending a lot at Christmas;

we were into gifts like mittens and scarves and scotch. Arlen and Maris had brought champagne and brandy in ribbons, and expensive tins of cookies, which went over huge and quickly disappeared, my mother objecting about champagne at such an hour while she packed away a few cookies and a snort of the brandy. Fergie gave everyone Red Sox stuff, even Maris, who gamely wore the jacket for the rest of the holiday.

Even though Taylor apparently had not approved of it because she thought they were hard on the ear canals, I gave Chase an iPod, which I'd loaded with all her CDs. I also gave her an iPod dock with a Bose speaker; she could blow Newton off its foundations with it, and probably would soon be trying. Chase gave everyone, I mean everyone, Juventus sweatshirts that she'd hauled in from the Jag in a green plastic lawn bag. They were thick cotton, obviously expensive, but money, after all, was not her problem. Naturally, being Boyans, we all immediately pulled them on and only exempted Maris in her new pitcher's jacket.

Anna had wanted to give Chase a puppy, but she asked me first and I nixed it. Maybe that was stupid. It was a tough call: if Chase had been twelve or even thirteen it would have been perfect. But I just didn't see her getting into feeding and walking and caring for a pet. It seemed like just another thing the two of us would start fighting about, like dirty dishes or too much soap in the washing machine. Neither Taylor nor I had ever been pet people, and something told me that Chase would not be one either. I couldn't bear the thought of some wiggly little dependent pissing on the hallway floor because no one got home soon enough to take it out for a leak.

So Anna gave her tickets to the Donnas in January at Avalon, a club near Fenway Park, after checking with me to be sure that a Donnas gig would work. Chase was surprised and pleased; but then we could all see her brow furrow for just a moment, and we knew she was unsure what she was supposed to do with the other ticket.

9.

After the third snowstorm of the winter, a few weeks after Christmas, I drove into Allston to see a friend who owned a classic car business. Among his personal collection he had an XK120. We'd done a little rallying together at one time; he always invited me to these "horses-doovers" receptions he put on to attract Harvard B-School types to look at his vintage cars. This proved very shrewd, since he seemed to be able to unload Ferrari Daytonas and Dinos as fast as he could source them, for big payoffs. I felt sick in my stomach as I walked into his showroom. A 1952 Aston Martin DB2 gleamed in the window. He must've known why I was there from the look on my face.

He'd often offered to buy the Jag. We both knew that if the car were cleaned up to a hundred-point standard that it could bring in six figures easy, but it needed work. Not a lot; most of the car's problems were endemic to the mark, not from wear and tear. The fact was, I simply couldn't live in Newton, work in Boston, and raise a teenage daughter with long legs and soccer gear while driving a two-seater. I also knew I'd already been a heartbeat away from sliding out on black ice into serious traffic once or twice with Chase in the car. And I needed cash, badly. I'd exhausted all my consulting collectibles; the work I was doing for clients at the moment was pretty low-yield stuff, and the doctor, PT, and counseling bills were killing me. The car had to go.

We made a deal on the spot. He gave me a good price: I could buy three new Jeeps for what he paid me. One was enough. He let me keep the Jag while he looked for a nearly new low-mileage Grand Cherokee for me so I could beat the taxes down a little. Driving home I felt like I was in a funeral procession. The engine purred its throaty song as if nothing was about to change.

"You sold your car? That's messed up."

"I couldn't keep driving a Jag around through snowdrifts," I said to Chase, already despairing of life in this conversation. We were driving into Boston to see Carrie for a routine knee check. Chase had almost refused to get into the Jeep when I picked her up after school. I couldn't fault her; I'd almost refused to drive it off the dealer's lot.

"That car was cool. I can't believe you sold it."

She sounded as pained as I felt.

I decided to tell her the other reason.

"Truth is, I needed the money. I could buy three of these for what I got for the Jag."

"You don't have money?"

"Well, this is a slow time of year for me. My work comes in waves – highs and lows, but it averages out OK. I'm just in a low right now. It'll pick up in the spring. Meanwhile, I just couldn't handle you and me skidding through another icy traffic light. Besides, this isn't so bad, is it?" We both glanced around the interior; she wrinkled her mouth.

We were heading down Route 9 into Brookline. The roads in late December were still mushy from the last snowfall.

"What happened to my money?" she asked.

"What happened. What do you mean?"

"I had money."

"Nobody spends your money but you."

"Gramma says you took it over." She looked out the window. "Is it gone?"

"Chase. Jesus! Of course it's not gone. I didn't touch your money. I can't touch it; it's all yours. Are you serious? The only thing your grandmother and I did was make it so you need my approval to get it."

We came to a stop at a traffic light and I turned to look at her. Now she was really pissing me off.

"You think we're going to let you zoom off to Chicago every time it suits you? Fifteen-year-old girls do not control trust funds. Your grandmother and I agree completely on this. And both of us monitor your account, not just me. I will never, ever touch any of your money."

She didn't look like she was listening. It occurred to me that at least we were talking about something, even if it was deeply offensive to me.

"Is there enough money for me to go back to school in Chicago?"

"Your grandmother would have to pay for that, but she can afford it, yes."

Traffic swirled around us as I drove slowly toward Children's Hospital.

"Is that what you want to do, go back to school there?"

"I didn't say that."

As we crossed over the Muddy River, Chase watched a pair of runners moving quickly along the sidewalk.

"What about like camp and stuff like that?"

"Chase, there's money available for you to do anything within reason that your grandmother and I think makes sense."

Actually, Maris had finally gotten the message that I wasn't interested in dipping into the family till. She had driven up a few days before to go over Chase's accounts with me. She'd also stayed to dinner. When she learned I'd sold the car, and looked around the house and noticed I hadn't bought any furniture, she asked me how things were going with my business. I told her this was my slow season.

"Are you concerned?" she said.

I told her of course not; there was no way I was putting a tool like that in her hands.

She just looked at me with her tight face and said, "I'm sure you'll work it out."

How different Taylor's family was from my own. My father would have reached in his pocket and pulled out a wad of twenties without a thought, even if he couldn't afford it. In my experience, people who have struggled to get by know they can live without it and remember all the help they've gotten and know how to give it back. People like Maris, for whom money has brought so much, feel a need to protect it because it's all they have.

"But I can't get cash with my credit card," Chase whined.

"No. We stopped that. But the money is there. I've told you when I've given you money that's been yours. And it's not always yours, you know; most of the time it's mine. Well," I corrected myself a little awkwardly, "that's yours, too. We're family. It's just from my bank account not from your trust fund."

"So if I want anything, I have to come to you."

"That's it. I thought we explained all this to you."

"And you don't have enough money to keep your car."

"I have enough money to take care of you even if you didn't have a trust fund."

"But I can't have my money."

I wondered why she was suddenly interested in money; I was sure it had nothing to do with my departed Jag.

"Is there something you want to buy?"

"I just want to know what happened to my money. And why I can't have it."

"If you stopped disappearing on me when it suits you, and did your homework instead of just listening to music, and acted like living with me wasn't a jail sentence, maybe we could negotiate something. But for the foreseeable future, no. If you want me to trust you to be responsible . . ."

"Bullshit."

She crossed her arms and slumped into the passenger seat.

"Well, bullshit is all you'll have next time you want to buy a train ticket."

I was beginning to think the arc of my romance with Carrie might have begun its descent, like a rocket, a little early. It wasn't a new experience for me; I'd been through a fair number of relationships that did the crash and burn sooner than expected, though it was usually me who sped the trajectory of descent. This time I felt like it was Carrie, and I wasn't too happy with that. She may have been a little too effervescent sometimes but she had this core of genuine knowledge and accomplishment that in truth I deeply envied. And she had lovely hair, eyes, in fact, all the equipment was excellent. I wasn't ready for it to flame out.

When she heard I'd sold the Jag, it seemed to bother Carrie much the way it bothered Chase. She wondered why if I needed a winter car, I didn't just buy one and garage the Jag until spring. I wasn't about to get into money issues with her. Carrie reminded me uncomfortably of Taylor, at least about money. She assumed it, and assumed everyone had it. I don't mean that she was mercenary: she was an orthopedist at what was arguably America's premier pediatric hospital, so her earning power was exceptional. And it wasn't as if she'd suddenly grown chilly or was slow answering my calls. In fact, most of the energy for our connection, at least so far, had come from her and still seemed to. It was sort of my usual way. I let these things happen to me with women more than I engineered them. But I wondered if all the turmoil with Chase was taking its toll.

A few weeks after the holidays, Carrie told me she had a weekend symposium in the Virgin Islands coming up in March and invited me to go with her. The islands, in the dead of New England winter? Of course I wanted to go. But I had a daughter I couldn't leave at home. With all the Boyans across the local landscape, it should have been easy to pass Chase off to Fergie or Trish or Anna. But it didn't feel right. Not that I felt I'd be encumbering them with her; it just seemed to me that before I could waltz off for a party weekend I needed to get more of a handle on my relationship with my daughter. It surely was a new feeling for me.

Carrie had said, "Oh, let Jenna take her. She'd love to have a roomie for the weekend!"

Chase's coach lived alone in a condo in West Newton, and probably would have been willing, maybe even eager to do it, since Chase seemed to be staying away from Jenna more than her recent injury merited. But I had to go with my gut and my gut said, "Stay close, battle it out, don't bail for the sun and fun yet." If Chase was going to be home miserable, I needed to be home miserable with her. Even if what was making us miserable was each other.

I pushed myself to remember the things Kate told me about Chase and the heavy burden of grief she was carrying. Maybe that was it: if my daughter was in pain, grieving for her suddenly dead mother, then I needed to be close, even if she didn't want me there. I had to remember I'd given her a choice where to live and she'd chosen me, even if her options weren't very plentiful. She hadn't mentioned private school again after our drive into Boston in the Jeep for her medical exam. Carrie had once told me I had to step up. Stepping up right now didn't include stepping out to the Caribbean. I tried to explain this to Carrie, but she said she thought I was being ridiculous, or making excuses.

She actually said, "If you don't want to go just say so," like a petulant teenager.

The phone conversation had the feel of a couple's tiff. I left her dangling on the Virgin Islands decision. It felt like a relationship make or breaker, but I couldn't imagine how I could leave Chase like that. The rhythm of daily calls and emails between Carrie and me stopped for a while. And I missed them. I left her messages. And she left me messages. The electronics were getting on famously.

I knew I needed to do something about Carrie, and of course I had ideas: coming up with corny projects and events was my stock-in-trade. But the draw of home weighed on me, the worst kind of unfinished business, like when you can't stop writing a letter of complaint in your head or you keep rehearsing a conversation you're worried about. I felt increasingly pulled to Chase. It seemed like the dark underside of her glittery soccer success. As captivating as it was to watch her excel on the field, the gravity of our daily tensions seemed to draw me in the same way. And held me, like a wild-eyed soccer fan caught in the grip of a game that was getting away from the home team, with the clock ticking down.

My daily interactions with Chase had taken on this power, as if every little thing mattered enormously. Our morning routine: struggling to get her to wake up by knocking on her door and listening through her repeated refusals until her feet hit the ground and her bathroom door finally closed. Breakfast: rolling my eyes pointedly in answer to her complaint that we never had food in the house, despite my packing it full of the things she ate on her own, and her eventually grabbing a bagel and wolfing it silently while I drove her to school in the car we both hated. Afternoons: rushing home from the train as early as I could get away so she would not be there alone, only to begin the battle to turn down the music, put away the food, close the hall windows, pick up the clothes on the stairs, open a book and study. Evenings were hardest: making something she would eat that at least had some semblance of value to it instead of her deliveries from Domino's and gigantic bowls of ice cream. My specialty was pasta – boil a bucket of water, throw in the angel hair, then slather it with jarred sauce, and chop fruit and veggies for her to dip in something. Nights were the easiest: we just exhausted each other, the bickering less difficult than the silences. Thank God for *Seinfeld* reruns and the soccer channel.

Into this family romance Megan Sullivan had entered, and if her presence meant little change in the tiresome comedy of manners between me and Chase, at least she was entertaining. Her own schedule demanded that her time could not be wasted; she tutored another student separately from Chase and also worked at the local Y as a receptionist, checking in members until late every night while getting her own homework done. Between the two of them, they caught a ride home from school every day, and Megan simply demanded that the two of them get down to work so she could make her next job. I would then drive her to the Y or the student's house, from which she somehow found her own way home. After riding for a week in the Jag, the first time she saw my ugly SUV she said, "So now you're ordinary like the rest of us." Which of course was pretty funny coming from her. She kept track of her tutoring hours with precision, and gave me the record at the end of each week, insisting on being paid immediately. Despite her kooky appearance, she had a tough-mindedness especially about money that admittedly taught me something about collecting from debtors.

"Why wait, I say," she remarked. "People aren't going to be more inclined to pay me a month or two later, and their convenience is really not my problem. Like I wait to be paid because someone says she doesn't have her checkbook with her? I say, 'Let's shoot over to the ATM right now, honey. I can live with cash.'"

About schoolwork, Megan was a gamer, just as she'd told us the first day she showed up. In each subject she was like a gambler working the point spread. Every teacher had quirks, expectations, points for homework and tests, and their own weaknesses, biases, and habits. Megan knew what these were and worked them. She was constantly giving Chase assignments for the next day, along with coaching tips.

"You're going to see Mr. Levy after school, but – and remember this – tell him before class, be*fore* class, that you're coming in this afternoon. You're going to go over these two problems," she slapped Chase's notebook page with equations on it. "Have him show you how to work out this one," she pointed, "then you're going to do this one right away, in front of him. I want him to see you doing it. And you're going to do it right because we're going over it right now, so you'll know it."

"Then why do I have to get him to show me?" Chase asked, her brow wrinkled in confusion.

"We want him to see you learn something right after he shows it to you. He loves to see himself actually making a difference. It's probably why he's a good teacher. You want him to feel good about your progress, like you're really learning from him. Besides, he's totally hot, so what's your problem?"

In French, she'd say things like, "Forget about the book; she's going to mark you tomorrow on your oral responses. I want you to memorize the answers I give you."

"But how do you know what . . ."

"Not to worry. Trust me. I got sources. This is just drill, girl. You're a jock, so let's drill."

Megan's gaming approach worked for Chase. As Megan recognized, Chase was an athlete to her core: competitive, intensely physical, always looking for ways to express herself by doing rather than talking about it. Megan's idea of school, at least the way she presented it to Chase, was like a soccer game: a challenge not of principles, or knowledge, or values, but one of tactics, technique, and sometimes even teamwork between the two of them.

"You hand it in early, before school; then I check her grade book at lunch. Don't ask. If she's given you credit for the assignment, it means she's accepted the topic so we don't have to wait until Monday. Then we're home free with three extra days, we're golden."

It was comical seeing the two of them together. They did all their work in the kitchen, Megan insisted on it. They sat at angles from each other at the counter with the work littered before them: Megan evaluating each assignment, cutting through a lot of it, and getting Chase to focus on some piece of the work that Megan decided was the shortcut. And Chase, her mouth perpetually wrinkled in disapproval, pushing herself to keep up. On the surface they looked so different: Chase long and thin with those pale muscular arms, and the long hair in the loose chignon flipping from one shoulder to the other; Megan's short hair poked in all directions and her body looked like warm dough: freckled, sagging, and moving with the slowness of dissolving yeast. Yet they were similar, like two weirdly matched twins: both fair-haired, fair-skinned, and both so focused. Megan pulled carrots from the refrigerator, or sliced red peppers or celery; she actually made me buy celery, and with blazing speed would whip up these dips of hummus and Tabasco sauce that were definitely tasty.

On nights when she didn't have to go on to her next job, Megan would stay in our kitchen and cook. These hours were "off the clock," as Megan put it, so I didn't have to pay for them. But a lot of the chat between her and Chase, which was really the one-sided chatter that Megan kept running, often revolved around whatever school assignments they worked on. I'd keep my distance as long as I could, but sooner or later Megan would call and it would be time to eat. Chase grudgingly helped a little with the cooking, mostly I think because she was hungry and enjoyed Megan's company. She had to chop, or stir, or find the right bowl. Megan didn't bother to teach cooking the way she approached algebra. Megan wanted something good to eat, and had learned the best way for her to get it was to make it herself. Her repertoire was limited, more by the cost of ingredients than anything, and in truth I wasn't too interested in paying for her learning experiences with a lot of trips to the meat counter.

The nights she stayed, we didn't eat expensive, but the meals were surprising. She liked to cook with chicken, even though the raw pieces disgusted Chase. Megan knew how to crank out recipes that sounded elaborate but were quick to prepare, like chicken piccata. We scarfed that down like three competing vacuum cleaners. She mostly stayed away from pasta because she complained about her weight. She also liked making soups, and would serve them with toast that she grilled in the oven with veggies and cheese on them, and as simple as it sounds, it was all quite good. In fact, part of the appeal of her cooking was the way she made it easy, much the same as her approach to school. Megan was all about directness; she worked the angles, making complexities seem manageable. It was exactly like the economy of movement in great athletes.

When Megan learned Chase had tickets to the Donnas at Avalon, she tried to buy one of them, so it quickly worked out that the two of them would go to the concert together. I think this was a great relief to Chase, who didn't want to go with me, for understandable reasons, but didn't really know anyone else that she could take, at least no one that wouldn't produce a lot of stress from me. Megan knew all about the Donnas, and generally seemed to approve of Chase's '80s music tastes, which were a legacy from Taylor more than anything. This legacy bothered me, not that I had anything against Blondie. It was the idea of Chase up in her room, listening for hours to music that Taylor played in her Beemer, that was troubling. At least the Donnas were current.

As a way of helping Chase organize her schoolwork each day, Megan began a routine of getting dropped off at our house instead of having her ride take her all the way to school. She'd come bustling in while I was making coffee, slice a couple of bagels or more likely put toast on the grill with butter and cinnamon on it, then flip open Chase's notebooks left overnight on the kitchen counter to see what work Chase had done. Chase – who may or may not have done her early-morning run – would come down looking blitzed and eat what Megan put on a plate. Often I would, too: Megan was the Olympic champion of cinnamon toast. She'd check Chase's homework and push her on things she had to do that day.

"Do I pay for these morning visits?" I once asked her.

"Yeah, you buy me breakfast. Consider yourself lucky."

One morning at the end of January, while Chase was finishing a shower, Megan was flipping through Chase's notebook as she waited for the oven to warm up. I was sitting at the kitchen table watching her. To tell the truth, I very much enjoyed having her working around the kitchen; unlike the rest of us, she seemed quite happy to be there.

"Bloody hell," she said to herself.

She was reading something in one of Chase's folders, and pulled the papers out of the folder pocket. She read it with her eyes narrowed, looked at the clock, and looked over at me.

"Would you mind if I used your laptop?" nodding her head at the ThinkPad next to my shoulder bag. She sat at the table and started in on the keyboard with the papers from Chase's folder next to her.

I couldn't see what she was doing from across the table.

"Something wrong?" I asked.

"No, it's fine," she said.

She seemed to find what she was looking for. Her eyes narrowed again as she read it, then she asked: "Can I take this upstairs for a minute?"

She took the laptop and the papers and went up to Chase's room. In a moment they were yelling at one another; I moved to the foot of the stairs to eavesdrop like every parent does.

"You're stupid if you think you can pull that shit and even if you do get away with it, it's bullshit," Megan yelled.

"Why don't you mind your own business?"

"It is my business."

"This has nothing to do with you. My father pays you to help me with my homework. I don't have to do everything with you and I don't need your approval!" Chase's voice rose steadily until she was yelling loudly.

Megan lowered her voice; I couldn't hear everything she said, but I distinctly heard her use the word "expelled."

At this point I thought, "Get up there." But it was almost a relief, having someone else yelling at Chase for a moment, like the times Jenna got on her, although unlike Jenna's challenges, this had nothing to do with the soccer field.

Soon Megan came slowly down the stairs. I quickly returned to the kitchen table, like a sneaky kid. She came in, put the laptop back on the table, the papers back on top of Chase's notebook, and looked at the clock. She turned off the oven and put the bread she'd covered with soft cheese and oregano in the refrigerator. Chase came downstairs, sweeping into the room like a giant predator. And picking up the papers on the notebook, she tore them in half, then in quarters, then tossed them into the wastebasket.

"I'll just take an F," she said.

Megan ignored her.

"Could we go?" she asked me. "We're late."

Megan said nothing during the ride, a rarity. She liked the banter as much as I did.

As they were getting out of the car in front of the school, Chase said to her, "So what am I supposed to do for English?"

"Tell her the truth," Megan answered.

"What's that supposed to mean?"

Megan turned to look at her for the first time since going through her notebook.

"Tell her you had a crisis of conscience. She'll buy that," she said with some venom. "She'll give you another day and it'll only cost you one grade."

She then spun on her heels and walked away. Chase shook her head in frustration and followed the feisty tutor into the building.

On the afternoons when Chase had physical therapy, I drove her to the health center where her therapist practiced and then either worked on my laptop in the waiting room or drove over to Starbucks to watch all the housewives in their exercise suits order nonfat no-foamers. Chase didn't like me coming into the therapists' working area with her, a slightly sweaty place where rows of benches like high cots were surrounded by an armory of equipment. Samantha was a young woman who worked with Chase for many hours, standing over her as Chase lifted, balanced, ran, twisted, kicked, or otherwise labored to strengthen her leg muscles. Samantha would usually just smile and tell me things were coming along or would give a short, positive report while Chase waited, tired and impatient to go to the car.

After a particularly long session, while Chase was icing down her leg on a bench, Samantha came out to the waiting area and sat down heavily next to me. Instead of the upbeat report, she rubbed her hand around her chin thoughtfully and said that she was concerned.

"She hasn't been working the way she used to at her rehab," she said. "And it's really not like her."

I asked Samantha how she knew this. The few times I'd asked Chase about her home exercise program, she said she did them all in her room, and since this had always been something she was hyper-intense about, I had no reason to doubt it. The only reason I even asked her was to try to make chitchat, and good luck with that.

"Her strength," Samantha said, "is not where it should be. She should be at least at 130 percent of normal, more like 150 or 160. But she's no further along than she was a month ago. She was at much higher levels last August before she got the green light to play."

One hundred thirty percent of normal sounded superhuman to me, but Samantha dismissed it.

"Not for an athlete at her level. We're not talking about normal parameters here. Not even normal ones for athletes. Chase has incredible strength, range, flexion, but I don't see her making progress; in fact, she's backsliding. And it's not as if her development has slowed; I think she's still growing. Her muscle density is still maturing."

I asked if this meant that something was wrong. Samantha shook her head, negative. Then she glanced into the work area to see that Chase was still icing, then looked at me pointedly and tapped her finger on her temple.

"Head case?" I offered.

"I think you should talk to Jenna Eisenbech. Chase has been at this a really long time; maybe she just needs some motivation. But I know Juventus has a bunch of really huge tournaments coming up soon, like March and April, right? Jenna really should know about this. If it's OK with you, I'll talk to her, too. I think we're at a critical point in Chase's rehab."

It occurred to me that Jenna had almost slipped out of our lives since the holidays. I called her that afternoon and left a message that I wanted to catch up with her. I liked Jenna, for all her intensity; it bothered me that we seemed to have disconnected a little.

Jenna's Toyota was in the driveway by the time Chase and I got home. We'd stopped at the Whole Foods market at Newton Four Corners, the only place Megan said we could buy half the things on her list. For some reason, Chase always seemed to enjoy the food shopping. She'd take the list from me on the way into the store and set off on her own, methodically working the aisles and clunking the produce onto the quaint old scales, as if the weight mattered. I hung around the back of the store pretending to look over the fish. When we got home, Jenna helped us carry the shopping bags into the house, then said the two of them needed to talk. I told them to use the family room since I had things to do, then went upstairs to try to listen through the floor. I couldn't hear anything, so I went for a run instead.

When I came back, wet and spattered from a cold night run on rush-hour roads, they were still at it. I didn't interrupt. I hung my windbreaker in the basement stairway, peeled off a wet layer of nylon, and slipped into the foyer. I could see them across the kitchen huddled in the family room. Chase was sitting on the couch, silent, bent over like a penitent sinner. Jenna on the opposite chair leaned forward close to Chase's face, talking firmly to her player. What can I say: I had to listen. Parents who are having trouble with a teenager would use brain implants if they had the technology.

Jenna seemed to be winding down from a blistering scolding. I'd seen her dress down players before and always wanted to hide in my car. A lot of her message sounded like sports clichés, but presented with Jenna's quiet fervor, they'd be daunting to anyone.

"You need to decide who you are and who you want to be," she said. "I need to know – right now – if I can count on you."

Chase's head seemed to drop lower and lower toward her chest.

"If you mean what you're telling me," Jenna said, "then it's time for you to cut the crap."

A part of me wanted to cheer Jenna on: cutting the crap was right and who knew the crap better than I did? I didn't want to let myself get into the indulgent mind-set that considered how tough this was for a fifteen-year-old girl to swallow. In fact, fifteen-year-olds are probably very well suited to swallow this sort of aggressive message. Chase seemed so vexed all the time, so ready to pull back from others and shut herself off. A clear statement of expectations and a message of concern from an adult she genuinely respected could only be positive.

But there was something in the picture that wasn't quite right to me. For all her size and strength, Chase was so young. If I looked above the broad shoulders in the Northwestern sweatshirt, I could only see her freckled face as the sad and struggling countenance of a hurt child. Everyone said, "You can't baby them. You've got to be clear, you've got to be tough." Well, I tried, all the time. Be on time, do your laundry, wash your face, ice your knee, call your grandmother, do your homework. I'd been working on not discussing things that were beyond negotiation and not repeating myself, just getting the messages out. I was short on consequences because there wasn't much that Chase seemed to regret losing or that actually limited her. But Jenna was different, Jenna had leverage. She could take away the thing Chase loved the most, and that was what she was threatening in the family room. Chase looked beaten-down.

"'You need to tell me right now: are you going to step up?"

"Yes."

"Are you going to be a part of this team?"

"Yes."

"Are you going to work on your rehab every day and follow Sam's program to the letter?" Jenna pumped her fist with these last three words: to-the-letter, pop pop pop.

"Yes."

"Can I count on you, Chase?"

"Yes, Coach."

"Are you sure?"

Yes. More fist pumping. I felt like pulling on a jersey and whacking the ball for the ol' team myself. The two of them were eye-locked.

"I need you, Chase. Are you going to be there for me?"

"Yes, Coach."

I walked Jenna out to her car. She looked toward the golf course and shook her head.

"You know she needs this more than any girl on the team," she said. She meant soccer, not the tough-love delivery.

"The tournaments this spring and especially this summer in Florida will be a fantastic opportunity for her, and it's what she wants. She's got to pull herself together."

"But what about all the other crap, Jenna?"

"This is her way through it, Tommy! This will center her. She's a *great* athlete. Her potential is unlimited. But that's a burden as well as a blessing. Don't imagine what's going on with her in soccer is separate from school or home. She's injured, and it's freaking her out and she's letting other stuff slip, too. Soccer has been that girl's life since she was four years old. If we want to get her through this, we all have to be on the same page – you know what I mean?"

"OK." I felt like saying, "Yes, Coach."

She smiled and gave me a long hug. It was surprisingly tender to tell the truth, and after a moment I hugged her back.

"Then don't be such a stranger," I said.

"You're right," she said, looking off again. "I've been pissed at her ever since she took off for Chicago. I know that's stupid but there it is."

While I was putting away the neglected groceries – I could already hear Megan scolding me about the chicken breasts – Chase went out for a run. She headed over to the golf course, even though she'd agreed not to run there at night in the dark. She was gone almost an hour. I was watching TV when she came back in. She went up to her room and showered.

I followed her up about an hour later because she hadn't come downstairs yet for food. Her door was open. She was sitting on the floor in front of her bed, in a T-shirt and pajama shorties, her long freckled legs stretched out in front of her. I went downstairs, got her a large freezer bag filled with ice chips and brought it back up, silently handing it to her.

"Thanks," she said as she put it on her right knee.

I risked overstaying my welcome and knelt down in front of her. Then I risked an even bigger gambit.

"You don't have to play soccer, you know." Her eyes widened like a startled deer. "Even if you don't, you'll still be the most amazing person I've ever lived with."

"Of course I want to play. Are you crazy? Are you totally and completely crazy?"

"Yes, I am crazy. Bonkers, to tell the truth."

The ice bag had slipped off her leg, and I picked it up and gently put it back on her knee.

"I just wanted you to know that even though we fight all the time, you're worth the battle to me, soccer or not."

She looked at me as if I was speaking Sumerian.

My sister Anna said I was completely crazy. A popular sentiment lately. Her evidence was that I was turning down a weekend in the Virgin Islands with "the new girlfriend" because I said I didn't want to leave Chase.

"That's depraved," Anna suggested, in her invariably patient goodhearted way. We were having lunch at a hole in the wall she liked on Washington Street in the South End, where they put sprouts on everything, including the napkin holders. I always hated sprouts; they smell like semen. But that wasn't the sort of joke I made to my sister.

I'd called her because I wanted to talk to her about Chase, what else. But somehow we'd gotten onto the subject of Carrie. I usually kept my love life separate from my family as much and as long as possible; the Boyans could be a bit much for someone new in my life to handle. My family tended to look at one of my dates the way a group of teenage girls look at a new girl's clothes. I told Anna about the inflated image I thought Carrie held of me and how the infatuation with the literary political man seemed to be coming back to earth right along with the struggling single parent.

"So go to St. John, are you kidding me? Then you'll know."

"Maybe I don't want to know."

I was eating a plate of French fries, dipping them in tartar sauce. She was working on a Caesar salad. I was winning the food battle; Anna was as skinny as Chase, without the swimmer's frame or the appetite.

"It sounds like you might be a little intimidated by this woman."

Like a lot of people, Anna often made statements sound like questions to cushion them, a kind of rhetorical deniability.

"No. I'm a *lot* intimidated by this woman."

She said something about how any woman would be lucky, the sort of gush I expected and secretly loved from my baby sister, then pushed me to let Chase come and stay with her. I said I might feel a little more comfortable if she went out to Newton and spent the weekend out there, but Anna thought this was the wrong way to go.

"You've been telling me how all she does is run and watch TV and hang around in her room. She needs to get out and see things, Tommy. I think you're trying to protect her too much."

"Right. She's got a boyfriend in a pickup truck with a juvie record as long as my arm and she flits to Chicago when it suits her. She doesn't need to get out more, she needs to take up knitting."

"Let me take her for the weekend. It'll work out, don't worry so much." This from the person who worried about everyone in the city who didn't have twelve pairs of shoes.

"And I think you ought to push yourself a little with this doctor; it sounds to me like that's what you really want to do. What've you got to lose?"

"My grip on Planet Earth?"

I heard a crash up in the bathroom while I was loading the dishwasher and ran upstairs. Chase had knocked a light fixture onto the floor and was standing in the hall looking agitated.

"A spider," she said.

I looked in the bathroom.

"On the ceiling." She pointed.

It was one of those truly ugly ones, with the hairy fat bodies and stubby legs. I took a couple of tissues and reached for it but couldn't quite get it. With that wingspan of hers, Chase could have done it easily. I got a stool from her room, picked the bug off the ceiling, and was about to drop it into the toilet.

"No! Not there."

I took the tissue wad into my bathroom and flushed it away. She was outside my room waiting for me with her arms tightly crossed: Who was this strange creature from another planet, who terrified midfielders with her speed and crashed through defenders like a locomotive, scared by a bug like a frightened six-year-old?

"Is it gone?" she asked.

"Out to sea."

"I hate spiders."

"All girls hate spiders."

She went into her room, started to close the door, then looked out.

"Thanks."

"Anytime."

I arranged a little evening with Carrie to make up for stalling on the St. John trip. She wasn't frosty when I called, but she wasn't swallowing her cell with excitement either. I'd already agreed to make the trip, and had hung in while she let me know in several different ways what a great opportunity I'd almost missed. So I knew I needed to do penance. On the phone I steered the conversation around to the Museum of Fine Arts and asked if she was planning on seeing the Hockney exhibit opening in a few days. She said she was interested but hated the crowds at the big shows, and tickets at reasonable times on the weekend were hard to get.

"Well," I said, all Mr. Casual, like I was coming up with the idea for the first time. "We might be able to go to a private show if you like." She was intrigued, so I said I'd work it out and told her when I'd pick her up.

A few days before the big exhibits opened to the public at the MFA and most major museums, corporate sponsors held private showings that were never crowded and could get pretty spiffy depending on the company and the show. While there were bigger shows at the museum this year, I'd heard through my newspaper sources that David Hockney himself was coming, which turned out a good number of the donors who had contributed a fair number of the paintings to the show. I'd known ahead of time that Bill Tillotson, chairman of the board of Carrie's hospital, owned a Hockney. So I called him and asked if his was in the show, and if he could get me and a date in to see his paintings without the crowd. He was also the chair of one of the big banks in Boston; I'd organized a fair number of do-gooder projects for his community relations and communications departments over the years: school partnerships, after-school activities, reports to the community on how drippy-generous the bank was for giving free tickets for Celtics games to churches in Roxbury. Bill was as gracious as I expected, and took care of it. We were in.

The show opening was a Saturday evening and had the feel of a gala. The event opened with a press conference that drew pretty good attendance from print and TV media. The press gathered in the lobby outside the long gallery where the paintings were hung. The lobby was set up as a reception for when the media finished. I knew a fair number of the journalists, especially those from the city papers. Before the press conference started, I dragged Carrie around and kept introducing her, which she seemed to enjoy.

David Hockney walked out from an inner room with the British-born director of the museum. He carried a cane and looked pretty good for his age – cool smile, shock of thick white hair, fair amount of British charm. He was dressed in a black sweater and a tweedy old gray jacket with a loose thing around his neck that looked more like an old-style cravat than a tie. He was game with the questions, though all of them were totally softball. After the press conference, the MFA director introduced him to me and Carrie, and he chatted comfortably with us longer than I would have expected. There were people in the group who were actually the subjects of several of the Hockney portraits on exhibit; they spoke to the press in side interviews, then mingled with the rest of us.

After the press event was over, the reception kicked in; it seemed more like a party than a media event. I'd put on a suit for a change and looked spiffy in blacks and charcoals, the Thirties gangster look that everyone wore but still looked good. Carrie looked spectacular. When Bill Tillotson pulled us over to his wife and friends, I knew I'd shut down Carrie's pique with me. We took a long turn through the gallery to look at the paintings. I'd done a little homework on Hockney so I wouldn't say anything stupid. As we moved along the walls doing the incredibly boring museum gape thing, I threw out a few little facty bits that scored with Carrie, kind of like bending a corner kick.

We had our picture taken by the *Globe*; I knew the stringer who took the shot. Bill and his wife naturally took to Carrie, and she enjoyed the attention. Like most CEOs, Bill expected everyone around him to be important, so her being a doctor in his hospital meant little. But when I told him she'd competed in the U.S. Figure Skating trials about twelve years earlier, Bill and his group were impressed. Carrie enjoyed it; she downplayed the achievement – after all, she'd finished about thirtieth – but she was there, she looked the part, and they were charmed.

Turns out, I knew other people there besides Bill. The president of the Massachusetts Senate smiled his way through the crowd. He went to high school with Fergie and I knew him quite well. He knew Bill; I introduced him to Bill's wife and to Carrie. But then he got into a routine about what was Tommy Boyan doing with a doctor, like I was vaulting a class barrier. He thought he was pretty funny and I wanted to kill him, but I managed to yuck him onto another topic and then tried to get Carrie away from him.

"So you and Tommy really know each other," she said to the senator.

"Intimately," the senator's wife said with attitude.

"No pillow talk, please," I said.

The buffet was excellent, the evening a success. As we were getting ready to leave, while Carrie milled around the crowd enjoying her new contacts, I waited in the coat-check line with the little red plastic thing. I'm not exactly sure why, but I started to feel like a total ass. What was I doing? Why all this mucking and finagling for a date with a babe I'd already been to bed with at least a couple of dozen times? I liked the Hockney paintings; why not, especially the big double portraits. But seriously. This had taken too much work, and it all felt so staged and phony: not the exhibit but me. As I stood there waiting for Carrie's coat, I knew I wasn't doing this just to impress Carrie; I did it to recover some idea of myself that had been taking a beating lately. Maybe Carrie's idea of me was troubling because this sense I had of my taking a downward turn was right on target.

Bill suggested we join them for a drink. He lived in Marblehead but had a condo at the Heritage, next to the Four Seasons, near downtown Boston. But his wife's friend said we should go somewhere fun – a slap at ol' Bill's digs but he seemed open to the idea. He looked at me like I was the idea guy.

"Ever been to Drago's Bar and Sociable?" I asked his wife.

Her friend had heard of it; her friend's husband said he'd been there a few times during Pats games on one of the Super Bowl run-ups. They knew it had a dive rep, but dives are chichi in a crowd like that, great idea, what fun, a night on the seamy side.

Actually, Drago's was in the South End, which was no longer seamy at all, so it really wasn't a risk, although it bordered on Southie. Drago's on a Saturday night got a pretty eclectic crowd, including enough stiffs from the burbs to cushion the regulars, who were really stiff. I'd grown up at Drago's; a lot of the people I'd learned to depend on in my life I'd connected with at one time or another amid the fumes from its sticky floors.

By the time we got there, it was late enough that the regulars were starting to season the crowd of tourists. The hostess gave me a raunchy hug as we went in the door, and this earned me more points with Carrie, who didn't seem to realize immediately that this was the place I'd told her about before. I took them up to the bar, dragging the five people in tow through the crowd like a conga line. When the bar crowd grudgingly gave us a gap, I introduced everyone to Jack Boyan. When I said, "This is my father," the exec with Bill laughed outright, thinking it was a joke. My father just stared at him until he realized I was serious. Jack Boyan is not a hail-fellow-well-met sort of Irishman, even though he is actually from the old country. He is more the clipped and cynical sort, which makes sense for the barkeep in a townie watering hole. He is bald and has a sagging face that makes him look like an old pug. While he sized up the two other men, Carrie stared at him. This was her boyfriend's father.

Dad aimed a thumb at her and said, "This the doc?" When I

nodded, he took a bottle from a cabinet behind the bar and put out a row of six shot glasses with one hand, no mean trick. One of the locals yelled, "Look out," while another behind us said something about the suits. He put another glass on the bar for himself, filled the glasses with the unblended, held his up to Carrie, and waited until my guests got the message and each picked up a glass, which seemed like about a week and a half.

"To my granddaughter," he said, "and her very pretty doctor."

He cleaned his shot with a flick of his wrist. I did the same. The others sipped. He set his glass on the bar and asked Carrie, "So what's wrong with her?"

"I'm sorry?"

"With my granddaughter. What's wrong with her?"

"Oh. Well, she dislocated her knee!"

She glanced at me. "Soccer's a rough sport, but she's brilliant!" She sounded like a beer commercial.

My father nodded and pointed to a wall behind us on the side of the bar near the step down to the tables and booths. There was Chase, in a blown-up shot taken by the *Globe* during the fall season, in her blue Newton uniform. Carrie clapped her hands like a cheerleader. "Fantastic!"

"I didn't mean her knee," my father said, but the others jumped into the soccer talk. Carrie seemed to prefer explaining soccer teams to Bill Tillotson over Chase's psychodynamics to my blunt parent.

I suggested a booth, and we went across the room to one of the six-seaters against the wall. One of the young waitresses came over and tried to get into the flirty thing with me, then took orders. There were a lot of tourists but there were regulars, too, including a table close by with some guys that didn't quite seem a social fit with the Tillotsons of

Marblehead. I began to think this was not such a good idea. The drinks came fast, with chips and salsa – a new thing for an Irish pub – and pretzels and a cheese plate, which I couldn't remember seeing lately. No one except me did any nibbling. They were still on the soccer, a safe subject. Carrie told a story about Chase at the all-star game. The table was impressed but a little bored. I was looking for an opening to start spouting a little more of my Hockney malarkey before it disappeared from my brain, but one of the bar regulars appeared at my elbow, name of Trippy for no good reason, sort of a walking beer slosh. And he was sloshing pretty generously.

"Tahhmee, where ya been keeping, we nevah see yahs," that sort of astute inquiry. I got up and took him to the bar and got rid of him, but then someone else, a guy I knew from high school, who was now a gas station manager, slipped in next to Carrie to flirt with her, just to rib me. I managed to get rid of him too after peeling his fist from Carrie's shoulder, but I could see it was getting to be time to go. They weren't barflies, just working men from Dorchester and Southie who drank together on Saturdays. The wife of Bill's friend seemed to be enjoying herself, lots of characters for anecdotes at her next dinner party. Her husband kept looking around and saying he thought he recognized the Red Sox TV color man.

"Most entertaining," Bill said as we left.

Yeah, right.

"I guess we should have gone to their place," I said as I drove Carrie home.

"No, it was interesting." Interesting: a comment that was always the exact equivalent of kiss, you're a corpse.

"So that was your father."

"That's me Dah."

"Well, that was interesting."

I wanted to flush the part of my brain with the Hockney in it down the crapper.

A Saturday night and I was at Fergie's watching a pay-per-view fight along with Fergie, my brother-in-law Dieter, and Joey McIsaac, a guy I'd known all my life, like a half brother, who was now the Boston fire chief. The undercard was sensational. The fights were going the distance, so the main event hadn't started yet when Chase called. It was after midnight; she was at the Avalon with Megan for the Donnas concert and needed a ride home. I told the guys I'd be back because I wanted to see the fight, even though I knew I wouldn't be; it was just too much of a schlep. And I wasn't about to skate out on Chase at one in the morning on a weekend: Who knew where she'd be when I got home.

She'd told me they'd meet me in Kenmore Square in front of the McDonald's. I pulled over across the street a little before the square. They were standing on the corner, Chase dwarfing Megan and taller than the group of boys surrounding them. Six boys, who all looked about high-school age, and one other girl. I didn't recognize any of them. They were clowning and making noise the way teenagers do.

I was curious to watch Chase among people her own age when she didn't have to push a ball around. She was clearly the center of attention, even though the other girl was small and looked from where I sat across the street to be very provocative – pretty and blonde and practically no clothes despite the February cold. Chase had the half smile going, and she was roughhousing a little, keeping a soda in a

McDonald's cup from two of the boys who were trying to take it from her. Good luck with that, guys. I zipped my window down and listened, though it was too far to make out more than their laughing and having a good time. Megan was on the perimeter, not quiet but not getting the attention, either. She noticed my car, waved, said something to Chase, and crossed the street, climbing into the back of the Jeep.

"Everything OK?" I asked, looking at her through the rearview mirror.

"It was great," she said. She talked a little about the Donnas and the crowd. She said it was mostly high-school girls and thought most of them were from Newton, which she found pretty funny. Chase was still surrounded by the boys. I asked Megan if the boys were from Newton, too.

"No, Brookline, I think," she said. "They kind of glommed onto Chase before the concert."

"Soccer fans?"

"No," she said, looking across the street, "just guys. She's kind of charismatic, you know."

I didn't know. Megan wasn't going to say anything else, but I pressed her. Chase was still across the street, so I asked what she meant by charismatic.

"I think it's like the way she holds herself back," she said.

I immediately thought of Taylor.

"She seems to have this thing going," Megan went on, "like she's keeping secrets or something; it's pretty cool."

Chase had seen the car and now waved.

"You think she has secrets?" I asked.

"Don't do a parent thing on me now, Mr. Tommy. It's not like some dark and deep secret; it's just the way she doesn't say things, like you have to work for her and it hooks you in, you know?"

"You mean she's self-possessed."

"Yeah, self-possessed." Megan seemed to like the phrase. "Maybe the soccer gives her that. I mean when a whole town talks about you like you're a movie star, it's got to do something to your head."

"Something good?"

"Hah. Good point. Maybe a little of both, the yin and yang of good and evil all in a soccer ball."

"Pretty deep analysis for a fifteen-year-old, Megan."

"Why do parents always think that fifteen-year-olds are four-year-olds?"

"So what does it mean for Chase to be charismatic?"

Chase pulled away from the circle of boys and started jogging slowly across the intersection.

"Well, it makes me want to cook something for her."

"You want to cook something for everyone."

"Not true. But I'd like to cook something right now, if you can take a hint."

Chase jumped into the passenger seat in the front and produced a CD from a pocket. "Could you play this?" she asked.

She slid the CD into the dash herself, punched the selector, the Donnas came on, and she and Megan sang "Take It Off" all the way out Comm. Ave.

10.

I was spending more hours in Boston than I wanted, trying to generate some client work to pay a whole windowsill of bills that were piling up in the dining room. I had several irons in the fire but they weren't heating up. The kind of work I did was usually seen as expendable unless there was some crisis; the bang that clients got out of my work tended to be fleeting. A story in a local magazine about what a good guy the CEO was to pay for some playground equipment that would outlast Stonehenge. How sparkly the senator and his wife looked at the annual fundraising dinner for the Nose-Wipers of the Pathetic and Poor. It often took a lot of work to organize these hits. I got along pretty well with the journalists I depended on to toss me a bone of coverage now and then, and every clipping was an entrée into the next client's office who wanted the same thing himself. But to earn a living doing little strikes like these I needed volume. It was better to have one really good client with a lot of complicated needs, like a developer who wanted to tear down a landmark to put up a Walmart. I could maintain a small fleet of leaky Jags with a few accounts like that, with enough money left over to bribe my guilty conscience.

Problem was I didn't have any at the present time, and I was avoiding even walking through the dining room. In years past, this never would have occurred to me as a problem. I would have just gone out a little less and skipped a trip here and there to Vegas. I always managed, and managed to do exactly what I liked. Obviously, things were different now. I wondered if I had it in me to do whatever I needed to do to be a parent.

Chase and Megan were working in the kitchen. Megan was talking through some edits on an essay, while Chase asked questions. It looked pretty intense. They hardly noticed me, so I went upstairs, changed, and went out for a run. After I returned and took a shower, they were still at it.

"This is costing me a fortune," I said to Megan.

"Worth every penny," Megan said. "She's as stubborn as a brick wall."

"Me?" Chase said, fluttering her eyes.

"Yes you, you stupid cow. Somebody better do some cooking around here."

"I could make bacon and eggs," I offered.

"Oh, goody," Megan said, "eggs like yellow water and bacon like driveway gravel. I nominate me for cook duty."

Chase raised her hand. "So moved."

Over very good omelets that we ate together at the kitchen table, I told Chase about my impending trip to St. John with Carrie.

"I know you're taking us," Megan said.

I told Chase she'd be spending the weekend with Anna in the South End.

Chase thought about that, wrinkling her mouth. "What're we

going to do?"

I debated not telling her what Anna had in mind; it seemed like a horrible idea, but my sister could be as stubborn as Chase.

"I think she sort of wants to take you to her work."

The two girls looked at me.

"To the homeless shelter."

"You've got to be kidding," Chase said.

"Nah-uh."

Megan asked about the shelter. I told her: the James Nevers Inn, near the edge of South Boston.

"They call the place Nevers," I said, thinking she might have heard of it; it was pretty well-known. Megan was curious, asked about Anna and what she did there. Megan had an agile mind and consumed information the way she ate eggs. We talked a little bit about homeless people in Boston, how bad conditions were, how hard my sister worked to help raise money and keep her clients in shoes and decent food.

"Can she come?" Chase asked abruptly, nodding at Megan.

"Oh, right," I said. "Girls hate to do things alone."

"Ha," Megan said. "Freaky the team player."

Chase shrugged. "You'll love it," she said to Megan. "You can cook them your famous yellow-water omelets."

St. John was less than excellent. The weather for the most part was crap, and Carrie had obligations because of the conference. There was a fair amount of socializing between sessions, especially at night, and it seemed like everyone at the resort was a doctor except me. A couple of the doctors had been at the dinner party at the Lowell mansion a few months earlier and tried to wind me up again on the topic of malpractice insurance legislation. We kicked it around but I didn't want to sound like a blowhard, and I'd grown tired of Carrie introducing me to people as an author and political consultant. My literary credentials amounted to spit.

I would not say that things were strained between Carrie and me since the night at Drago's, not at all; but they were by no means more intimate. She sensed something, and asked questions every now and then, like, Is something wrong? I hate that question. I mean, if you've gotta ask. She even asked about the night at Drago's. Maybe it was me. I'd been in enough relationships to know when one was winding down and the bobbin on this one was probably already showing. I felt like Carrie's opinion of me, or at least her knowledge of me, was on a downward curve and would sooner or later hit the ground with a thud.

Carrie enjoyed talking to her colleagues about Chase and soccer. She knew the sport from the very special angle of a person who puts players back together. Nearly all her patients at the sports medicine clinic were serious about whatever sports they played, and Carrie had clients with names a lot brighter and better known than Chase's. I knew she had a growing fondness for my daughter that extended well beyond doctor-patient, and even beyond what I might have expected of her for the daughter of a boyfriend. When Carrie touched Chase, stroking her hair and saying "hey baby" with a purring voice, Chase always melted a little; and Carrie knew how to make her smile better than anyone else did.

I knew from past experience that Carrie was husband hunting. The men she'd been dating for some time had all no doubt been sized up for marriage and child potential. I knew she'd been sizing me up the same way. I could tell there were items on the minus side of her ledger. Sure there were pluses, too: everyone loves a comic. But I knew

I couldn't court her by continuing to feed the illusions or maybe just the aspirations she had about me. I'd long ago come to terms with the reality that I was not going to be a famous journalist and that I might not be able to push my life much beyond the flack-and-grift trade that had become my specialty. OK, maybe an article here and there to feed my own illusions. But increasingly the reality of having a daughter, the demands, the money weighed on me, not as an unwanted burden, but – even though it sounds totally cornball – as a kind of life-focusing responsibility. The whole weekend on St. John I thought about Chase. I called my sister often enough for Carrie to roll her eyes. I didn't care. I kept imagining my prep-school WASP-raised daughter living up to her nickname and freaking out at the pee-besotted pants and booze breath she'd be surrounded with for three days solid. If I tried it myself, inside of three hours I'd jump in the Charles and consider it an improvement.

Sunday evening Carrie and I kissed goodnight in her apartment in Brookline and said some courtly and goofy things and I drove home. I was glad to get there; it was late. Anna was sitting in the family room watching CNN and Chase was upstairs asleep. I went up and checked on her. Anna made tea while I was upstairs. I'd told her for years I was a coffee drinker but she was more Dorchester than I was; she pushed tea with milk at everybody.

Anna was bursting with stories. As she talked, the delicate features of her pretty face sparkled with energy.

"They were fun, both of them!" she gushed.

I'd told her before the weekend that Megan would have no trouble at Nevers, but that I couldn't imagine Chase there. She had too much of Taylor in her and maybe too much of me. Predictably, Megan went right to the kitchen and impressed everyone.

"That girl can cook!" and Chase tagged along, shy, withdrawn.

Most of the people at the shelter were men, as always, running in age range from low twenties to well into their seventh decade. "It can get a little depressing," she admitted, as if she had to say it, though I'd been there often enough, for about six seconds a visit.

But Saturday morning, after they'd spent most of the evening helping out in food service the night before, Chase found the gym, a small box that got infrequent use except evenings during the athletic program and often served as a place to smoke when it was cold outside. Chase started shooting baskets, and slowly a game picked up.

"She played, she reffed, she organized, she really got into it, Tommy."

She explained: most volunteers were women who found it hard to take the banter of the men, and while Megan gave as good as she got in the kitchen, Chase reacted differently.

"Oh sure, at first she was a little intimidated; she didn't really know what to do in the kitchen and kind of stood around. But when she got to the gym, she started playing, and she didn't mind the teases and you know she can handle the sports stuff."

Chase worked in the gym all weekend. She found a soccer ball and got a lot of the men and some of the women to actually play, a minor miracle as Anna called it. "She got me to play!" Anna said, bouncing on the couch. "It was really fun." Anna said Chase showed off a little here and there with the balls and had a good touch with the regulars: she didn't push or cheerlead or encourage. "She just kind of got out and did it and they got into it with her."

Anna laughed. "You should've seen her slamming the volleyball at a few of those bruisers. They'd slam it right back at her and they all knocked it around like it was the Olympics. These guys hate to be seen as pathetic. She took them on. She teased them back." Anna said one of the regulars claimed it was the first time he'd worked up a sweat in the winter without a heating grate.

"Tommy, here's the thing: the director offered her a job."

"You're kidding."

"No. A serious, paid, part-time job. It won't pay much but it's a real job."

"Doing what?"

"Working in the gym: running games, getting the men and women off their butts a little bit. They usually hate people who do that work, they don't like to be pushed into things. But Chase was just a big kid with attitude who could play anything, so they took to her."

"Wouldn't it make more sense for her to just volunteer now and then?"

"Well, maybe, but don't you think it would be good for her to have some responsibility? It won't be a lot of hours. She can work that out. She can take the train into town a few afternoons a week and on the weekend; we can get her a T pass. I think she wants to do it."

Anna was working me. "I hope it's OK with you. I really think you should let her do this."

I didn't know how to react. Of course I was delighted that she'd had a good weekend. But I told Anna that Chase had a lot on her plate. Her grades had improved since Megan's arrival but there was still a long uphill climb. And Jenna was putting a lot of pressure on Chase to work with Juventus, which meant practice four days a week, plus her rehab, weight training, team meetings, on and on. Her club demands were already a full-time job, and the tournaments were coming up. "I just don't know when she'll find the time," I said.

"Is time ever really a good excuse?" Anna asked, a little school-marmishly. "People make time for what they want, don't they? Maybe she'll have to make choices. But I think you should let her make those choices. Don't you think?"

All my life I'd loved my little sister more than anyone on Earth.

"Of course I will," I said. "What about Megan?"

"Megan can come any time; she's great. I don't think there's money for a job there for her, not yet anyway. I love her by the way. Talk about a full plate: she is one busy girl. I don't think we could afford her if we had the money."

Anna got up off the couch and walked around the family room.

"You should have seen her, Tommy. She was . . . " Anna sought the right expression, "she was totally into it. She got those guys and ladies humming their butts off."

"I'm surprised. Amazed actually. She's a teenage girl from a private school."

"That's not all she is."

"You mean she's also an athlete."

"No. I mean," Anna spoke carefully, "that maybe she's felt a little homeless herself lately."

Anna could see that this zinged me. "Don't take it that way, Tommy. You've just got to give her time. She'll find herself, I know she will. I think she found something this weekend."

The life of serious teenage soccer players, whether she's at the national level or struggling to make a club team, is incredibly demanding and cuts deep into everything else they need or want to do. It's a year-round obligation, intensely competitive, and sometimes isolating, because there is often little connection between where players live and the clubs where they play. Juventus had players from

Rhode Island, New Hampshire, and western Massachusetts as well as the eastern Massachusetts suburbs. A lot of parents value the demands on their children, especially for high-school-age girls, because sports have a way of providing a focus that otherwise might be on Party Boy Pete and his bottle of poppers.

For club players, the pressures can have a make-or-break quality. All high-school students – and their parents – spend a tremendous amount of emotional capital worrying about college: competing for grades, stockpiling activity experiences, and grooming for the SATs. For student-athletes, the complexity and pressure of this process is compounded exponentially. Playing Division I in college is a full-time job, an employment commitment. College coaches look for players the way headhunters look through business schools and law schools for major partnership firms. Young athletes must constantly showcase themselves through their clubs, at highly selective club tournaments and on regional Olympic Development teams that can be cutthroat, political, and heartbreaking. Most athletes on the club soccer treadmill have known that all their work since they were first singled out at the age of six, seven, and eight has been aimed at prepping them for their sophomore and junior years in high school. Those are the recruitment years, and the process can be grueling for everyone involved.

So it was with Chase as spring approached. Her injured knee continued to require rehab for several months, after which she needed to retrain herself aggressively to build her conditioning back up to the level she'd been at before her ACL tear nearly two years ago. Juventus undoubtedly would benefit from a marquee forward like Chase, but the team still had a roster of other players with talent and the perseverance to manage their own injuries. Chase also was under pressure from the state's Olympic Development program. Although she hadn't tried out for the team the previous fall, they wanted her and offered her a bye so she could play in the spring. She had to attend Sunday-morning practices twice a month throughout the winter. This meant the two of us had to leave the house before six in the morning to be at the college in western Massachusetts where the training was held. She had to spend a full day running through repetitive drills in dusty gyms with girls who desperately wanted to show themselves to be better than her.

At home, her schoolwork was a daily issue: she had to overcome a base from her prep-school years that was not adequate for the work at Newton High, and she had to grapple with her desire to bolt from the class or the homework and do something physically satisfying whenever the academics frustrated her. Added to this were the hours she now spent at the James Nevers Inn playing games with homeless men, which she seemed to enjoy more than soccer. All this activity while achingly missing her mother and trying to figure out where she stood in a new school, a new club, and a new home, with a very different parent than the one who had raised her.

When Chase's third report card came home with Cs and C-minuses I went back to the high school to see Chris Winberg. The popular dean was as gracious as ever when I came into her office in the afternoon armed with Starbucks lattes. I thanked her for Megan, and we told Megan stories for a few minutes; there was no doubt the brassy tutor had value for Chase that far exceeded any effect she was having on Chase's schoolwork.

We went over Chase's grades course by course. She'd checked in before the meeting again with Kate to get a general sense of how Chase was progressing, and said reassuring things about Chase, even though we both knew her schoolwork was basically lousy. She also let me know without saying it that her teachers were giving Chase a lot of leeway, some because they knew she was torn apart by her mother's death, others because she was a top athlete. I said we'd take all the help we could get. Chris was more concerned about how Chase was holding up amid the stress than she was about the grades.

Chris knew all about the demands on top athletes and wondered if it wouldn't make sense for Chase to back off a little for six months. But she understood the big-picture college clock, too. She was intrigued to learn about Chase's job at Nevers.

"I can see that," she said, her eyes a little far-off when I told her Chase seemed to be good with homeless men. But she asked the questions I was asking myself constantly, which only made me wince at them more when I heard them from her.

"How can she do it all and not crack?"

I told her I couldn't get Chase to make choices. She wanted to do things, she didn't know how to pace herself, and she felt like she was a failure if she pulled back on any of it except schoolwork.

"She's like one of those models you read about," I said, "who weigh a hundred pounds and feel like their career is on the line if they eat a bagel. When she lets up, she's overcome with guilt; when she doesn't, she's exhausted."

"Teenagers don't understand they have limits on their ability; they only see the constraints we put on them," Chris said. "They want it all. A lot of them have learned from their parents that they have to get it all."

She told me a couple of ugly little anecdotes about parents who went crazy because their kids dropped from an A to a B, as if their futures were tossed in the great college dumpster.

"So what do I do?" I said.

She smiled. "What do you want for her, Tommy?"

I said something about wanting her to be happy. She didn't accept that; it was too much of a cliché that could serve as cover for all sorts of pressures. We kicked around who it was – me or Chase – who was upset by a report card with C-minuses. We talked about who Chase felt she was playing soccer for. I had to admit I felt an almost drug-like buzz watching Chase play and train, especially when she surpassed the other girls. Chris just nodded. I didn't have to defend myself by telling her how important soccer was to Chase; she already knew that.

"It sounds to me," she said carefully, "that if she can't back out of some things, then it's your job to make those decisions for her."

She knew how hard that was; she said she had a teenage son who wanted a music career. Good luck with that. I told her I didn't think I could make those decisions, that Chase had to own them herself or she'd blow. She wouldn't let me regulate her on how much soap to put in the washing machine.

"It can happen anyway," Chris said about blowing. "It's too much for anyone."

And so Chase and I churned our way through the mornings and evenings, testing limits, battling over stupid stuff, never quite drawing lines in the sand with each other but never really settling in comfortably, either. We were still houseguests in each others' lives: Chase desperate to hold herself together and at the same time escape, and me just as desperate to hold onto her while struggling to believe that everything was not on the brink of toppling over.

We were not big on birthday parties in my family, so I was genuinely surprised when I came home from work one evening and got jumped when I flicked on the family-room lights. It wasn't a big do, thank goodness, because I was tired from spending a day trying to generate new business, to absolutely no effect. Carrie had organized it. Jenna and Kim were there together, and for the first time it dawned on me that the two of them might have more of a relationship than just coaching. Away from the team they acted like a couple. Megan was there and had cooked chili, which sounds pretty low-brow but she knew I loved it, and made cornbread that was so good I wanted to put my face in the baking tray. Megan and Chase had made me a cake, a gigantic thing with thirty-nine candles. The cake tasted great to everyone. Carrie had even gotten my brother and sister-in-law to come, and Anna, who brought flowers. It was pretty touching, actually.

Carrie had not met my brother or sisters before. Carrie was charmed by Anna's sweet directness. Fergie was entertaining: he kept teasing Chase about her run to Chicago. He told a story about describing her to the Boston Police as a soccer player.

"I was getting nowhere, then I remembered: Boston's a hockey town," Fergie joked.

He pronounced hockey like a true Bean Towner, as if it rhymed with wacky.

"They suggested we let Chicago have her. So I switched her sport. I told them she was the female Cam Neely; next thing you know I'm getting recruiter calls from BC High. So I signed you up, OK? You'll love hockey, Chase: nobody talks because they have no teeth and you get to hit people with sticks. It's the real you. Practice is tomorrow. At four in the morning. Bring your mouth guard."

The high point of the party happened after my sister Trish showed up with her husband, Dieter. Getting them out of Boston was a rarity; in fact, getting any of my family into the burbs seemed a miracle. But they came, and Dieter brought a Boston cream pie he'd made because he knew I loved it.

When Megan looked at the cake, and then tasted it, she stared at him and said, "You *made* this?"

Trish told her he owned a restaurant in Boston. Megan blinked, and said, "You're Dieter Kohler?" So Megan started ragging me for keeping this a secret – she was truly a food groupie – and then she and Fergie started riding Chase and me pretty hard. The two of them were very funny together. They both had an instinct for how to deal with Chase: they had her laughing so hard she had to run to the bathroom, the ultimate comic victory with a female audience.

After the party, Carrie cleaned up with Megan and Anna, then Anna drove Megan home. Carrie stayed. She went upstairs to talk to Chase after she had gone up for the night, and then came down looking like something was still cooking. She led me by the hand over to the couch, said sit down, then pulled a thin present wrapped in blue from under it. I'd gotten a few presents with the cake, most with a joke to them, except my sister's flowers and Chase's present. Chase was taking a class in ceramics and gave me a blue lump that looked enough like it might have had four suggestions of wheels to clue me in that it was a model of my Jag. It was such a flop I almost laughed, but made a fuss about it and put it on the mantel. Fergie told her not to quit her day job.

Carrie's gift was of a different sort. Inside the wrapping was a folder, inside of which among other things was an Air France envelope: two tickets in June to Paris. I noticed immediately that they were first class. I'd flown first class once in my life, on my honeymoon to Italy with Taylor, and only because Taylor's father sprang for the ride. I could have used that cash. The rest of the folder was hotel stuff, restaurant reservations, tickets to museums and glitzy events. The trip would have paid for a little sister to the Jeep in the driveway.

I had enough of my wits about me to react with enthusiasm. Carrie was excited the way people get whenever they give a present they know is a big deal, sort of nervous and smug at the same time. But soon she sensed something was amiss, even though I was trying to hide it.

"What is it, Tommy? You don't want to go?"

"Of course I do."

She looked at me closely. "Fess up, Sport. What's eating you?"

I wanted to say nothing but she pushed, and finally I thought, do it.

"There's something I have to tell you."

"You're *married*" Before I could react, she laughed, another of her gotchas.

"No, not lately. But I am broke."

She didn't understand. It probably didn't relate to anything in her experience. I explained: my consulting work had been slow, I hadn't been able to sell my condo, I had a lot of expenses, and I was in a bit of a rough patch. I told her this had nothing to do with her or with Paris, that I wanted to go very much. Who wouldn't?

I said, "It's just, the first-class thing, you know? I'm just not feeling very first class lately."

I could see my stock as husband material rocketing toward the crapper. Before she could ask questions, I decided to lay it out for her even more clearly. I told her I thought she had a lofty view of me but that I didn't think I quite fit the picture. I hadn't published any more of those short stories she liked in a very long time and I wasn't a political consultant, as she put it; I was more of a grifter for little public relations deals here and there with a few companies and politicians that let me handle things for them that they could probably do for themselves. I told her I'd sold the Jag because I needed the money, not because of life in the suburbs.

"The trip to Paris is paid for," she said, still a little befuddled, trying to find a connection to her gift. "Does it bother you that I make more money than you?"

"God, no," I said. "Not at all. It's not about you, Carrie. Except that I want you to know who you're dealing with here. I'm not trying to pull a sad sack routine. I've got some temporary money issues, and when I saw the first-class tickets I just felt a twinge of something. Guilt or anxiety or envy or assholery. That's all. I love the present. The trip will be unbelievable."

She sat in deep thought for a little while. When she reached for the ticket folder in my lap, I pulled it away from her. She got up, went over to the kitchen, and started wiping the counters with a sponge. I knew enough to keep my mouth shut. Whatever she said that night wouldn't matter. What happened after that night between us would tell the story.

"I'm guessing your financial worries started when you became a single parent?"

I thought about that. I didn't want to blame anything on having Chase. I just said I'd had ups and downs in the past, and this was just a down period.

Carrie didn't seem to be buying this.

"Your whole life basically changed overnight," she said. "You spend unbelievable amounts of time with Chase. You don't even like to go out for pizza if you have to leave her here. When have you had the time to get any work done?"

"I can't lay this on Chase."

"So you're unhappy with the work you do and you don't make enough money. Is that what this is about?"

I nodded, reluctantly, because it sounded so dull.

"Then I guess you are pulling a sad sack routine."

She put the sponge aside and sat on one of the counter stools. She wasn't looking at me. Anna had loaded the dishwasher, so I went over and turned it on. When I glanced at Carrie, it looked as if her eyes were clouding up with tears.

"You know, I had dreams and things in my life that didn't work out, Tommy. I wanted more than anything to be a great skater, and no matter how hard I worked at it I couldn't do it. I finally realized I just wasn't good enough. That was a very hard thing for me. Everyone for so long made me feel like I was the next Katarina Witt, and when it came down to it, I wasn't even close. So I quit."

She pulled her long hair back off the side of her face and leaned against the counter.

"I decided to be a great doctor. And I'm doing fine, I know that, but it's not what I thought it would be. It's competitive, and I don't mind that part. But it's repetitive and political and sometimes the people I have to deal with are so mind-numbingly stupid I want to start breaking legs instead of fixing them. And I work my ass off. I find myself dreaming all the time of moving back to San Diego and starting a skating club. A winter sport in San Diego," she said, shaking her head. "The hard thing about dreams and having to come back down to earth one day is that it turns out it's more difficult to do the ordinary things. I made choices. So if I'm not happy then I have to make different ones. It seems to me that you're disappointed about some things in your life but you're just floating along doing this and that and hoping things work out for you somehow, but it's not happening. Maybe you need to start making some choices."

Isn't it amazing how when things sometimes seem to be turning up they suddenly have a way of turning right back down? Gravity lurks under all of us. I sort of remember reading somewhere in college that Bertrand Russell once calculated the probability of gravity. He said the likelihood of a chair rising off the floor was one chance in ten to the tenth power and then that number to the twentieth power. There would be more zeroes in that number than all the soccer goals ever scored in the history of the sport. But I suppose it offered hope. Maybe things didn't always have to come crashing down. Or maybe they did and I don't know squat about Bertrand Russell.

Newton only had a half day of school and Maris had driven up from Connecticut to see Chase. I was tied up at the Boston Public School Department and came home around seven, tired and a little irritable. Maris met me in the kitchen. I could hear Chase playing music up in her room. The volume was very high, and based on our track record, I wondered if something was wrong.

"We had a bit of an argument this afternoon," Maris said, looking a little anxious as I hung up my jacket in the kitchen closet.

"Welcome to the club."

"Yes, well." She looked at her manicured hands and hesitated.

"Spit it out, Maris, even though I didn't cook it."

She smiled at that but only a flicker.

"She was telling me about this new job she has, at the homeless shelter."

I thought to myself, uh-oh.

"Which of course I was very positive about."

Come to think of it, Maris came from generations of bleeding hearts, and she probably did think it was good for Chase to slum it now and then.

"She said she was hoping to work there this summer when she didn't have soccer obligations. I mentioned that I had been hoping she might consider spending the summer in Jamestown. Now I didn't say the whole summer, I just suggested perhaps a part of the summer."

We hadn't talked about the summer; my radar started beeping.

"So we got into a bit of an exchange about spending some time in Jamestown."

The McKinleys had a spread on the water in Jamestown. I'd been intimidated by it several times.

"She could work in one of the homeless shelters in Jamestown," I said, but Maris missed the joke entirely.

"Of course, I said we'd love to have you come, too. But for some reason she got very upset. It was only a suggestion."

"She has a hair trigger about anything to do with Taylor."

"Well, thank you for saying that."

Maris sat down on the couch in the family room. It seemed like Manhattan time and I got to it.

I could see there was something more, but she'd decided to wait until I handed her the cocktail. As always, she ate the cherry first, which for some reason I found comical.

"Well I think I did a very stupid thing."

Sip.

"We argued a little about the summer and her coming down. I wasn't talking about anything permanent, my goodness, just a summer visit. But she blew up. She said she thought I was trying to take her away from here. Tommy, I assure you . . ."

I cut her off. I didn't have the energy to argue with her.

"Don't worry about it," I said.

"*Thank* you."

Big sip.

"But she refused to hear it. She started crying and storming around; it was a little ugly, I must say."

"So what was the stupid thing? Aside from trying to explain anything to a teenager?"

She tried to smile, then got to it.

"I mentioned her mother's letter. The letter Taylor had written to you, the one that I gave you a few months ago."

I tried to put together what this meant and must have looked puzzled.

"I told her that Taylor had explicitly said she wanted her with you and not me and that I would never go against Taylor's wishes."

Right, I thought. Then what were all those custody shenanigans?

"I don't know how it came out, it just did. I said something about Taylor writing you a letter to that effect. She thought at first I meant the will, but I said no, that there had been a letter. Of course I regretted it the moment I'd said it, but it just kept getting worse the more I tried to back out of it."

Maris sighed deeply. "I think she now believes there is some secret letter on her fate that we've been withholding from her."

I didn't bother to point out that it was obvious Maris had read the letter just as I'd suspected. I thought about what Taylor had written to me.

"I can't show her that letter," I said.

She sipped her drink slowly, then looked at me for a long moment.

"Absolutely not. Though I would certainly understand if you did."

"It would tear her apart."

"I completely agree with you."

"We could both lose her. She idolizes Taylor."

"More than she ever did when," she breathed deeply, "when they were together."

We talked about Taylor and Chase, and how much Chase had been grieving for her in different ways. Maris asked me what I wanted her to do. She had planned on leaving that evening but would of course stay if I thought it would help. She felt she could not just run out after making such a mess. I thought about it and said I thought it was OK for her to go, that Chase and I getting into our daily routines, such as they were, might be the best thing all the way around. That I would act like the letter was basically just a reiteration of the will that Chase had heard and that was it.

Maris went upstairs with the intention of saying goodbye, but the music volume did not come down to earth.

After Maris left, I was hungry. It was an off-day for Megan, and even though the freezer was now loaded with things she'd put away in oddball containers, I had no idea what to do with a lot of it; there were all these indecipherable notes. When Chase finally came downstairs, I asked her if she wanted some bacon and eggs. She shrugged, about as strong a yes as I ever got from her. While I was trying to fork out all the eggshells I'd dropped into the egg bowl, she loomed up next to the stove.

"You got a letter from my mother."

I looked at her, blinking.

"You did. Gramma told me."

"Oh," I said, acting like I'd just remembered and it was no big deal.

"That was just some details about custody. All that came out in the hearing in Chicago, remember?"

"No. This was a letter. You got a letter about why I needed to be here with you. You know you did."

Here we go, I thought. I turned off the burner on the stove and wiped the egg off my hands with a potholder mitt. I leaned back against the stove, almost frying a shirttail, then moved a step away from her and sat at the counter.

"What's the matter, Chase?" I asked.

"Don't try to charm me out of this."

"I wouldn't think of it."

"I want to see the letter."

"You don't think your mother wanted you to be with me?"

"I didn't say that! I just want to see her fucking letter."

I recalled enough of the details of Taylor's letter to be certain that sharing it with Chase would be a disaster. Taylor had taken on a mythic status for Chase, whose room was now practically a shrine to her mother. Every photo of her that Chase had been able to unearth from the boxes sent from Evanston was now taped to her walls. Copies of her books were displayed like bestsellers, holding a more prominent place than even Chase's beloved *Harry Potters*. She wore Northwestern shirts and gear all the time. The only people she seemed to text with – and unlike most teens, Chase rarely sat at her computer in electronic conversation – were people she'd known in the Chicago area. Chase was vulnerable enough that her mother's actions and decisions described in the letter could influence her own future values and experiences. I couldn't do it.

"What did your grandmother tell you?"

Chase could barely contain her impatience.

"She said my mother wrote you a letter explaining why she wanted me to live with you instead of her. I want to see it."

"Are you looking for reasons to leave here again?"

It was a stupid thing to say, but I was trying to redirect her away from the actual letter.

"I will if you don't show me that letter."

I felt like she was actually trying to physically intimidate me. She was only fifteen but make no mistake, this was a formidable presence. I was on a stool, and she came closer, hovering over me like a linebacker ready to sack. I had not yet seen her this intense. I had to do something. Sometimes a little truth would be enough.

"Your mother's letter was really personal to me, Chase. It wasn't just about you. There are things in there that I feel are between Taylor and me and I'm certain your mother would not have wanted you to read it. I feel like it would be wrong – "

"My mother told me everything. You don't have anything between her and you. You were history. My mother and I shared everything. Everything!"

This last she yelled so loud that her spit hit me in the face. She was shaking.

"Chase," I said, trying to calm her down. She turned and strode out of the kitchen. She came back immediately, still shaking.

"You don't think I know everything? I know everything. I know why she left you. You beat her! You hit my mother! You beat my mother and she had to run away to protect me and that's why she never wanted me to come here to visit you! And it wasn't just some lawyer's trick like you told me when I was ten."

She'd closed the distance between us again and was hovering over me threateningly. I thought of getting up and stepping around the counter, putting something between us. I had to just stay on the stool, and not respond in kind. I knew I couldn't tell her at this moment that her accusations were untrue; she would never hear it. A big part of me wanted to slam the letter on the counter and say, "Go ahead and read it,

Kid." But then I'd most certainly lose her, in one way or another.

"I want my money," she demanded.

I started to say something and she cut me off.

"No. I want my money. I'm not staying here. I'll go to Gramma's. I've got friends at home. You can't make me stay here."

"I know that."

She glared at me for a full ten count.

"Then let me see the fucking letter!"

"OK. All right. But – " She threw up her hands in protest.

"But I want to do it with Kate."

She wasn't expecting this; it seemed to push her back a little.

"I want Kate to be there when you read it. That's all I ask."

"I feel like you're up to something."

"I am. I'm trying to protect you from some things that might hurt you."

"Yeah . . . you!"

"You've been here long enough to know that's not true."

"I want to read the letter."

She said each word as if it were a separate sound bite.

"Then let's call Kate right now and set it up. She's wanted to get the three of us together for months. I'll give you the letter when we're there and you can do anything you want with it. If she thinks it's OK."

"Oh no, forget it. You'll manipulate her like everything else. I get the letter or I'm walking out of here forever."

"OK. But in her office. I'll call her right now."

"I want to hear what you say to her."

"I'll put it on speaker."

She glared at me, again for a long count. She was considering, worrying the angles. Her face looked pale and tired. She'd developed this way of wrinkling her mouth so often that there were creases around her lips, the sort of lines a much older woman might have from too much beach.

"Call her," she said.

Kate agreed to see us right away, that evening, and at a little after eight we walked into her big Tudor house. Already changed out of her professional clothes and into jeans and a sweatshirt, she looked more friendly, less pinched. Chase and I sat at opposite ends of a four-seat couch. Kate sat in her swivel chair facing us. I'd told Kate on the phone as Chase listened why I felt we needed to see her right away: that Taylor had written me a letter, Chase wanted to read it, but there were things in it that I felt would be difficult for Chase to hear. I told her that Chase was determined to leave home if I did not let her read it and that I believed her. I said I'd committed to showing Chase the letter in her presence. She simply said to come at eight.

When we first arrived, Kate wanted to talk to Chase privately first before sitting with me or dealing with the letter, but Chase refused, and went in and dropped onto the couch. Kate studied us a moment and asked me why I felt that Chase was not ready to see the letter. She was working the conversation toward creating options but Chase was inflexible. I admitted I'd considered destroying the letter but that it might one day have legal value and I couldn't. Kate finally asked if she could read the letter first. We both looked at Chase, who nodded. It struck me what a force Chase could be, that she could impose her will on two adults to such an extent. Even though a part of me felt like dropping a piano on her head, I felt this rush of respect for her, for the way she could hold her own.

Kate took her time reading the letter, which covered five pages in Taylor's neat, tiny hand, then refolded it and put it back in the envelope. Kate then asked me if I could explain to Chase why it was that I didn't want her to read it.

I looked at Chase and said, "In the letter your mother talks about very personal issues between the two of us that I'm certain she never intended for anyone else to read. There are things between married people that have to stay private."

Chase wrinkled her face in disapproval. She wasn't buying it. I had to give her more.

"Your mother admits to making mistakes and doing some things that she was sorry about.

I guess I'm worried that you'll feel like this is some kind of betrayal. Or that we're all ganging up on you."

I looked at Kate, feeling a little desperate.

"I guess that's it."

"That's bullshit," Chase said. "My mother didn't make mistakes that she wouldn't tell me about. You're the one who made the mistakes."

But she was looking intently at Kate, as if to read her reaction to the letter.

"I told her about you," Chase said to me. "About the way you treated my mother and why she had to run away from you."

The two of them went back and forth, Kate trying to draw Chase out on what she was feeling, while Chase demanded to see the letter for herself. Kate then tried to get Chase to talk about exactly what she would do, step by step, after reading the letter if it made her feel badly. Chase denied, Kate pressed; we seemed to be at an impasse.

Somewhere along the way, Kate said she felt Chase needed a little help calming down, got up and left the room, and came back with a small vial of pills and a glass of water.

"I want you to take one of these," she said, handing Chase a tiny white tablet. Chase refused and was about to toss them, but Kate said firmly, "No pill, no letter."

Chase swallowed it, sipped the water, and said, "I want to read my mother's fucking letter now."

Kate gave her the letter. Chase pulled it from the envelope and read it, half turning her body away from me and Kate. Kate handed me the vial of pills. Our eyes met and I could see her concern, which strangely made me feel great relief. In the kitchen earlier and on the ride over, I'd felt this growing panic, a sense of being utterly alone and not having a clue what to do. Now someone else was involved and seemed to be silently agreeing with me.

The letter was Taylor's attempt to explain to me – should the explanation ever be needed though she hoped it would not – why she wanted me to get custody of Chase. It was an extension of her drawing up her will; she'd left it with the attorney who had called me last May from Chicago. How Maris got hold of it I could only imagine. Taylor had been prompted to write both – the will and letter – shortly after her second husband left, because she wanted to confirm without any question her wishes about her estate and her child. She wrote very clearly of her desire for Chase to be with me, not Maris, and most definitely not Dale Ellis, should he ever desire to seek custody. She wrote that she did not feel Maris was ready to take on the challenges of raising another daughter.

But it was not a public document; her will had said all of this except that it had not said so specifically that she did not want Chase to go to her grandmother. It was also a personal message from her, though as always with Taylor, it was not gushy. She apologized for the way in which the divorce happened, and deeply regretted the accusations she'd been advised by several lawyers to make to assure that she got custody of our daughter rather than sharing time between us. During the divorce, it troubled her greatly to see that her accusations of my beating her had caused me such pain. She wrote that she knew I would never have done such things. But she tried to excuse her actions. She wrote that she did not believe I was mature enough back then to take on the responsibility of helping to raise Chase. She was afraid I would undermine the firm limits she believed Chase needed. But she sensed that I'd matured since then and that Chase always enjoyed her visits to Boston.

She also acknowledged, to her credit, that she'd been wrong in the way our marriage had ended. The affair with the Harvard postdoc had been her way of getting out of something she wasn't ready for, that her infidelity was stupid and cruel and inexcusable and that she'd regretted her mistakes, if not the end of our marriage, ever since. She acknowledged that she'd then gotten herself into a marriage with someone far less compatible than I'd been who turned out to be a nightmare.

She went on to say something about her intention, which she'd obviously not followed up on, to give me the letter regardless of her circumstances: "to clean the slate," as she put it. She closed by saying that she believed I truly loved Chase when she was a child and that I would be very proud of her as she became a young woman.

Chase took so long reading the letter that my mind wandered to stupid things – whether I'd left the eggs out, if I'd mailed the rent bill yet. Kate looked out the French doors toward the dark garden. When it was clear that Chase had finished reading, and her eyes had been focused on a spot on the carpet for a while, Kate quietly asked Chase if the two of them could take a few minutes while I sat in the waiting room. Chase almost imperceptibly shrugged, and I got up and left the room. It seemed like hours that I'd been sitting there, and I was taken aback to see that it was only a little after nine o'clock.

It was well past eleven when Kate came to the door and asked me to come back in. Only once during the more than two hours did I hear anything from inside: Chase began yelling, saying repeatedly that it was all bullshit. I wondered if she meant the letter, or life in general, or something Kate had said to her. I confess there was a part of me that felt vindicated; I'd known since my first conversation with Kate that Chase had told her I'd abused her mother.

There were times when I'd actually thought of showing her the letter. But even the most obtuse blockhead would have known if they could see Chase looking at her mother's books or pictures that this would be a very bad idea. Chase would read her mother's confession that she'd lied about me to get control of our daughter and that our marriage ended because she had initiated an affair. Chase was old enough to appreciate at least in some way the banal cruelty of infidelity. But Chase's entire moral compass would be thrown out of whack. I told myself that in time, not a lot of time surely, we'd be able to tell her. I'd actually thought of giving Kate the letter before, not just to help her understand Chase a little better, but to exonerate myself from any nasty assumptions. Which is why I suppose that I hadn't done it. It might have seemed defensive. I wondered if Chase could ever fully believe what her mother had written.

Chase was curled up on the couch, her face red and sore-looking. I took a hard chair and put it near her. Kate said she'd summarize for me a few of the things the two had talked about.

"Chase and I," she kept saying, as if the two of them had reached a series of agreements, but Chase didn't look like she agreed with anything in the world. Kate and Chase had agreed that Chase would come to see Kate every day after school for the next week or so. That I would give Chase the medication twice a day for a few days to help her relax and not feel so terrible. That Chase would not under any circumstances drink alcohol while on the medication. That Chase would continue to live with me in Newton and not run away or do dangerous things.

Chase agreeing not to drink while on the medication disturbed me; I gathered that drinking was something the two of them had been working on in their sessions. This disturbed me deeply.

Kate summed up for me what she and Chase had talked about. She said she thought we all understood how difficult the letter must have been for Taylor to write, and how everything she'd done was to love and look after Chase the best way she could. She said that it seemed she'd been given some very bad advice by a lawyer, and that this had been painful for me and for Taylor, so much so that she wrote the letter. She said that she and Chase both understood that Chase's home with me was safe and comfortable and that we were having a lot of good experiences. She said she was very sure that Chase was a strong person and would work hard to understand everything they'd talked about that night. She closed by saying Chase had promised to go home and stay with me and not do anything foolish.

I made the hand phone sign and mouthed, "Can I call you?"

She nodded and said, "Your father wants to call me tomorrow to talk and I think that's a good idea. We all need to talk a lot with each other."

Soon we left. On the drive home, I put on the radio just to fill the air between us with something more than Chase's silent sorrow.

11.

A few days after Chase and I met with Kate, on a Friday morning, I was sitting in my office waiting for a callback from the superintendent of the Boston schools. I'd drafted a proposal for him to reorganize and update his communications department. It wasn't the sort of job I wanted. It would mean long hours and interminable meetings, but it had legs, even if the payoff wouldn't be great. I was digging as fast as I could. I'd managed to sublet my condo through the summer, which would pay my rent in Newton. For years I rented a small office near the Massachusetts State House and purchased part-time secretarial help as part of an office pool. And even though I got a deal because I knew someone who knew someone, my working expenses were piling up along with all the others. When I got a call from Bill Tillotson's bank asking through his secretary if I could make a meeting that afternoon at Children's Hospital, I was juiced. I thought it might be another PR bone. I pushed the secretary on the reason for the meeting. She futzed and putzed and finally told me it had something to with malpractice legislation and that the head of a doctors' lobbying group would be there.

After agreeing to the meeting, I had a moment of panic. Had I badmouthed some well-heeled lobbyist enough to be forced to defend my weekend bullshit on St. John? I had a few hours to learn something about the issues so that by the time the meeting rolled around I wouldn't have to fake it if I got pressed.

At the meeting, Bill put me on the spot: in front of the director of the hospital and the head of a thirty-thousand-member doctors' group that promoted legislation to change malpractice insurance rules. Bill said he heard from several of his doctors that I had ideas about the issue. For all sorts of reasons, the membership group had not been able to get the right kind of support, meaning the personal commitment of the Speaker of the House, along with a push from the President of the Senate. I thought they wanted to pick my brain, meaning free consulting, which was fine with me: freebies in my line paid off later. But after a fair amount of back-and-forth, the membership president offered me a contract to represent his group and take the lead on promoting new insurance legislation. It was a fat deal, potentially the biggest of my life. He'd checked me out with the Speaker already, who apparently had spread it on a little thick. The Speaker and I ran the Boston Marathon together for years and I'd always been careful not to run away from him. So he didn't run away from me. In fact, while we were talking in the hospital boardroom, a secretary came in to tell me the Speaker himself was on the phone.

"You want this, Tommy?" he asked, after Bill motioned for me to take the call.

"Only if it's gonna work, Jimmy. I don't want to chase windmills, even for lobby bucks."

"I think we can work something out."

So it was done. On the way out, after we all shook hands and told running stories, I held back to talk to Bill. I wanted to ask him who set this up. But I didn't really have to ask.

All that afternoon it rained very heavily, and by the time I returned from work, our basement was flooding. I'd lived across the street from a river in Boston for ten years yet never had to slosh my way into a cellar to salvage personal stuff before. I only thought to check it out because someone at work asked if my basement was a flooder. Turns out it was. We didn't have a lot of personal stuff in the house, but there were those boxes from Chicago with Chase's belongings in them, along with some book boxes and old college stuff of mine. Chase was at a Juventus meeting, so I was home alone. The basement wasn't too bad, maybe an inch of water here and there, but it was still raining. I made about a dozen trips up and down the narrow stairway, lugging boxes upstairs and emptying them in our unused dining room. I spent some time going through a couple of book boxes: the paperbacks on the bottom were ruined. I tossed them into a plastic yard bag.

Some of Chase's stuff had also gotten wet. I unpacked the boxes of old soccer equipment and spread them out on plastic yard bags to dry out; since the stuff was old, I wasn't concerned about it. I probably should have tossed it all since the box included old shin guards. Nothing on this earth smells worse than used soccer shin guards.

I took more care with the box filled with handwritten training logs and the two boxes crammed with videos. The brown cardboard boxes got wet on the bottom but it looked as if their contents were dry: in her never-ending quest to package and protect, Taylor had sorted the logs into smaller white cardboard file boxes that fit perfectly, and the videos in similar boxes of a different size. Boxes in boxes; that was my ex-wife right there.

I was curious about the videos. Each one was in a plain white jacket, labeled according to place and date. From the covers, they all appeared to be about Chase, all of them having something to do with soccer. I popped one in my VCR and turned on the TV. There was Chase, I guessed about eleven years old until I checked the date taped to the video cover. She was nine, dressed in shorts, T-shirt, and cleats. She looked like a tiny, grainy version of the much larger and impressive person who now lived with me. She had that same brow furrowed with intensity; her hair was tied only with a single band, so instead of a tight chignon the pony tail exploded, mad hair everywhere.

The video jacket said the film was at an indoor field house at Northwestern; Chase appeared to be in a soccer clinic with other athletes, all of them girls. The camera must have been on a tripod, because though it panned from right to left following Chase, it didn't do much else. Chase was running soccer drills with a ball, taking shots, and taking instruction like the other girls from two adults in warm-up suits. It all seemed so intense. Chase was by far the youngest; the other girls looked to be three or even four years older, though my judgment on these things was dubious. It may have been parental pride, but Chase looked better in the drills than all of them. The camera stopped and restarted several times, filming different drills in several places around the big field house. Occasionally, Taylor would appear on the film for a moment or two and obviously was making the video. Sometimes her voice could be heard calling to Chase during a drill. Taylor looked young, pretty, in her tense unsmiling way, and very fit, wearing a sleek warm-up.

I fast-forwarded through the tape, to see what else was on it. At the end was a scene where Chase was standing in front of the camera, the gym empty behind her. She was answering questions put to her by an invisible Taylor. It was an odd little interview. I was struck by the strange intensity of Taylor's repetitive questions and Chase's recitation-like answers. *What did you work on?* Traps and one-touch. *What did you do well?* Traps. *What was good about them?* The ball dropped in front of me, it didn't bounce. *What do you need to work on?* One-touches. *What was wrong with your one-touches?* They weren't – they didn't go right. *Your accuracy wasn't good?* Yes, my accuracy wasn't good. *What are you going to do about that?* Practice. *What else?* More practice? *Are you asking me?* More practice.

A lot of the tapes were of games, with their dates, locations, scores, and other basic facts logged on the video jackets. There were also tapes of Chase working out: in weight rooms with trainers, though I couldn't always see the point of them, unless they were to show off how diligent and strong Chase was becoming. There were outdoor clinics with Chase in them, working out with adults. There were also scenes shot on an empty football field, where Chase and Taylor worked out alone. Taylor for the most part would be behind the camera calling out at times while Chase ran shuttle runs and suicides. Occasionally, Taylor would appear on film.

I was struck by how hard Chase was working, and how aggressively Taylor was driving her. The more I watched, the more apparent this became. Taylor would make her repeat the drill when she was unhappy with the times. I skipped ahead. In scene after scene, Chase was running, dribbling, or kicking against a tennis practice wall, while Taylor barked commands, read times, and pushed Chase to work harder.

I put another video in its place, then another. The two large cardboard boxes filled with videos covered a period of at least six years.

They seemed to begin when Chase was eight; and the last ones I could find were when she was nearly fourteen. Most were games and events such as training clinics, but there were a fair number that were just with Chase and Taylor working on skill drills or fitness work. The Taylor who appeared in these private tapes was much more imposing than at the clinics or games. At times, when Taylor appeared dissatisfied with Chase's performance, especially after a clinic or game, the question-and-answer sessions at the end took on an edge that was troubling.

The logs in the other box were handwritten in blue-lined journals, in Taylor's small, neat script. Taylor had meticulously kept a record of Chase's soccer: her games, her minutes played in each game and position, her stats. There was a record of each week of Chase's training sessions, those she did with the team, along with her running and fitness training done on her own. Her weight and height were recorded at much less regular intervals. There were also pages devoted to Chase's diet, quick little notes logging what she'd eaten during the week, in much less detail than the workouts but still tracked. There was virtually no personal comment in the logs; it was all data. At first I thought I was looking at some sort of data for a research project in which Chase was the guinea pig, but there seemed to be no other information to support this and nothing evaluative beyond grading the different workouts on a one-to-five scale.

The obsessively detailed quality of the films and logs did not surprise me. I'd lived with Taylor for more than five years, married to her for three, so I knew her penchant for organizing, recording, tracking everything. She could never, ever buy a tank of gas for her car without calculating the mileage she'd gotten, and kept a neat little pad in the glove box of her car to do it. What did surprise me was the way Taylor interacted with Chase in some of the films. She was this looming presence in a dark warm-up suit, in and out of the pictures while Chase drove herself, pushing, coaxing, and disapproving or demeaning her when she was not satisfied.

I'd spent a fair portion of my life being coached in athletics: I ran track and cross-country through all my years of school and ran for the Boston Athletic Association for years after (and am still a member, though who has the time anymore?). I've seen a lot of coaches with the in-your-face style of motivation, chewing out athletes, pushing them in workouts, barking from the sidelines, generally being a little frightening at times. Taylor was no worse than a lot of coaches. But Taylor was not Chase's coach. During the years of these videos, Chase was a member of at least one soccer team, usually more. She had coaches. The films and logs gave a picture of someone obsessively driving her own child, with great seriousness of purpose. The extent of it, the degree of it, the high seriousness of it all – was nuts. It was really nuts.

OK, someone might say this was my ex-wife I was looking at; that former husbands, after a particularly nasty little divorce, might not be the most reliable judge of ex-wife behavior. And I was not experienced in the world of youth soccer. But even with that caveat, I could not see anything in these excessively organized and carefully filmed scenes of encouragement and intimidation that could fit anyone's idea of the normal parameters of parenting. The films were disturbing. I tried to tell myself maybe these films and all this obsession was not so bad as it looked, because I didn't want to think of my daughter as in some way damaged by them.

Jenna's Toyota pulled into our driveway followed by another car driven by Kim. As Chase came running into the house, I quickly turned off the television and pushed the boxes to the side of the couch out of view. As Chase ran upstairs, Jenna came into the house. She needed a check for the upcoming tournament in Washington. While I dug out my checkbook and wrote out a check, Chase came thundering back downstairs and ran out to Kim's car. The two drove away. Jenna explained they were returning to the practice field and were going with others for pizza. Jenna was not joining them.

"Can I show you something?" I asked her.

"Wow," she said as she looked through the workout logs. At first she was excited, as if Taylor had compiled something that might have had a treasure in it. When I began showing her the videos, she was less interested at first. She'd seen a lot of games on tape and training videos before. But then the same thing happened to her as it did to me. She stood back from the TV, a workout log in her hand, and watched as I fast-forwarded one of the videos to give her a sense of what I'd been watching.

"Huh," she said after a workout on a track where Taylor had been timing Chase.

"Way too young," she said after a session in the weight room, her eyes narrowed as she watched the film of a young Chase on her back doing bench presses.

"Whoa," she said, watching one particularly grueling session on the empty football field in which Taylor drove Chase to near exhaustion.

"Let me show you one more," I said. It took a minute to find the video I wanted, and then to back up to the scene I'd just watched. In it, Chase is sitting on the ground, holding her legs, her face white with fatigue. Taylor is berating her, telling her she's pathetic, that she hasn't been working hard enough. Chase is rocking slightly; she looks as if all the blood has been drained from her body. Finally Chase slowly gets up, and the moment she is up on her legs Taylor yells, "Go!" and Chase begins to run again, scooping in a ball as she does and running toward the goalposts on the football field. I backed it up to where Chase was on the ground looking up at her mother and paused it.

"Jenna, have you seen anything like this?"

Jenna sat down on the couch opposite the TV, her eyes still on Chase's blanched face.

"Well," she said, glancing at the open logbook page still in her hand. "I've seen a lot of crazy parents, believe me. I mean I've seen things you wouldn't believe. Parents charging refs on the field, or worse, waiting for them in parking lots. Parents chewing their kids' faces off after games, or even during games from the sidelines. I've seen parents slap their daughters for missing a penalty kick or driving away and demanding they run home because they didn't play well. Parents of athletes can get pretty intense."

"Is this . . ." I gestured at the TV screen, "the same as that?"

She thought a moment. I sensed she was being careful more than thoughtful.

"I've known a lot of parents who worked out their kids privately. That's pretty common."

"Like this?"

"Well, I can't say. I wasn't there."

I was about to say something sarcastic but she cut me off.

"This is just all so intense and organized, you know?"

"Yah think?"

I clicked on the video again, with Chase looking desperately up at Taylor in exhaustion.

"It's kind of spooky, actually. I've seen actual abuse . . ."

"Would you call this abuse?"

"Oh, I don't want to go there," she said, and began to explain herself while the video played, and then Jenna stopped abruptly. We both turned around. Chase was standing in the kitchen, looking across the room at the television screen, wide-eyed, her entire posture as if frozen by a sudden ice age. For a moment, Taylor's voice was the only sound, telling Chase that she was pathetic. I couldn't help noticing that Chase standing there in her warm-up suit looked so much like Taylor lurking off to one side on the TV screen. We had no idea how long she'd been standing behind us.

"Chase," I said, and hit the pause button.

I expected her to bolt, to just tear out the door and leg it off up the street, as she'd done before. She didn't. She glared at Jenna and me from across the room, then turned and stalked upstairs. I heard her stomping around the upstairs hall. It sounded like she went into my room but in a moment she was back downstairs and banged out the front door. Kim's car was out front rather than in the driveway, which explained why we hadn't heard them pull up. As Kim and a car of players waited, Chase strode across the lawn and climbed into the back seat.

Jenna and I looked at each other.

"That's a relief," I said.

"I don't know," Jenna said. "Did you see the look on her face?"

"Like we betrayed her?"

Jenna didn't answer right away.

"Someone betrayed that girl," she said, looking back at the TV screen. My tall ex-wife was frozen in a pose, standing over our daughter as she excoriated her for not playing hard enough.

"I hope," Jenna added, "I haven't done the same with her."

I persuaded Jenna to stay for dinner after Chase left with Kim. She seemed willing, but was relieved when I told her I'd heat up soup and enchiladas that Megan had made and frozen. Megan was always very fussy about the microwave, and probably would not have approved of my using it on the frozen food. But it was terrific. Megan learned I loved Mexican and had begun to indulge me. I had a six-pack of Dos Equis in the fridge that Jenna and I polished off in no time. Jenna was good company, and the way she loved and genuinely admired Chase despite all her moody explosiveness was endearing to me. We talked more about the logs and videos; she asked a lot about Taylor and our marriage. I was glad to talk about it. I felt deeply guilty about going through Chase's stuff and being caught looking at the very private scene between her and her mother. I couldn't even begin to figure out why Taylor had wanted all those games and workouts on film, but that was Taylor: the few things she cared about would often engulf her. I'd actually been one of those things, for about a week. Chase and her soccer had become a consuming passion.

It must have been about nine o'clock when Kim called. The pizza dinner had ended some time before and a few of the girls had connected with their boyfriends and headed into the city. She said Chase had gone into Boston with a mixed group and wanted us to know because Chase had seemed upset and withdrawn all evening. I wasn't too happy about the boyfriend idea, since Jenna and I both knew that she had seen Kevin Lassiter at least a few times during the winter, even though I'd done my best to frighten him away. I tried several times to call her cell but she wasn't picking up. I texted her but got no answer.

At nearly eleven o'clock, I got a more upsetting call. It was Megan, saying she'd just talked to Chase and she sounded "messed up," as Megan put it. Chase was in Boston, she wasn't sure where, and thought she was with "that man she talks about," meaning Kevin Lassiter. Jenna and I were a little buzzed ourselves but the call pulled us both out of it. I made coffee.

Chase running off was not new any longer and neither one of us was about to panic. She always seemed to emerge unscathed, even if once it had been a third of the way across the country. Jenna's main concern was about drinking. I'm sure she was worried about Chase's safety but she was also probably thinking about some Juventus violation that might keep her out of the approaching tournament. I didn't ask. My concern emanated from Megan. Chase's friend and tutor was usually level-headed, remarkably so for her age, probably because she worked so much. If she was worried about Chase, maybe there was reason. Jenna began calling the other girls who had been at the pizza dinner with Chase.

Jenna learned that the junior girls had driven into Boston to a party somewhere downtown, possibly a club. Jenna yelled several times at the girls on the phone. She reminded one junior that Chase was still fifteen, which seemed to end the conversation with the effect Jenna wanted. By eleven thirty we'd learned that Chase had been at a party in Allston near Boston University, and some of the girls were at an Allston club but no one was sure about Chase. Jenna and I drank more coffee and reassured one another that the girls were probably not doing anything that high-school girls didn't ordinarily do. Which actually was precious little reassurance.

I think at this point, despite Megan's concern, our greatest anxiety was about Chase's reaction to our seeing her mother berating her on film. The Juventus players all had a club curfew that Jenna was pretty strict about, so we expected Chase to be dropped off by midnight or that we would at least know where she was. Chase hadn't pulled the old standby "I'm spending the night with X" routine, naming a friend who probably used the same excuse to her parents. But we both half expected it.

A little after midnight, one of the juniors called Jenna. Jenna suddenly said, "Oh, fuck," to one of her players, not typical of her. She then demanded, "Where? Where is she? Where are you right now?" then turned to me.

"Allison says Chase was picked up by the police."

I took the phone from Jenna and talked to the Juventus defender, who was also on Chase's high-school team; I knew both of her parents. Allison said there had been a party at a house near Boston University and the police came. There was an argument and Chase was put in the car with "that guy she sees," meaning Kevin Lassiter. Allison sounded like she might have been a little drunk; she was quite agitated and was frothing with a lot of useless information.

"Did they put cuffs on her?" I asked.

Allison didn't know. I asked where she was calling from and she gave me a credible address. She said the police drove off with Chase, Kevin, and several other people at the party in two cars.

When Allison was off the line, Jenna, now very anxious, looked a little panicky and said, "What in the world do we do now?"

I got up to leave and told her I wanted her to stay in the kitchen, to use the land line and keep her cell open.

"What are you going to do?"

I was about to say I was heading into Boston, but the house phone rang, and I grabbed it. It was Chase.

"Dad?" she said.

It sounded so odd to hear her call me that. I don't think I'd heard that since she was three years old. To tell the truth, I wasn't sure what she called me lately, I think it was usually Tommy, but at that moment she could have called me Shitbag as long as she stayed on the line.

"Where *are* you?"

"I'm at the police," she said.

She was breathing heavily, like a child trying to get control of herself, fighting the urge to cry.

"I've been arrested!"

When I asked again where she was, she just said, "At the police station!"

"Let me talk to a policeman," I said.

After talking to a duty officer briefly and explaining I was Chase's father, a man identifying himself as a police sergeant got on the line. I asked him his district: unlike a lot of cities, Boston did not refer to its neighborhoods as precincts but as districts. He was in D-14 covering the Allston-Brighton area. When I asked if there were charges, he said there would be and wanted my name. We had to go around in a circle a little bit about our different surnames because he thought for a moment that Chase had given him a phony name and ID. By this point, I just wanted to get off the phone and get moving. I told him I was on my way in. Before I rang off, he said the charges were potentially serious.

"What does that mean?" I said.

"Assaulting an officer and attempting to sell narcotics."

"*What?*" I demanded of the police sergeant.

But I got little more out of him other than that she was in a holding area awaiting booking with several others. I told him she was fifteen and he said a juvenile officer was present. I hung up and started for the door.

"I'm coming with you," Jenna said.

"Great, you drive. I've got work to do."

While Jenna drove us toward Brighton in her Toyota, I worked my cell. I called the two people I knew who could make a difference; I told them in shorthand what was happening. And in the fifteen minutes it took Jenna to get us from Newton to Brighton, I'd managed to get them both moving in my same direction. To tell the truth, I didn't care right then what Chase had or had not done. This was Boston. There was no way in hell my kid was going to get busted for some piece of shit drug charge, and the rest of the charges the sergeant had threatened sounded like nothing more than typical authoritarian crappola.

I knew the D-14 Allston-Brighton District station well; it was on Washington Street in Brighton, very close to where I went to school at Boston College. It was the station where a lot of rowdy college parties came to a close, several of which had involved me over the years. I showed the duty officer at the front desk my ID and was told I'd have to wait to get into the holding area, and that other parents from Newton had also been notified. He pointed out three people standing in the small waiting area near the front door. Two of them, both men, looked familiar. I'd seen them somewhere around a soccer field but I didn't think they were soccer parents. While I was introducing myself, my cell rang. My sister Anna was calling me back with the information I needed. Then she said she was on her way and would be there in ten minutes. I left the Newton parents and Jenna and went back to the desk.

"Is Joe Duggan here tonight?" I asked.

The officer sized me up for a moment then nodded. I said I wanted to talk to him. He asked me who I was, even though he'd already written down my name.

"Tell him Anna's brother Tommy is out here – and he's ripshit," I said.

He acted as if I'd just said something he heard five times an hour all his life and picked up his phone.

"He'll be right out," he said.

I felt a little better knowing someone. That's the way the world works, by the way, whenever there's a problem with government or public agencies. It's not what you've done, or even who you are that matters; it's who you know. And that in a nutshell was my stock-in-trade.

Joey Duggan, a detective lieutenant, came through the door behind the duty desk, smiling, hand extended.

"Tommy!" he said cheerfully. "What the fuck!"

When he saw the Newton parents, he toned it down, pulled my hand in close to his chest, and asked how I was doing. Joey used to date my sister Anna a thousand years ago and looked like he'd had a beer keg surgically attached to his stomach since then. He waved to the duty officer and in a moment we were deep into the station. In a large open area filled with desks and a small wire-fence cell area at the back, there was a group of police, some in uniform standing at the back. Three young people were seated next to desks in the corner of the room. Chase was one of them. Kevin Lassiter was standing in the wired-off "cooler" cell. Chase was smoldering, her eyes furrowed in anger, she looked as if she was about to erupt. Two other girls were nearby, one of whom looked familiar to me.

Chase saw me and stood up from the desk.

"Hold it," one of the police said.

When I got to her, I put my arms around her. She was so tall I was hugging up. She was so tense, she could hardly respond. Though she smelled a little of cigarette smoke, I couldn't smell any alcohol on her. I turned back to Joey Duggan. He introduced me to the officers nearby, but before we could get into a conversation about what to do next, a familiar voice boomed across the wide office.

"That's my *niece!*" Fergie called out, sounding just playful enough not to offend the authority of the place. He crossed the room in his best work-the-room style and started shaking hands with the police. The mood of the room changed with the arrival of the well-known city counselor. Jenna followed him across the room. He must have scooped her up when he swept through the lobby. Fergie gave Chase a cheek kiss, then stood for a while with his arm around her waist as if to send a message to everyone in the room. Chase stood with her arms crossed and her forehead lined from a deep scowl of anger.

We began putting together what had happened. The police had responded to a complaint about a loud party where teenage drinking had been reported. At the scene they found several youths in possession of alcohol and one person – Kevin Lassiter – in possession of narcotics that he had been attempting to sell. When Fergie patiently asked what this had to do with Chase, the arresting officer said that the narcotics belonged to Chase.

The officer placed a small vial of pills on the desk around which we were all standing. Chase, looking at them wide-eyed in surprise, said, "Those are mine!"

"Right," the officer said.

He explained that Kevin Lassiter had been selling the tiny tablets to people at the party for twenty bucks a tab. It was the anti-depressant medication that Kate had prescribed for Chase a few days earlier. The bottle was nearly empty. We all looked at the bottle, but Chase, looking back and forth a moment between the desk and the wire cage, suddenly jumped up and screamed at Kevin, "You fucking asshole!" and started toward the cage in fury.

"Stop it, Chase!" I snapped.

Amazingly, she actually stopped. She looked at Kevin as if she wanted to tear his leg off and beat him to death with it, but she listened when I told her to sit down. Jenna went behind her and put her hands on her shoulders.

Chase was so angry that we had to rely on the other two girls, neither of whom was from Chase's soccer team, to help us fill out the story. There seemed to be some question about whether Kevin was actually selling the medication or just giving it away, a point that Fergie carefully had them repeat. Chase said she had no idea that he had taken the medication. The police asked me about the pills and I told them. Chase's mother had died recently and her therapist had just prescribed them for her. When one of the police asked me if she was allowed to be carrying the medication around, I lied. I said yes. In fact, at Kate's suggestion, I had kept the medication myself and just given her the prescribed dose twice a day. Chase must have taken the vial from my bedroom before she left the house after seeing her mother on the videos.

"Were you drinking, Chase?" I asked.

She shook her head.

"No – because of those," she said. "Kate said not to."

I wasn't sure I believed her but she sounded credible. I remembered Kate's warning to her not to drink alcohol. It occurred to me that Chase, upset when she left our house, may have taken the pills with her precisely for that reason, to get a buzz from the combined effects. She didn't seem to have been drinking, but then an evening in a Boston police station could sober up even a Drago's regular.

"They were all drinking," one of the officers on the scene said.

"Then why aren't they all here?" I asked.

Fergie stepped in. "I'm sure there was drinking at the party," he offered, "but I think it highly unlikely that Chase or her friends were part of it. This girl," he said, addressing Joey Duggan, "is a high-school All American soccer player. The rest of these girls are on her team," which wasn't true but no one corrected him.

"I know kids are kids, but," he shook his head, "I just think this might be a case of being in the wrong place at the wrong time."

During this back-and-forth, Anna arrived. She smiled shyly at seeing Joey Duggan and the two hugged.

"You look spectacular," he said, and I couldn't disagree with him.

When Chase turned and saw Anna, she started to melt, and by the time Anna got to her Chase's entire affect had changed, from barely contained fury to full-body sadness. Chase had half a foot easy on my sister but sagged into her arms like a rag doll. She began sobbing. Like a child, her resolve turned to jelly. Anna held her and said it would be all right. After a minute, Anna steered her into a chair and sat next to her, still holding her close. The two other girls standing nearby as if catching the contagion began to sob quietly.

Anna knew several of the police on duty and her appearance changed the tenor of the conversation more than Fergie's arrival. With Fergie we were important; with Anna we were friends. Now the only question was what to do with Kevin Lassiter. Technically, no one had been booked yet. Kevin was in the cage because he clearly was under the influence of something. Fergie suggested that maybe he had taken Chase's pills himself and that he might need medical help.

Soon Chase, the two Newton seniors, and Kevin Lassiter were walking out into the waiting area with the rest of us. The parents reacted differently. The girls were greeted with relief and concern, while Kevin Lassiter's father was barely able to contain his fury.

Joey Duggan introduced himself and told him that while no charges were filed this time, Kevin had gotten the break of his life. Then picking up on something Fergie must have told him, Joey, in all the splendor of his quarter century in the Boston Police Department, leaned into Kevin and growled ominously, "I'd stay away from Chase in the future if I were a smaht boy like you."

Out on the sidewalk, the other parents thanked me and my brother and sister. I think everyone there, especially the four young people, even Kevin, who was still high, felt like they'd ducked a bullet. I introduced myself to Kevin's father and pulling him away from the sidewalk, told him that his son was too old for my daughter and I wanted whatever there was between them to end. He nodded; he'd heard Joey and got the message. Kevin watched us, looking dopey-eyed. I didn't think there was a lot of hope for him but I was certain that he was not going to take my daughter down with him.

My sister and brother both hugged Chase and in a moment we all scattered. Chase rode home with Jenna and me. I turned around to talk to her in the back seat, asking her how much she'd had to drink. Once again she denied it, pretty convincingly: Kate had told her not to take her medicine with alcohol. So why had she taken the bottle with her? She looked down at the back of the seat in front of her, and shrugged. I asked her how many tabs she'd taken. Two or three. I asked her why. She just shrugged again.

Jenna dropped us off at our house, got out of the car, and gave Chase a hug, then a brief scolding, then left. Inside, Chase started for the stairs to head up to her room and I said, "Hold on there Quick Draw," and told her we needed to talk. She followed me into the kitchen. The videos were still in the opened box on the family-room floor. I asked her why she wanted to take more of the medication than was prescribed. When she didn't answer, I said, as calmly as I could, that the next thing she had to do was answer that question, and that I would wait. I got up from the counter where we were sitting and started making tea for Chase.

"I know you hate her," she finally said. It was an indirect answer but I got it.

"Never," I said. "We made you together."

She glared at the kitchen counter.

"She really helped me," she said. "With soccer."

Her eyes were tearing up. She got up from the counter, and thinking she was bolting I almost told her to sit down, but she was just getting a tissue from a box nearby.

"Do you think, sometimes, it was a little too much?"

"No!" she fired back. "That's what you have to do if you want to be any good! She really, really helped me."

"Well, you're a great athlete. The proof's in the pudding," I said, not wanting to upset her any more. She clearly felt a need to defend her mother, so in a way she had answered my question. She sat in silence for a while; I poured water into her tea cup.

"She really loved soccer," Chase said. "And math. She was really, really beautiful. I don't think you know how wonderful she was." She began tracing the granite pattern of the counter with her fingertip. "I can't believe she's dead."

I told her that after our honeymoon, Taylor had relentlessly tracked down every photograph that anyone had taken during our wedding and reception, and put them together with all the snaps from our honeymoon into a set of albums.

"We had such fun with those books. They were the most incredibly organized wedding albums in the history of the world," I said, laughing.

Chase got up from the counter and went upstairs. In a moment she was back in the kitchen. The three bound albums, that I don't think I'd actually opened since the day Taylor had first shown them proudly to me, were in her hands. She put them on the counter. Slowly, we began looking through them.

After a little while, however, we stopped; the poignancy of the photos of her young mother began to erode the brief recovery of her self-possession. I closed them and said that we should look at them another time when it wasn't so late. She sipped her warm tea.

"I messed up," she said after a while.

"Yeah, you did."

I told her she was grounded for a month except for soccer practice. Then I added, with feeling: "The next time you go anywhere without my permission you won't play soccer either for a month. And that is non-negotiable. Do you understand me?"

"Yes."

"And if you see Kevin Dickhead again, I swear I'll lock you in the basement and starve you. I'm not kidding."

She half smiled. I had the feeling Kevin Dickhead was already history.

"Do we understand each other, Chase?" I asked her again, not sternly this time.

"Yes." She nodded a couple of times as if to underscore it to herself, then looked out across the front lawn toward the golf course. "I feel like my whole life has been spinning around," she said.

"It has." I smiled at her. "Mine, too. It's not boring."

"No," she laughed, "definitely not."

She looked at me out of the side of her eye.

"I'm sorry. It all just seems so horrible sometimes. Like nothing matters."

She leaned on her elbow and propped her chin with her hand.

"I see these people at the shelter all the time; they are so pathetic," she said.

Just a few hours earlier, we had both heard her mother say that to her in front of a camera.

"I feel like I just want to slap them and say, 'Get it together and stop whining!' I know that sounds terrible but I do. Then I think I could be them. Like when I went back home to Evanston and the house was totally empty, I felt like I had nothing, like everything just disappeared out from under me. That must be the way they feel. That must be what it's like to be one of the Nevers. Anna says that's why they drink so much, because feeling alone sometimes can be so painful that it's better to feel nothing."

I couldn't think of anything to say in answer that wouldn't reveal how it wounded me a little. Then she looked at me, full face – a rarity – and said, "Thanks for coming for me tonight."

I told her a story about a time when I was in high school and was picked up by the police after a fight at a football game.

"My dad came down to the station and pulled out the stops to get me out of there. He made me sound like the best kid on the face of the earth. And they let me walk, just like you did tonight. And then when he got me home, he kicked me in the butt, literally, with his big ugly shoe, really hard, like five times. It hurt for three days."

"You want to kick me in the butt?"

"Absolutely."

We sipped tea. It was after two o'clock in the morning. I felt exhausted but not ground-down, maybe even a little elated. Here was my daughter, so big at fifteen she towered over most men and dwarfed them with the size of her shoulders, who loved *Harry Potter* and was afraid of spiders, and always needed to run away when something hurt her. I reached over and put my hand on her back just below her neck and stroked it for a little while. She didn't object.

"You hungry?" I asked. She nodded. "I could make bacon and eggs," I offered.

She half smiled and said, "Maybe I better do it."

Part Three: Florida, July 2006

12.

Juventus has not played well in its first two games at the national club championships in Orlando. The intense Florida heat in July has taken its toll on the girls, who look bedraggled at their early-morning wake-up. For the second day in a row, the team has a game at eight in the morning, meaning that players and parents have to be awake and at least heading for breakfast by six. When I call Chase's room a few minutes before six, Amy, the Juventus captain, sounds wide awake.

"The Bicycle Girl is not moving, I think she's dead," Amy says as if playing to an audience. Chase does not get along well with any of her club teammates, including the garrulous captain. In the last few months, at club practices and the few games that Chase has managed to play, I've heard her referred to as the Bicycle Girl, but without affection. At least it's better than Bike Dyke. I can only imagine Chase, lying in bed while the other girls race to get ready for the game, wanting instead to hide under the covers. Although able to get up in the dark to go out and run on the golf course at home, here in Florida it seems as if the dog-season weather has sucked the will out of her young body.

Juventus faces the Red Devils from North Carolina in the morning game. With a record so far of one tie and one loss, ordinarily Juventus would be eliminated from advancing to the semifinals later in the afternoon. But a series of surprises to other clubs have given Juventus a statistical chance to move on to the semis, if they can post a win against the North Carolina team. Jen makes this clear to everyone in the small function room off the coffee shop where the team spreads out for a quick breakfast.

As I sit at a table by myself with a cup of coffee, I'm so tired I feel like someone has scraped the insides of my eyelids with a spackle knife. The night before, Chase was the last player to return to her room, nearly an hour after the last of the other girls quietly came back from elsewhere in the hotel. She hadn't been in her room when Jen went in to look for her earlier, a kind of informal bed check a little before the actual curfew she'd set for all the players. I had the feeling that Jen was giving Chase latitude; or maybe she was giving herself latitude, needing Chase for the game this morning and not wanting to bench her for a curfew violation. I only knew that Chase had returned, because I saw her walking to her room from the elevator. I sent her a text asking if everything was OK, a fatuous question she answered with a question: "Is it ever?" not a very reassuring response.

Liz sits down at my table. Liz's daughter is Amy, the team captain, who plays defense, so there is no competitive thing between the two of us over whose daughter gets playing time. She has a plate full of those little Danish jobs and offers me one. Victor, another parent, joins us, with a plate heaped with bacon and scrambled eggs that look all wet and revolting, as if I'd cooked it.

We talk about the game coming up; Victor explains the complicated tournament scoring formula, which could result in Juventus advancing if they beat the Red Devils. Victor asks pointedly about Chase's knee, about the fiftieth time I've been asked in the last eighteen hours, ever since Chase's play the day before proved undistinguished. Chase has probably been asked the same question even more often. Since the parents of every player have spent at least a couple of grand just for this tournament, and since this is a major potential showcase for their daughters in pursuit of college aspirations, their concern about a highly touted player underperforming may seem reasonable. Actually, I don't think it is reasonable. I think it's a little wacky, all this intensity of focus on colleges and the girls' individual performances. Some of these people, like Victor, have enough money to buy a chunk of some college all by themselves. For some, the passion is more about status and bragging rights than dollars; for others, it is as if the girls being evaluated makes them uncomfortable, as if it is a direct reflection upon themselves as parents. For still others, it is simply a wish to have their children realize their dreams to play soccer in college. I'm hoping I'm in that group; I'm not immune to this anxiety. But it still is wacky. I keep waiting for the stairway metaphor, the one about needing to step up.

"Aren't they supposed to have super-defenders?" Liz asks.

"Both are Region One ODP," Victor says, knowingly. "Chase better be on her game or we won't even get a shot off."

Easy for him to say, his daughter is in the backfield playing stopper.

"She's not the whole offense," Liz says, reading my thoughts.

"Yeah, but this team hasn't exactly been staging a shooting clinic, either."

When the game is under way, it looks to my untutored eye that Juventus is indeed outgunned. But the Juventus keeper is having a career day: save after save keeps the game scoreless throughout the first half, as Juventus is unable to convert on several chances. Once again Chase has not started, and has been subbed in and out for short minutes, her play largely undistinguished. At one point in the first half, it looks as if she might be able to create something: cutting across the midfield, she takes a pass from Amy, wins two fast fifty-fifties, and beats the first defender for a possible shot. But at the last second, she fakes the shot, pulling out the NC keeper, and taps the ball to her left to a trailing Juventus midfielder. The midfielder takes the shot, but her foot is too low on the ball: it whacks off the crossbar. Chase's header off the rebound sails into the keeper's outstretched hands.

As the Juventus front line moves to get back into position for the keeper punt, Jenna screams at Chase from the player sideline, "Take the shot, Chase, for Chrissake!"

The game remains scoreless, and we hear along the sidelines that the team from Sonoma that beat Juventus the day before has lost to the Pennsylvania all stars. With a few other strokes of luck, a win could propel Juventus into a semifinal game late this afternoon against the defending national champions from Dallas. The news stirs the Juventus supporters along the sidelines. Somehow the scuttlebutt seems to have reached the players on the field; Juventus picks up its game and for the first time in three tournament games begins to control the play.

For much of the second half, Chase has been sitting on a ball away from her teammates on the players' sideline. Across the wide field from us she looks all knees and shoulders. I find myself doing what a lot of other parents of players do, timing her sub-turns, keeping a running calculation of her minutes in my head. I expect that Jenna will put her back in for at least the last fifteen minutes of the game, even though I know part of her motive for benching Chase is to punish her for what she has called a lack of commitment.

Chase is subbed back in with twelve minutes left to play.

Immediately, one of the defenders, who has been roving freely when Chase is not on the field, drops over to cover her one on one, as she has done throughout the game. Each time the ball is sent to Chase, the North Carolina left midfielder doubles down to cover her as well. The NC defender on Chase is a fast, stocky sixteen-year-old who grabs at Chase's shirt and shorts whenever Chase is between her and the ref's line of vision. The game is still scoreless.

With less than five minutes left in the game, the Red Devils almost score. The Juventus keeper makes what will be called the save of the game, reversing direction against a double attack and perfectly anticipating the North Carolina shot. The save lifts the sidelines and charges the Juventus players with excitement. Amy takes the throw from the keeper and lofts the ball across the field; Chase steps back, takes the pass, cuts past two NC players, and takes off down the sidelines with a burst of speed. She slices through the midfield ahead of her teammates as the left middie and the stocky defender converge on her. Chase fakes a pass, then suddenly shifts to her left and accelerates harder, and as she accelerates, she flips the ball with her right foot high over the defender's head. The defender lunges awkwardly, sticking out her hip trying to pivot toward the ball, and she catches Chase hard on her right leg. Chase for an instant appears to be tackled, in midstride, a solid hit. She pitches forward, out of control, both of her legs swept out from under her.

And then it happens, so quickly we can only truly understand it hours later, after seeing it replayed on film shot by scouts from the coaching tower. As her right leg goes out from under her, with her great momentum driving her forward, Chase uncannily lifts herself into the air: like a gymnast in a floor exercise executing a high forward roll, she flips through a complete somersault, and spinning airborne as she comes out of the rotation, she strikes the ball hard with her forehead. The ball explodes off her head through the air and shoots past the keeper's outstretched fingertips, just missing the far post and striking the high corner at the back of the net – an utterly astonishing goal.

Chase cannot stop her momentum. She lands hard on the pitch and rolls through another somersault, this one on the wet morning grass. Her ecstatic teammates converge as if to pile on top of her, and then pull up; Chase is down, and not moving. The beaten keeper looks on, hands at her side like a helpless witness to a traffic accident. Jenna is already running hard across the field. I just stand on the sideline, open-mouthed, a series of grim scenarios running through my head like a slide show. This cannot be happening, not again.

Then Chase is moving her legs; then sitting up. Jenna, on her knees bent over looking earnest, now looks to the sideline and finds me. She holds out a hand. Thumbs-up.

Once again, the Juventus players leap into the air, hugging, laughing in celebration. As Jenna helps Chase to her feet, the silence on the sidelines breaks into jubilance. Chase stays on the field. The referee signals play to resume. Chase moves awkwardly at first, and seems hurt, but soon begins to regain fluidity. Although the Red Devils mount a furious counterattack in the last minutes, the ref soon blows the whistle and Juventus gets the win.

Appearing at my elbow, Victor leans close to me and says, "So the Bicycle Girl does it again."

Maybe I'm too sensitive, but it seems to me that there's more resignation in his voice than warmth.

It would be unfair to characterize the reactions to Chase among some of her teammates as resentment. That would be too strong. However she has performed so far in the tournament, the team's reactions to Chase have always been ambivalent at best. Athletes generally have a "show-me" attitude to others, especially about new teammates. While Chase has been on the team for a year, in fact she has only been an active player for the past two months, because of her high-school season and then her knee reinjury, which needed therapy during much of the winter. She played in a few friendlies during the spring, and a tournament in Washington on Memorial Day weekend, but missed the big summer tournament at the end of June. So in a way she is still a new player, largely untested in pressure situations among her teammates, an unknown in the course of play. Soccer is a game where players must learn the moves of their teammates, their speed, the ways they react both on and off the ball. This takes time. During the first three games of this tournament, a lot of missed passes – both from and to her – were undoubtedly a function of this learning curve. So the rest of the team watches her from a distance, friendly but not friends yet, a little wary because of her silent, almost surly affect, and puzzled, at best, by her renown as a one-time national-team player.

The elation of the win over North Carolina only increases when we learn on the bus before leaving the field complex that Juventus will advance to the semifinals against last year's champions. While players and parents congratulate Chase on her game-winning goal, the high praise is reserved for the keeper, who has justifiably earned everyone's attention for her spectacular shutout. Yet the news of the game has spread back to the hotel, and by the time the team bus rolls back under the carport, a cluster of players, parents, tournament officials, and scouts recognize the team when they come into the lobby, as if they'd already won the tournament. A lot of the attention is aimed at Chase. Mostly it is just a lot of "great game" comments, long looks, and pointed fingers. But to the Juventus players, Chase is getting too much recognition, given her uneven play, while the keeper walks through the crowded lobby without notice.

Jenna has called a full team meeting immediately in the small function room before showers. She wants chaperones and parents there as well. She has to be pleased: even just making the semifinals will give the team a lot of ranking points, which will move them up significantly in the national-club team rankings. This means more top tournaments, more travel invitations, and more attention for the players and coaches from colleges and from potential sponsors.

But Jenna's edginess from the day before is still evident. She quickly runs through a list of expectations for the team over the next several hours. It is only half-past ten and the Dallas game is scheduled for after four. There is a lot of downtime; she wants the players resting in their rooms. Chores for parents are assigned: water cases in from the bus, takeout lunches ordered, light lunch, no turkey, no sodas – and rest. She wants everyone in the lobby by three, in uniform, ready to board the bus.

Only after giving her instructions does she comment on the game. She's unhappy with the way the team played. Her list is a long one, of missed assignments, collapsing offenses, this player and that player holding the ball too long. She praises the goal-keeper briefly but emphatically. She gives Amy as team captain the chance to speak. Amy says much the same thing as the coach, though she doesn't single out individual players for bad play and is more effusive about the keeper. At the end, she sounds like a high-school cheerleader, pushing the team with the usual clichés. Chase's name is not mentioned; she's not singled out for bad play nor praised for her goal. I'm relieved on both counts. Jenna ends the meeting by saying a few things about the Dallas team, notably, that they have an even more formidable defense than the Red Devils. At this she looks at Chase, sitting on the floor at the back of the room. Chase is tracing her finger on the sole of the flip-flops she wears between games, looking as if she hasn't heard a word. At the end of the meeting, the girls slowly separate and head to their rooms.

While the parents begin to sort out the assignments, Jenna comes over to me and says, "We need to talk."

We decide the best place for privacy is my room. She wants Chase, too. We follow her down the hall single file like a chain gang. When I put my hand on Chase's shoulder, I can feel the tension in her; she doesn't shrug it off. We sit in chairs at the balcony end of the room; Chase slumps uncomfortably in one of the upholstered chairs, her long body too big for it. Chase and I both know what is coming, another "step-up" talk. I also know why I'm there for this one. Jenna has been annoyed at both of us for weeks, ever since we missed the Las Vegas tournament in June. We couldn't go because a different trip had come up.

After my meeting in April with Bill Tillotson at Children's Hospital, my new contract to work the State House on behalf of the doctors' collective took off. I expected a lot of grinding hours, which I thought I was ready to do, but it didn't turn out that way. I knew just about all the members of the Boston delegation to the State House pretty well, though I'd never worked with them as a group before. It took very little time to get the doctors' legislation moved on the floor, and with the help of the Speaker of the House and the President of the Senate, a new piece of legislation was passed into law at the end of June, hours before the lawmakers' vacation recess. In truth, I hadn't really done much work and none of it heavy lifting: a lot of phone calls, and lunches, and cell chats, but I didn't spend hours bird-dogging congressional staffers at the State House and I didn't make any political contributions. I just helped a few friends to see that the law made sense to their constituencies, packaging it as a bit of a slam at the insurance companies. Since everyone hates insurance companies, it was a piece of cake. I think my new clients were surprised; they expected me to milk the contract a little, which I could have done. They would have been delighted if I helped bring in the law in a year, or even made progress and lined up a done deal for two years out. Two and a half months blew them away. So they deepened the contract, and put some money and security in my pocket for the first time in way too long.

The person I really had to thank for the deal was miffed at me but didn't stay that way. The morning after my first meeting with Bill Tillotson, I walked over to her office; she was in surgery, so I went to the hospital florist and got her a basket of peonies. She called that night and told me I was an asshole about the Paris trip. Then she made me a better offer.

"What if I turn in the first-class tickets and get four in coach?"

"A little group grope?"

"Well, we could if you like," she laughed, "or maybe we could take Chase and her friend Megan?"

When Megan realized she was actually going to Paris, her kookiness reached new limits of audacity: the thought of all that rich food affected her brain so much she changed her hair color four times. Carrie changed our reservations from the Crillon to a small Left Bank hotel and traded in a few expensive extras she'd planned for the two of us. Megan got to take a couple of cooking seminars while Carrie and

Chase went shopping, and the four of us ate handsomely at storefront restaurants catering mostly to locals. Chase had been to Paris several times with Taylor, but always as part of travel soccer. This time, the closest Chase got to a soccer ball was when the four of us took a train to Marseilles: along with tooling up and down the Côte d'Azur in an absurdly small rental for a couple of days, we went to the Marseille Velodrome to see Olympique Marseilles play Real Madrid. The only exercise the four of us got during the trip was the interminable walking around Paris and morning jogs around the Luxembourg Garden, pretty comical choreography since Megan ran with us. Chase and Megan mostly spent nine days in France cavorting like puppies.

The Friday evening of our second weekend, three days before our return, the four of us went to dinner at a small family place near the Ile St. Louis that we'd decided after several meals was our favorite. Sitting at a long table just inside the door were Maris, Anna, Fergie, Carolyn, Jack Boyan, and my mother. Another of Carrie's surprises, though this one thankfully was paid for by my brother. My father offered the first toast – which had something to do with the failure of our country to export genuine American soup spoons – and all ten of us were in the bag by midnight. Fergie and Megan achieved new levels of public assholery, which Maris seemed to enjoy almost as much as my mother did.

At the time of our trip, Jenna readily understood our reasons and seemed to accept our going to Paris instead of the club outing to Vegas. Her deep affection for Chase was beyond question. But Juventus had not done well in the tournament, and the club had very high standards for the commitment of players to events that the team as a whole had voted to attend. Parents grumbled; there was a flurry of team emails after the tournament, parents and players whining about "some players" not being fully committed to the team. Since Chase was the only uninjured player who didn't go to Vegas, there was no decoding involved.

Sitting in my hotel room, Jenna does not lecture us this time, or give one of her rah-rah talks. She asks Chase how she felt about her play for the past two days. When Chase tries to shrug her way out of it, Jenna insists.

"I sucked," Chase says.

Jenna looks at her closely. "Your goal should tell you what you're capable of doing. That was an absolutely brilliant goal. But you gave me twenty seconds. You were on the field for thirty minutes. The rest of the time you looked as if you couldn't be bothered."

For a moment the clanky air conditioner is the only thing in the room willing to talk. Jen leans in to Chase and puts her hands on Chase's knees.

"You have four hours until we leave here to play Dallas. I want you to use the time to think about who you are, and what's important to you. I don't want you to suit up, Chase," she says, and pauses, long enough for Chase to look up, now attentive. "I don't want you to suit up for the game unless you want to be part of this team, and give it everything you've got, the whole game. If you're not into it, or you feel out of shape, or you've got other things going on in your life right now, that's OK." She squeezes Chase's knees. "I'll still love you. And I'll be there for you as your friend. And you can always come back and play for Newton in the fall if you want. You still have your junior year. Maybe you just need the summer to think. Or maybe you've had enough of soccer for a while and need to take a year to do other things. The world won't end for you if you don't play soccer. But please, please:

don't suit up if you don't want to be out there. Just decide, and I'll back you up. So will your dad. It's that simple, honey."

Chase looks down at the floor. Jenna gets up, and I walk her to the door.

"Maybe you're right, Tommy," she says so Chase can hear as well. "Maybe she needs to take care of other things now. That trip to Paris should tell all three of us what Chase needs right now." She smiles and gives me a hug, and as she does she whispers in my ear, "Take her home, Tommy, she's miserable." She lets herself out.

"Can I use your shower?" Chase asks.

"Of course," I say. I look at her game bag on the bed. "You want to just hang out here and take a nap? I'm going downstairs anyway."

"OK. Thanks."

I leave her and go downstairs to find a decent cup of coffee. Jenna's whispered comment feels like a punch in the liver. Maybe Jenna is right. Chase has been under terrific pressure since she was eight years old, from her mother, her school, her few friends, everyone who knew her, all over a game. It 's nearly impossible not to get swept up in the seductive excitement of watching her play when she's on her game. There is no denying she has unusual gifts. For her not to use them seems wasteful, like leaving a sports car in the garage or sending a beautiful French meal untouched back to the kitchen. There is also the money. Like every other club parent, the possibility of a college scholarship is something for me to worry over, like a sensitive knee, to be nursed and indulged. Chase has been through a lot in the past year, but in the last few months she has begun to come out the other side of it. Paris was wonderful. And her job at Anna's shelter has given her days when she's come home on the train eager to sit in our kitchen and tell stories. Chase a talker, going on and on about something besides

Harry Potter: imagine that! The thought of her being miserable now, after discovering new things at home that have excited her, makes soccer seem more like a disruption.

In the coffee shop I run into Liz, Vic, and a few of the other parents. After worrying over what the girls will eat for lunch and ordering pizzas delivered to Amy's room, we decide to cross the highway and walk to a Friday's for lunch, no players invited. I feel as if I'm tagging along under false pretenses. The conversation never once deviates from soccer, mostly the games played and the one coming up, but also the tournament, the scouts, colleges, the running conversation of the trip revolving through yet another iteration. When someone asks how Chase is doing – always a bit of a loaded question since no one is satisfied with her play despite the game winner – I lie and say she's icing her knee and resting but stonewall when they ask if she's injured.

It is after one thirty when I get back to the hotel. It occurs to me that Chase has not eaten, so I call the room to see if I can bring her something. She doesn't answer the phone. She might be asleep; I head down the hall, tap on the door and go in. She's not there. But her suitcase is on the bed; she must have retrieved it from the room she has been sharing with Amy and two other players. Her game bag is on the floor, along with her cleats, shin guards, and uniform, all tossed into a white garbage bag, ready to be packed for the plane. Her few toiletries are on the bed in a plastic sandwich bag.

I call her cell a couple of times but she's not answering. Down in the function room, Jenna is there with Kim and Andrea, the team manager, and a few other parents, going over tournament details. Jenna looks at me quizzically; I just wave and head back out. I don't want to tell her I can't find Chase again. I call Amy's room and ask for her. Amy says they haven't seen her since the morning, when she moved out. Amy sounds annoyed. I wonder if Chase has said anything to her, but it is highly unlikely. She would never announce she is leaving to a player before telling her coach.

I walk around the hotel, checking places where soccer players are congregating. She is not at the pool, or down in the arcade or the weight room. Half her team has gathered in the coffee shop, eating sandwiches. Girls from the Dallas team are there, and there seems to be some tension building among the players already: a few straw wrappers are shot across the tables, a few snarky side comments draw private laughs.

It is after two. I stop at the front desk and ask if Javier Couto is registered at the hotel. The cow-eyed young woman behind the desk smiles, writes his room number on a card, and offers the house phone on the counter. A man answers.

"Javier?"

"Not here."

I tell him I'm Chase Ellis's father and I'm looking for her. I think I hear the man laugh slightly, a knowing sort of laugh that makes me want to beat him to death with the phone receiver. I tell him I've got a plane to catch, and for the first time think to myself that maybe I ought to be calling the airline to change our flight.

After a pause, the man says, "Yeah, he met her, they went to the bar or something." Then he adds by way of explanation, "She called him."

The hotel is big and has at least three places that might be called the bar. I finally track them down in a lounge off the pool where drinks are served on both sides of a wall of French doors. Javier and Chase are sitting in a pair of deck chairs aimed in opposite directions, facing each other. He's drinking a beer and talking expansively. She looks surprised to see me. She's drinking lemonade.

"So, what's up Javier?" I say.

Pulling up a stool, I sit very close to him. I haven't met him yet.

He doesn't act like a man caught in a bar with someone's fifteen-year-old daughter. He says, "Oh, yes, yes!" when he realizes I'm Chase's father, and extends a hand. A waitress smiles when he flicks his fingers and she jumps over to the bar to fetch us each a beer.

He is not so much talking to me as everyone in the lounge within earshot. He asks if I saw Chase's goal, and without needing an answer, sails into a description of it and of what a wonderful player Chase is. He says it looks even better on film, which makes no sense at all. He has a kind of European sensual energy that is contagious; as he talks, he is either taking short sips of beer or scooping handfuls of bar nuts into his large mouth. He's one of those guys who is always putting his hands on someone: he's as comfortable grabbing my forearm while he makes a point as he is squeezing Chase's hand when he turns to her. He's a big, warm Portuguese athlete with big brown eyes and white teeth. He's probably too shameless to have even thought about doing anything wrong.

He says he's already written his evaluation of Chase and put it on the coaches' website, which means that any college coach around the country can log in with their password, enter Chase's name, and read how a World Cup player has described her play. He announces that this was a very stupid thing for him to do, even though this is what he is paid for. He should have written terrible things to scare everyone off, so he can bring her to Michigan with him. He's being playful; he wants Chase and me to know he is doing good things for her.

I tell Chase we have to get ready; I don't say for what. As we get up to go, Javier stands and puts his arm around Chase's shoulders, shaking her affectionately.

He says, "You will remember what I have told you? You remember?"

Chase nods. "I am very serious, I will not forget. You must not forget, either," then gives her a hug, a double-cheek kiss, and he and I shake hands again. I still think he's a bit of a slimeball but at least he's a charming one.

"What does he want you to remember?" I ask as we walk back to my room.

"He wants me to go to Michigan," she says, "and play for him."

"Does that interest you?"

"Not really." She wrinkles her mouth. "I'm sick of playing for everyone else."

I debate asking the next question, then go ahead.

"Then why did you call him?"

"He's the only person that's been friendly," she says.

"Have you been friendly to anyone?"

She looks at me as we walk into the hotel atrium.

"I guess not," she says after a moment.

When we're back in the room, I close the door and look at her.

"So what are we doing, Chase?"

"Going home."

She looks at me as if this is as much a test as it is an answer.

"OK." I go over and turn off the clanky air conditioner. It's almost three o'clock. "I'm going to need to call the airport," I say. "You're sure?" She nods. "Do you want me to tell Jenna or will you?"

"I'll do it," she says.

We decide she'll find the coach, while I'll take care of the flight seats. We will meet downstairs in twenty minutes at the side of the hotel, next to the miniature golf course, where the shuttle service to the airport stops. She can go out the side entrance right off her room and not have to run into the team bus. She picks up her suitcase from the bed and her various bags and leaves.

The airline tells me there are seats on the next flight to Boston, leaving in about two hours. I don't actually book them. I keep thinking, maybe this will turn around again. I can't imagine facing Jenna or any of the other parents after this, just walking out on her team with one or possibly two games left to play. Not that I'll have to face them. If we leave now, we're done with Juventus. I'm sure Chase knows this, too. It feels like bad parenting to encourage this sort of bailout. But I am also sure that there are times when you just shut up and back your kids, even if you think they're making a bad choice, especially if you've given them the choice to make in the first place. Chase has let herself be dragged from one soccer experience to another for so long. It's time she owned it or quit. Even Jenna can see the pressure is making her miserable.

The Juventus players are gathering in the lobby when I go to the desk to check out. The Dallas team is waiting there, too. The baiting game between the two sides seems to have gotten a little uglier; clusters of girls from both teams are eyeing one another and pointing, joking a little too loud to keep the comments private. The Dallas players are especially loud and confrontational. They look gigantic to me: not just tall, but powerful and cocky. They are after all the national champions. Jenna comes into the lobby while I'm at the front desk. She moves the team outside, then leads them away from the front door to a small lawn at the far end of the building to wait for the bus, out of harm's way.

I don't see Chase come downstairs. When I've checked out, I head out the side door to meet her at the shuttle-bus stop. She's not there, nor at the miniature golf course. I wait briefly, then decide to stand in the lobby where I will have to see her when she comes down from the room. The Juventus parents who were waiting in the lobby have moved outside and have joined the players at the far end of the building. I can see the club bus still in the parking lot; the driver has just stepped in and will soon pull up to the carport. I feel horrible about leaving.

Then I see Chase. She's standing outside in front of the hotel, under the carport. I feel a moment of panic: she's waiting for me on the wrong side of the damn hotel, the last thing I want right now is to run into the rest of the team while we're about to slip out on them. Some of the Dallas players have gone outside to wait for their rides to the field; they are standing a little off from Chase under the carport. When I jog through the front doors and hurry over to grab her luggage, I see that she doesn't have any. She's dressed in her Juventus uniform, her game bag in one hand, her cleats in the other. So she's turned things upside down again. She is just standing there like a warrior, facing the cluster of Dallas players, who are all looking back at her but saying nothing, no jokes this time, no whispers. On her face is a calm, almost faraway look, as if focused on some distant point beyond the players in front of her. It is a look I've never actually seen before except in a famous photograph.

She sees me and flashes her half smile.

"I'm ready," she says.

More About the Author:

Ted Dooley grew up in Pennsylvania with an abiding interest in literature, poetry, and writing. He moved to Boston as a young adult, and for many years worked with emotionally troubled children. He eventually became the senior advisor and writer for the Superintendent of Schools in Boston, where he demonstrated his gift for connecting with constituents and local politicians.

Ted was the father of two children, one of whom played competitive soccer in high school and through college. A devoted parent, Ted regularly attended his daughter's soccer games and traveled with the girls and their parents up and down the East Coast. He always found time to write, completing *The Bicycle Kick* the day before his sudden death.

Ted's family is thrilled to publish his immensely readable and engaging book, which depicts so well Ted's exceptional wit and love for his family and life.

Made in the USA
Middletown, DE
15 December 2018